HIGH PRAISE FOR
SUSAN DUNLAP
AND THE
KIERNAN O'SHAUGHNESSY
SERIES

"DUNLAP IS THE LEADING PROPONENT
OF GUTSY, NON-TRADITIONAL WOMEN
WHO NIMBLY TREAD IN HE-MAN
TERRITORY."
—*The Washington Times*

"O'SHAUGHNESSY IS VERY MUCH A NEW
BREED OF INVESTIGATOR . . . as exciting an
offering as we've seen all year!"
—*The Plain Dealer* (Cleveland)

"[KIERNAN O'SHAUGHNESSY] IS . . .
FUNNY, AND AUTHORITATIVE."
—*San Francisco Chronicle*

"Susan Dunlap evokes the sensual details of
her characters and their environment
with singular talent."
—*The Sunday Herald* (Monterey, Calif.)

"SUSAN DUNLAP IS ONE OF THE BEST!
[She] spins a satisfying story and in the tough-but-
tender Kiernan creates a likable new sleuth."
—*The San Diego Union-Tribune*

SUSAN DUNLAP

NO IMMUNITY

A KIERNAN O'SHAUGHNESSY MYSTERY

A Dell Book

Published by
Dell Publishing
a division of
Random House, Inc.
1540 Broadway
New York, New York 10036

The trademark Dell® is registered in the U.S. Patent and Trademark Office.

ISBN: 0-440-22480-2

Reprinted by arrangement with Delacorte Press

Printed in the United States of America

Published simultaneously in Canada

February 1999

10 9 8 7 6 5 4 3 2 1

OPM

For three inspiring women of Pioche:
Martha Lauritzen
Betty Gemmill
Jean Orr

Many thanks to Martha Lauritzen,
superb guide to Nevada.

To John Arndt for his oil expertise,
Bette Golden Lamb for her medical expertise,
and Toby Gottfried for her guidance with research,
and to Linda Grant and Marilyn Wallace
for their thoughtful
and perceptive comments.

As always, I am indebted to my superb editor,
Jackie Cantor, and my agent, Dominick Abel,
for their support, insight, and integrity.

CHAPTER

1

HE NEVER SHOULD have trusted them to Louisa. You don't leave two defenseless Panamanians who speak no English, no Spanish, no nothing with a woman who just dumped you.

Whom *you* dumped.

But Louisa was the only one here in Las Vegas who had shown any interest in Juan and Carlos. And she was a doctor.

What other choice was there, Grady Hummacher asked himself again. He could hardly baby-sit two teenaged boys while fifty million dollars oozed through his fingers, could he? The charter to Panama would have taken off without him. Anyone would have told him "Go!"—even the boys, if they could have.

But the sudden flight to Panama and back in two days had wiped him out. He hadn't slept down there, and all the way back he'd worried about the boys.

The steering wheel slipped as Grady cut left, away from Las Vegas's McCarran Airport. Pickups roll. He'd rolled three of them in his thirty-seven years. If he'd had any sense, he would have sworn off trucks after the first one. But he loved the lurch when he screeched around a corner on two wheels, that split second between flipping and straightening out, between life and death. He'd thought the boys might be frightened, but they loved it too. Sunday on the way to the picnic he'd had the truck up over a hundred. They were grinning, the two of them. They hadn't grinned like that since the first time he brought them out of the Panamanian rain forest and into the hotel in Yaviza.

The hotel was a no-star place, but to two deaf teenagers from a rain forest tribe, walking into the lobby bar with the neon lights had been like catapulting into the future. They'd shrunk back against the wall, sure, but Juan hadn't stayed there long. His eyes had widened in awe, then zeroed in on the glowing colored tubes. Transfixed by the magical lights, he had reached for Carlos's hand, and the two of them had inched forward to touch the neon tube.

Juan was so curious, so resourceful. Maybe the part of his brain that had never processed sound sharpened his views of each hanging branch, the minute variations of the underbrush, the varied consistency of the mud in every scintilla of his tribal rain forest. He was a topographical map locked in a silent drawer. Hummacher had spotted his potential the first time in the rain forest. He was so quick. Without hearing or language, Juan was the best guide in the tribe. And it had been so easy to get him and Carlos visaed in on the exploration company. Here in Las Vegas, they could have doctors, teachers, whatever they needed. And there wasn't the danger of another geologist in Yaviza discovering their skill—and *his* find.

No way could he have guessed they'd get so sick here. Was it flu? Germs to which they had no immunity? One of those viruses you see on the six o'clock news? Or was it some microbe they brought into the country?

Hummacher squealed left. A horn shrieked in his ear. Cut too close. But he'd almost missed the damned parking lot. He slammed on the brakes, leaped out, and ran across the empty lot to Louisa's clinic door.

His feet felt funny, like they weren't making it all the way to the ground. Two endless air flights in two days, charter or not, was enough to give you rubber legs.

Door was locked. What the hell type of clinic was Louisa running here? Hummacher shivered more fiercely and glared at the dark, empty parking lot. Well, okay, it was late. But if she had the hombres here, she ought to be with them. What kind of doctor would leave them alone? He loped around the side of the stucco block building.

Light in the back. That's where they would be, then. Couldn't see in; window too high and those damn cacti Louisa had been so proud of planting in front of her windows. Nature's barbed wire, she'd called them. He leaped, smacked the window grate before he fell back, catching his sleeve on a cactus spine.

No response.

Of course they didn't hear it. They were *deaf*. If Juan could speak, the first question he'd ask would be, "Are you the village idiot?"

Hummacher ran back to his truck, flashed the lights on and off, on, off. Waited. Nothing changed. Were they too sick to notice?

The back door was weak. Dangerous, he'd told Louisa. Easy to jimmy. Easier to bang through. He started the engine, shifted into first, and hit the gas.

He was onto the macadam in one bounce, inside the clinic in two. The alarm shrieked. The place was lit up like a casino. A white-on-white casino. He ran down the hall, flinging open doors.

"Hombres! Carlos! Juan!" No answer. Of course no answer, idiot!

They were in a tiny examination room, lying on the floor like rags. Neither looked up. Not normal. Somehow—maybe they felt the air move—they'd always known when he'd come in, even if their eyes were closed. Christ, they should feel the alarm; half of Vegas could hear it.

He grabbed Juan's shoulders. The boy's eyes opened and faded closed. He was burning up. "Damn!" What the hell was Louisa doing letting them burn up?

The alarm seared his ears. Carlos rolled limply onto his back. Hummacher gasped. The boy's face was masked in blood.

He scooped the boy up and ran for the truck. Dammit, why didn't he have a shell on the back? He couldn't put the hombres in the open bed. The cab seat was too small, but it would have to do. He dropped Carlos in, and raced back into the clinic. The braying alarm rasped his skin. He almost missed the rise of the police siren.

Juan's skin looked as if it had been inflated, his wide face ballooned, his neck swollen out to his ears. Grady gasped. The boy was bleeding from the eyes. The alarm screamed. Grady picked Juan up and ran, tripping over the doorstep, grabbing the banister, landing hard on the asphalt.

The siren died, then rose, loud as the alarm.

Hummacher jammed the gearshift into reverse. "Hombres. Have to get them out . . . get them safe. To a real hospital."

They lay like rag dolls, half off the seat. He hit the brake, shifted to first, and floored the pedal. Their heads banged against the door panel.

He made the first right, flinging their heads into his lap. He braced them with his arm and took a left. He'd lost track of where he was. Vegas wasn't his city. Off the main streets he was useless. Didn't matter. Only mattered to slow down, look innocent.

He pulled the boys closer. They felt like hot coals against his jacket. They didn't even groan. God, he would have felt better if they'd groaned. He should never have brought them here, exposed them, made them sick. The windows were shut tight and the air was thick. He was so tired. He grasped the steering wheel harder and squinted into the dark, looking for a hospital sign.

They had been fine at the picnic just two days ago. Louisa had said they'd love the spot. An acre of lush green, a veritable rain forest, three hours north of Vegas. Who would think any amount of cash could create that? When the hombres saw it Monday, they'd rubbed their faces against the thick, meaty tropical leaves, they'd rolled in the soft ground, their eyes had the same sparkle of that first sight of neon.

They'd been so happy. Why wouldn't he expect things to work out for them here?

His head throbbed, his thoughts were tumbling over each other. He had to concentrate. In a few minutes he'd have the boys at a hospital and everything would be all right.

Hospital. He couldn't go there, and he couldn't leave them there to be turned in to the INS. If Juan and Carlos were contagious, the INS would round up everyone with a sniffle in the barrio and fling them over the border before they could pull out a hanky. For sick immigrants, particularly ones with questionable papers, a hospital was the last place to be.

Then where? It was so hard to think. His apartment? No, definitely not there. He couldn't swear he'd be safe there himself. And he had to get back to Yaviza to finish negotiations. "Fifty million dollars," he said aloud, as if the vibrations made the words more real than the two searing, sweaty heads and the blood soaking into his jacket. His share would buy them every doctor in the state. He just needed a couple days more, then he could nurse them around the clock.

He jerked to a stop at a red light. The street lamp shone down on their swollen, bloody faces. "Oh, God," he muttered. For an instant the panic dissipated. His mind was clear and he knew he'd been feeding himself a line. What the boys had was no flu. He had never seen anything like it. He had heard of plagues in South America that swept through villages leaving everyone there swollen, bloody, and dead. They would still be spreading if the villages weren't isolated and the governments hadn't closed the only roads to lead in or out.

The boys, he had to focus on the boys! If he took them to his apartment, they'd die. But if this was some strange virus from the rain forest, the Las Vegas doctors could do nothing but shake their heads while the hombres died. And they'd keep him quarantined to see if he died too. The panic squeezed him tighter. "Oh God, there is no answer." Maybe back in Panama . . . rain forest . . . someone would   know . . . something.   Roots . . . bark . . . tribal healers, they'd know.

He shook his head clear again. Of course he couldn't take the hombres back to Panama. He could never slip them onto a flight, sick as they were. He had to get them someplace safe here in Nevada. Whom could he trust?

He did know a place. Not the exact location, just the number. In Nevada there were plenty of people who needed to disappear. Girls outrunning pimps, guys too far into the mob, gamblers who'd ratted out one friend too many. Plenty of trade for a safe house. Two sick kids would be peanuts.

He headed north. He knew not to call till he got there.

2

"I NEED YOU on this autopsy, Kiernan."

"No 'Hello, how are you? How've you been for the last five years?'" Kiernan O'Shaughnessy fingered her short dark hair and leaned forward on her desk. When she'd last seen Jeff Tremaine on the plane out of the epidemic site in Africa he had been tall, blond, and despite months in the equatorial sun, pale and burning with anger. Anger at her. She had been at the makeshift Lassa fever hospital only a month, but pictures of the patients staggering down the slippery slope of fever, terror, convulsions, and death still invaded her dreams. Even now, when she'd bolt awake, it would take her a full minute to realize she was safe at home in her La Jolla duplex and the hot film that coated her body was not blood, merely sweat. But those terrified faces never left her. She wasn't a woman to indulge in what-ifs, but when she thought of Africa it was always, *If only we'd had enough ribavirin to stop the virus reproducing. If only we'd gotten it sooner. If only . . .* For Jeff Tremaine the problem had been simple; he merely blamed her.

Jeff Tremaine might need a forensic pathologist, but

she'd have sworn she would be the last one he would call. "I'm a private investigator now. I haven't done an autopsy in five years. And I've never been licensed in Nevada. Find yourself a local forensic pathologist."

"There isn't one in the county."

"Get one up from Las Vegas, then. A pathologist from there will have seen everything."

The buzz on the phone line seemed to grow louder. After a moment he said, "I can't chance word leaking about this death."

"Why not?"

"I'll tell you when you get here."

"Aren't you being a mite paranoid?"

"Not inappropriately so."

"That's what they all say, Jeff." Kiernan stifled a laugh. Her med-school class had had no dearth of candidates for Class Paranoid, but Jeff Tremaine had not been one of them. Against the liberal backdrop of San Francisco, Tremaine had seemed a throwback to the days of gingham curtains and Dwight D. Eisenhower. His goal had been to return home to eastern Nevada, settle into his father's office on Main Street, and minister to every mining casualty and sick baby within a hundred-mile radius. As far as she knew, he had never marched against the military or protested a parking ticket. He was a play-by-the-rules guy; he kept the rule book in his pocket and he had been affronted every time someone—student, patient, hospital administrator, or faculty member—had ignored it. In his four years in San Francisco Jeffrey Tremaine had been affronted a lot. He was the last man she would have expected to volunteer for anything as dangerous and quixotic as a contagious-hemorrhagic-fever project on the far side of the world. "Look, Jeff, surely you can tell me what you found in this body—"

"I can't. That's just it. I don't know."

She sighed, and tried another tack. "Why me?"

"Because you were in Africa, and"—the buzz on the line was stronger, but his gasp for breath was still audible—"because you know how fast things can spread."

Her breath caught. She felt the hot sweat on her back. "Call the health department, Jeff. Right now!"

"I can't be sure."

"They'll make that decision."

"It's more complicated than that."

"If you're talking about anything like Lassa fever, you don't have a choice. You call them, or I'll do it myself."

There was a hoarse, scratchy sound on the line; it took her a moment to recall it as his odd, nervous laugh. "And you'll tell them what, Kiernan? That a crazy colleague of yours somewhere in Nevada is worried about an autopsy? Come, see for yourself. If it weren't vital, you know I wouldn't have called . . . you."

That much she did know was true.

"You can fly into Las Vegas. I'll meet you at the airport."

"No," she said with a sigh, giving up as much to curiosity as to urgency. She didn't trust Jeff Tremaine enough to let herself end up three hours into the desert without a car of her own. "I'll get a rental."

"Bring double gloves and a full head mask," he said before hanging up.

CHAPTER
3

"**AND YOU'RE GOING?** To Nevada? Without taking a fee?" Brad Tchernak smacked the serving platter so hard on the table that the skewered, fig-stuffed Canadian quail almost flew to the floor. Ezra lifted his shaggy wolfhound head and tensed his muscles in readiness.

At barely five feet and not quite a hundred pounds, Kiernan was nowhere near Tchernak's size. But, as she'd taught herself early on, authority was not physical but mental. She let a moment pass before saying, "Yes, I'm going. This is a courtesy to a, uh, colleague, not an agency case."

"What about your time? Does this guy, this doctor, think that just because you're not part of the exclusive medical fraternity anymore, your time's worth zip? Clients could call while you're gone. Ongoing cases could go sour. Investigation waits for no woman. This could mean big bucks lost while you fly off to play around with an uh—colleague."

"Boundaries, Tchernak! You'd think a former offensive

lineman would have a clearer concept of the meaning of out-of-bounds."

"When I was playing football, the quarterback stayed in the pocket," he reminded her.

"I am not in your pocket. I'm your employer." Before Tchernak could get to the real focus of his pique, she added, "You were in the process of serving dinner."

He pursed his face in what she assumed was the fierce look he'd aimed at defensive tackles across the line of scrimmage. Tchernak had been invalided out of the pros before the era of trash talking, so his threatening glare must have been his entire preamble to each play. That scowl, under a helmet and above shoulder pads the size of a 747, doubtless was once a fearsome thing. But now, with a wreath of wiry brown hair capping brown eyes as big as Ezra's, an oft-broken nose that pulled to one side when he laughed, and a ripped T-shirt on a hundred pounds less of sleek muscle, the effect was no longer terrifying. It was endearing.

But this was an inopportune moment to mention that. She watched Tchernak stride into his half of the duplex. If the way the man had played football was anything like the way he worked for her, he must have blocked the defensive tackles down the field and into the bleachers. There was a time when she would have said Brad Tchernak had been the second best addition to her life, the first being Ezra, her wolfhound, whose loyalty was severely strained by the meaty smell on the table. She had advertised for a house-keeper and ended up with a gourmet cook who adored her dog. Adored her work. And her. For ninety percent of America's women, and men, that would have been heaven. Sometimes she wished she were in that majority. But then she had seen the truth.

It had been revealed in two epiphanies. The first had been right here in her living room. She had been sitting outside on the balcony rail watching the deep apricot sun settle into the green-gray Pacific. Her eyes were adjusting to the indoor light when she walked into the living room and spotted Tchernak on the sofa, his wiry brown hair unfettered as he leaned forward, elbows on knees, whiskered chin cupped in palms. Beside the sofa lay Ezra, paws crossed, whiskered chin resting on forelegs. The physical resemblance she had noticed before. But that was the first time she registered that they were brothers under the fur.

She hadn't yet felt it appropriate to mention the similarity to Tchernak. But she thought of it when Ezra eyed her food, sniffed at her work papers, stood beside her bed with his big brown eyes staring at her lovingly, his head tilted to one side. It was only through consistent discipline that she'd kept him off the bed.

The second great realization was that Tchernak could never be trusted off leash. He had taken the job as house-keeper-cook-dogwalker to "find himself" after the sudden end of his football days. The man was so quick to learn her tastes, to take over the *affaires de maison*, she had assumed he was a pro instituting his new quarterback's regime. What she had forgotten was that great offensive linemen work on instinct. The lineman makes his move first. He clamps hands on the defensive guy's jersey regardless of the holding penalty, he leg-whips ignoring the fifteen yards it might cost. For him the rules are mere impediments. Linemen who never deviated from the playbook were second string. Tchernak had been elected to the Pro Bowl.

Kiernan did love breaking the rules, as long as the rules in question weren't hers.

"So, tell me more about this vital phone call you just got." Tchernak loomed—six feet four inches—over the table.

It was irrational to resist talking about it, as if it made

the danger less, but she ached to put off the specter of disease for another few hours. She cut a piece of quail and chewed, savoring the sweet meat as much as possible under her cook's demanding stare. "Great! Quail was an inspired choice. And your glaze!"

Tchernak shrugged away the diversion as if he had forgotten he had made the dish.

"Jeff Tremaine was in med school with me," Kiernan admitted.

"And that's enough to make you drop everything?"

"He's never asked a favor before."

"So of course you can't wait to see what the big deal is."

"Got it."

"You can't just—"

"It's *my* agency, Tchernak; I go where I choose!" Ignoring his hurt expression, she forked another piece of meat, then gave up and let the fork slide to the plate. "Jeff's talking hemorrhagic fever, like the epidemics that swept through Africa and South America. He's probably panicking over nothing; it wouldn't be the first baseless conclusion he's jumped to. But if he's right, if he's got anything like Lassa fever up there, it's a crisis. It would spread from town to town, and if it hit Las Vegas, even if it's a virus we knew how to treat, there wouldn't be enough of the drug in the world to treat all the people who'd get sick."

"You mean this is like the Ebola epidemics?"

"There are a whole range of arenaviruses—Lassa fever, Junin, Argentine or Bolivian hemorrhagic fever. This could be any of them—deadly stuff, passed from rodents to humans through scratches, bites, and abrasions, or, and this is the scary part, Tchernak, sometimes through the air."

"You mean a cough on a bus—"

"Exactly. With airborne contagion no one is immune. But I don't know what Jeff Tremaine's got up there in rural

Nevada. It could be a new arenavirus, one of the RNA viruses we've never heard of, or something entirely different. Or Jeff Tremaine could have gone off the deep end. I'll get a flight first light and catch the midnight special back."

Tchernak pulled out his chair and sat. "Okay, one day. I'll hold down the office in your absence."

She felt the sides of her neck tighten protectively. Leaving Tchernak in charge of her hard-gained agency was like leaving Ezra to guard the quail. Even with the best of intentions he might decide a leg or two wouldn't be missed. "Okay, but follow the instructions I—"

The phone rang and she leaped for it. "Hello?"

"Is this Kiernan O'Shaughnessy? O'Shaughnessy Investigations?"

The call was not her business line; it came through on her unlisted number. "And you are?"

"Reston Adcock, Adcock Oil Explorations. Remember me?"

There was no point in asking how he got this number; the arrogance in his voice said it all. She certainly hadn't given it to him. She remembered that, and him.

Tchernak was chewing very slowly, ear cocked in her direction, meat hanging from the fork he held absently at half mast.

"Here's my problem. A guy who does some work for me, Grady Hummacher, he's gone missing. He was supposed to be here this morning at ten. He's not the type to forget. I've called his place all day, even had my girl check the hospitals."

"And did your *girl* call the jails about this Grady Hummacher?"

Of course Adcock missed her sarcasm. "Yeah, them too. Grady can be a hotdog, but he's no fool. Not the type to drink and speed."

She pictured Reston Adcock: big, his skin burned a permanent tan from years in the oil fields, muscles just beginning to sag, hair just beginning to gray at the temples, blue eyes squinting, as if looking for whatever angle he could find. "So if Grady Hummacher is really missing, as opposed to merely having skipped a meeting with you, he's been gone less than a day, right?"

Adcock's voice was now just a mite sharper and she could tell he was restraining the urge to snap. He was not a man who restrained himself often. "It wasn't just any meeting Grady missed. That meeting was key, for me, and especially for him. If it were anything less, I wouldn't be calling a detective."

"An out-of-state detective whose fees are substantial."

"Right," he said without pause.

Tchernak put down his fork and shifted his head in front of her. *Grady Hummacher?* he mouthed.

Adcock's office was in Las Vegas. It would be an easy stop on the way back from Jeff Tremaine. An easy fee to justify the trip, she thought. But no; she definitely did not need a fee that badly. "Mr. Adcock, since you called me at home at dinnertime, I'm sure you'll understand if I seem abrupt. Clearly you are not looking for a standard straightforward missing-person's investigation or you would have gotten someone locally who would know the possibilities for mishap much better than I. Your need is more complicated than that, and more immediate. I have a pressing commitment, so there is no way I can help you."

Tchernak cleared his throat.

"I don't want someone else. I need the best."

"I can't be in two places at once."

"Grady Hummacher's missing! He could be lying dead somewhere. Look, I'm asking for your help."

Tchernak pointed his finger at himself.

She hesitated, then said to Adcock, "You and I have

different standards. People are too expendable to you. I'm not going to endanger my agency working for you again." Before he could start another round, she hung up.

"Me!" Tchernak shouted. His wiry hair bristled. He looked like he'd stuck a finger in the socket. "Grady Hummacher, right?"

"So?"

"I know a Grady Hummacher. How many can there be?"

"In the oil industry?"

"I think so."

"You *think* so? Just how well do you know Hummacher?"

"He was at State with me, a dorm counselor my freshman year."

"*Your* counselor?"

"On the floor above me."

"So it's more like you knew *of* him than actually knew him?"

"No, I knew him all right. And I ran into him in the airport a month or so ago and we caught up."

"And did he say he was planning to skip a meeting with Reston Adcock?"

"Grady's missing, huh? You know, Kiernan, this is a perfect case for me. I mean, I know the guy. I—"

"Tchernak! I've already turned down the case."

"We can—"

"If Adcock's really worried, he'll be on the horn to someone local by now."

"I can—"

"Tchernak—"

"I'm good at detecting, you know that."

He had handled each job she'd grudgingly allowed him, and better than she had imagined. He could get anyone within a hundred miles of San Diego to open up. Women found him adorable, like the biggest puppy in the litter. For men, they remembered the offensive lineman who tossed Kevin Greene on his butt three times in one quarter. He was the all-pro lineman with the good instincts. *Get over your need to be the boss, Kiernan. Take him and give thanks.*

Her throat squeezed in so hard she could barely force words out. "That's not the problem, Tchernak."

"What is the problem, then?"

She took a breath. "I worked in the coroner's office. I don't do well in bureaucracy. I don't like to take orders—"

Tchernak grinned. "Yeah, right. You like to give them."

She nodded, took a longer breath. She expected Tchernak to go into a riff on her love of command, but he didn't. He loomed silent, waiting. The air in the room seemed to thicken and everything slowed. Ezra let out a moan, but neither of them looked at him. "The thing is, Tchernak, I don't like to share. I wasn't one of those kids who got a strawberry ice cream and said to all my friends, 'You want a lick?' I like—I need—to have things be just mine. This is my agency. It and what it's gotten me are all I have. I can't give it up. Or share it."

Tchernak started to speak, but she stopped him.

"Don't tell me you'll always take orders, you'll be just an employee. As it is, I'm afraid if I forget to check the letterhead each morning, I'll find 'O'Shaughnessy Investigations' has been replaced with 'O'Shaughnessy and Tchernak.' Or more likely 'Tchernak and O'Shaughnessy.' "

Tchernak didn't seem to move, but his mouth had tightened. He bent toward her, hands braced on thighs, glaring as he must have at the defensive tackle. "You just want someone to keep house, cook, and walk your dog."

It was of course exactly what she wanted. A more diplomatic woman would have equivocated. She nodded.

He lifted his chair, put it under the table, walked to the door of his flat, turned, and said, "I quit."

CHAPTER

4

RESTON ADCOCK TAPPED his finger on his polished teak desk. It was a thick finger, one muscled by work. A finger that should not be dialing his own phone. That's what he had a secretary for. He hated being held captive while the phone rang, while the guy at the other end took his own time to get to the receiver. Adcock wasn't a man made for waiting. *He who waits . . . waits,* and Reston Adcock had no time to waste. He stared at his finger, noting the dark lines in the creases, the stains of the oil he had discovered, oil he had rubbed into his palms and on his face and neck and bare chest in joy the first time he'd found a seeper. He'd screamed and laughed; he'd rolled in it then, the black anointing oil of riches.

He thought then that he'd never want his hands clean of it, that if it never washed off, he'd be a happy man, a happy magnate, a merry mogul. But it had washed off, and he'd gone after his second strike with only "greater reputation" in his pocket.

Twenty years since then. He'd lost count of the strikes. And the oil companies he'd worked for, the times he'd quit and set up on his own, the times he'd gone back on payroll. The Mercedes and the Chapter Elevens. The wives and the kids. And the college tuitions.

And Grady Hummacher. Where was Grady? The guy could have been himself twenty years ago, smelling oil in his sleep, sniffing it out for the joy of rubbing his hands in it. Hummacher had the best nose in the business. Loved the jungles and deserts, the wilder the better. Wanted to scale the highest peak on each continent, row the oceans, stand atop the earth and pound his chest, and stop to wink at the gods and men. And the girls. Adcock understood it all. No wonder he loved Hummacher. But he should never have trusted him with details. You don't pound your chest with paper and pen in hand.

At least he'd had the sense to demand reports from Hummacher so that he couldn't be left totally out of the loop. Still, he never expected Hummacher to miss this meeting, the one that would set them both in gold. Grady was a party guy, but he wasn't a fool. No matter what shape he may have been in, he'd get himself in *here* today.

Unless he opened his mouth in the wrong place.

Dammit, he had to have the detective. He wasn't about to ask her again; he didn't operate that way. He needed some leverage. He could—

The phone rang.

"Adcock Explorations."

"Is this Reston Adcock?"

"Right. You?"

"Kiernan O'Shaughnessy's associate, Brad Tchernak. I think I can help you."

CHAPTER

5

THE SWOLLEN, BLOODY, terrified African faces had filled Kiernan's dreams, and she'd jolted up time after time, sweat-drenched and disoriented. The alarm woke her forty minutes earlier Saturday morning than if Tchernak had been driving her to the airport. The van company insisted on unloading passengers a full hour before their departure, not the twenty minutes any sensible woman preferred. The twenty minutes that always drove Tchernak crazy. If he hadn't quit, he'd be pulling out of the driveway right now, describing how far off the ground her plane would be by the time she made it to the airport. It would serve her right, he'd be adding; any competent business-woman should have the maturity not to make a contest out of every flight departure.

She smiled at the memory as she strolled to the gate for Las Vegas. She would miss Tchernak, no question about that. But he had been an aberration in her life. She was meant to be alone, she'd known that since she was twelve and her sister's death left her with parents dead in spirit, and the Catholic community who no longer spoke to infidels like the suicide's sister. Tchernak was as close to family, to belonging . . . But life moves on. This was best for both of them. And at least Tchernak had agreed to take care of Ezra in her absence. "No reason why *he* should suffer," Tchernak had said by way of exit line as he disappeared into his half of the duplex. She'd watched him reach out, hand on the edge of the door, the urge to slam illustrated in every tense muscle. But of course he couldn't. Ezra liked to roam through both units, keeping tabs on both his people.

Her eyes filled. Quickly she blinked back the threat of tears. She'd find Tchernak a place close by; Ezra could still see him.

The sour coffee and airplane pretzels arrived, supplanting the prosciutto-and-Emmentaler quiche, sourdough bagels, mixed melon slices, and still-hot espresso Tchernak would have sent with her. She silently acknowledged the gastronomic depth of her loss. She was hungry, but she would wait.

When the plane landed, she sprung the overhead compartment door while the stewardess was still on the speaker warning of luggage shifting during the trip. If the terminal at McCarran offered food, it was camouflaged by the blinking colored lights, the clanging bells and whirling winner sounds of the banks of slot machines. The very air seemed laced with caffeine, and everything about the place screamed, *Hurry! Last chance!* She'd wait till she picked up the rental car, cleared town, and spotted the first real food cafe along the road.

Minutes later the Las Vegas Strip rose from the sand like a plastic mirage, and was gone again before she could believe it had been there. There were one or two more city exits and then: nothing. No exits, no access roads, no gas or even a rest stop, much less real food. The only comfort was that her cell phone would not be ringing with nagging calls from Tchernak. The rumpled hills lay beside the highway like dying elephants laid tail to trunk. Once she turned onto 93, her only decision was made. Next stop would be the town of Gattozzi, and Jeff Tremaine; but that wasn't for well over a hundred miles. The blacktop shot out straight ahead, bisecting the high desert; the morning sun seemed to bleach the land colorless. To her right, jacketed power lines ran like covered bridges in the air. In the nearly treeless, waterless, uninhabited desert the meticulously protected power lines were baffling.

An hour and a half into the drive she noticed a narrow strip of green pasture, ponds, cattle—southeastern Nevada's answer to the Nile Valley. Thirst had settled like blotting paper in her throat. She longed to pull the car over, run into the pasture, and shove in among the slurping cows.

Jeff Tremaine had talked about the land here, but oddly she hadn't pictured it like this. She'd known it would be brown and dry, but he hadn't mentioned the subtle, seductive browns and violets in the distance, the isolated green strip of ranches and cottonwoods, the miles and hours that separated men from their deeds.

It was after eleven when she spotted the prefab truck stop inaptly called the Doll's House. Unless those dolls were beneath the red light in the no-frills motel behind. In the cafe she hit the Dolls' bathroom (Guys' was around the corner), grabbed the two tallest bottles of water in the cooler and a bar of waxy chocolate Tchernak would gag at. "Why are the power lines covered?"

"Huh?" The boy proffered her change.

"The power lines, they're jacketed, all the way from Las Vegas."

"Oh, the shields? Birds were shitting on the power lines. Acid rotted 'em out. But these shields saved the day.

Coated with poison. You check out the ground below?"
He giggled. "Chorus line of corpses."

She swerved to avoid a decaying crow as she pulled onto
the highway and now recognized the gray and black lines
that lined the road. On the horizon sun-bleached dirt
darkened into red rock. Against it the piñon pines were
greener, the rabbit sage bright yellow, and the gravel and
stones not gray but silver. She passed through one small
town and close by another that probably hadn't changed
since 1950. Pioche, the old mining town, sat too far up the
knobby tan hill for close viewing, but she could still see the
wires that had carried the ore buckets from the dead mine.
There was an odd completeness to these tiny isolated
places, as if the ensuing years and outside world were
merely tales told beside the hearth.

When Jeff Tremaine had talked of coming back here, it
had sounded like life without the possibility of parole.
Now, as she turned off the highway onto Gattozzi's Victorian main street, she wondered if she had heard Tremaine's
initial description with urban ears or if dry grass and duty
were all he'd been able to see back then.

First Street slithered up the hillside, a two-lane main
drag largely unchanged in the hundred years since pros-
pectors and thieves shot it out in the muddy road and died
on the covered wooden sidewalks. The wind and dirt had
turned painted facades gray. The Gattozzi Saloon—
Rooms by the Night, Week, Month—was a tall-windowed
Victorian that must have outlasted its paint job by seventy
years. Across the street a one-pump gas station beckoned
drivers with promises of water, soda, sanitary supplies. Under the covered walkway signs in windows announced
Sam's Supplies, Masting's Hardware, The 47th Street
Deli. Kiernan smiled appreciatively as she pulled in by the
red-and-white oilcloth-covered tables of the whimsically

named cafe, walked back down past the Tin Nugget Bar to the door stenciled Jeffrey Tremaine, M.D.

She stopped outside, taken aback by the poverty of this weathered storefront. Was this the venerable practice he had taken over from his father? She had pictured it operated out of a venerable dwelling of the saloon's vintage. But this was a spot available to anyone with a hundred dollars and a load of collectibles on the back of the truck. How little she really knew of Jeff Tremaine. Even her assumptions were turning out to be wrong.

The dry wind strafed her cheeks and she could smell the dirt and dust in it, unforgiving of those who stood too long waiting to decide. The November sun pricked weakly at her shoulders. She had to shove hard to open Tremaine's door, and nearly leap out of the way as the wind thudded it closed behind her.

A woodstove crackled in the far corner, and a woman and child, both in jeans, sat on the nearest seats, across the room from the receptionist's counter.

"You Dr. O'Shea?" the gray-haired receptionist asked.

"O'Shaughnessy."

"Dr. Tremaine may be at lunch. The mortuary'll be unlocked. Autopsy room's in the back."

"Customers aren't likely to walk out, huh?"

Outside, the wind seemed stronger, and winter had settled in under the sidewalk awning. Between her death-ridden nightmares and Tchernak's quitting she had forgotten about winter. La Jolla winters merely meant more tourists on the beach. She pulled her brown bouclé jacket tighter around her ribs, but she didn't feel any warmer. The jacket, black shirt, and brown pants made up her "every possibility" suit, created by her dressmaker to suit her five-foot frame. Her running shoes pretty much destroyed the image, but Jeff Tremaine hadn't called her for her image.

The Constant Mortuary was one storefront wide, like Jeff's office. Trade might be constant, but it was clearly not lucrative. Indeed the door was open. She stepped into a paneled room with a riser at one side. The viewing room had no one on view. "Jeff?" she called, pushing open the door to the back.

No answer. She considered and immediately discarded the idea of tracking Tremaine down at lunch. Not with the body so close, and the chance that one glance would prove Jeff had overreacted—again. She tried one door, then the next, and walked into a small, close room unbrightened by its one window a few feet from the next storefront. The air was close, and the grit on the window lock suggested it hadn't been opened in years. The body would be in the fridge.

CHAPTER 6

THE RECEIVER WAS slippery in Brad Tchernak's hand. He'd been up all night pacing back and forth across his studio, around the chest press and stationary bike, from the kitchen to the garage door, and for a two-hour stretch he strode along the beach. Kiernan couldn't be bothered with the Adcock case; and she couldn't be bothered with him. A perfect match. He'd come to that conclusion a dozen times in the last few hours. Her ethical standards were too pure to take on Adcock? On the gridiron he'd faced off against plenty worse than whatever Adcock was. No problem. Still, now he could hear the crack in his voice as he said to Adcock, "I knew Grady Hummacher—"

"O'Shaughnessy's the one I want. She charges a bundle, I know that. I'll pay it, but I'm paying for the best. I don't deal with underlings."

Sweat was running down his back. Christ, he had bent over at the line of scrimmage when the disks in his back were bulging so bad the fans in the stands must have seen them, and he hadn't sweated like this. And as for Adcock, had the guy forgotten Kiernan blew him off? Was Adcock

arrogant, or an idiot? He wanted to tell him to go to hell.
But this case was a once-in-a-lifetime chance. A big-money
case like this could set up Tchernak Investigations.
"Kiernan's out of town—"

"Look, I've got a guy missing here. He could be lying
dead in the sand by now. I told her—"

"She's dealing with an epidemic. North of Las Vegas.
That's a no-wait situation. Contagious hemorrhagic fever," he added. Wouldn't hurt to lay it on, big-case-like.
His brow was sweating like Niagara. Maybe Kiernan was
right; maybe he wasn't cut out for this kind of work, not if
he went to pieces like this on a phone call. He put his hand
over the mouthpiece and breathed in through his nose. He
sounded almost normal as he said, "You're Grady's boss,
that right? He missed a big meeting with you two days
ago."

"Right. If you know Grady, you know that flying close
to the edge is his style. But he's not a flake, and I'll tell
you, this was one helluva vital meeting for him."

"And for you?"

There was a pause before Adcock said, "Right."

The sweat all over Tchernak's body suddenly felt cold,
refreshingly cold. Reston Adcock had blinked. "I'm glad to
help you, Mr. Adcock. I liked Grady. But I want to be
thorough; I'll proceed as if I were a stranger. I'll start with
what you've got in his personnel file. And of course what
you know about him yourself."

Adcock sighed. "I was hoping to get O'Shaughnessy on
this right away. Like I said to her, Nevada's a big, empty
state. You make the wrong decision here, you forget what
you need, it's easy to die before someone figures out where
you are."

Was Adcock going to whine about Kiernan forever?
"Oil exploration's no desk job. Grady knows more about
survival than ninety percent of mankind. Are you sure—"

"Listen, Grady Hummacher left Panama and arrived back here at McCarran a week ago. Tickets were on the company; I know he used them. He came in Friday. I was out of town till Wednesday. I scheduled him for Thursday at one."

"He didn't show?"

"No call, no nothing."

"You didn't call him?" Guy like Adcock would be on the horn by one-fifteen.

"Of course I called him. Had my girl try him then, Friday morning and afternoon. I like Grady; I gave him the benefit of the doubt. Then I started to worry. Grady could have stopped off, had a couple drinks, made a wrong decision. . . ."

"Adcock, I know what kind of guy Grady is, what he'd do, things he'd rule out by reflex. The guy lived above me for a year. I can . . ." He forced himself to stop and take another breath. "But if you'd rather wait till Kiernan gets back tomorrow— No, tomorrow is Sunday. Give her till Monday morning to be back in the office—" He could hear Adcock's breath, a Niagara of its own.

"Yeah, fine, Churner—"

"Tchernak."

"Yeah. I wait two days, I might as well call the mortician. So, yeah, come. Go through his apartment, think like he thinks, see if you can come up with any lead. Grady's apartment's in my name. This is all legal. How soon can you get here?"

Tchernak glanced at his watch. He glanced around the studio he'd lived in for over a year, the first decent place he'd had since he left football, with the first job off the gridiron in which he felt like he was living again. He owed Kiernan a lot. He'd miss her, and—he leaned over and scratched the head of the big dog lying at his feet—he'd miss Ezra.

But it was her own fault, right? Right.

"I'll catch the ten o'clock flight and be at your office before noon." He broke the connection, paused, and dialed the woman who took Ezra in emergencies. There was no telling how long he'd be gone.

CHAPTER
7

THE AUTOPSY ROOM in the Constant Mortuary was suitable for its main purpose, embalming a body for a quick good-bye. On a scale of one to ten, San Francisco ranked about eight, the makeshift facility in Africa one, and this place about three. It didn't have a dirt floor, and Kiernan felt obliged to give it a point for that. But even the smaller county where she had worked as the forensic pathologist provided a room three times this size, with a fridge room double this, and the freezer where "long-term residents" were kept at ten degrees was as big as this space. Here there was one troughed gurney, one set of sinks, a fluorescent tube on the ceiling, and a rattling exhaust fan that would render the autopsy tape almost inaudible.

She shook out her mask, a plastic apparatus akin to a tent covering face and neck, pulled it and the gloves on, opened the fridge door, and hauled out the gurney. The dead woman lay ashen and half draped on the cold metal.

Unwillingly, Kiernan stepped back against the support of the wall. She wrapped her arms around her ribs as if that

could ward off the chill she felt. Ashes to ashes. Cold ashes
when the fire is dead.

She clasped her arms tighter, but the shaking wouldn't
stop. The cold. She pushed the gurney back in the fridge,
stepped into the hall, and ripped off her gear. She hadn't
felt like this in five years.

The dead woman was nothing like Hope Mkema. The
dead woman looked Hispanic; Hope had been African.
Here the winter air seemed to float in currents of its own
will, circling legs, icing neck, licking her spine. When she
had stood over Hope's body five years ago, in the brick-
and-tin hospital in Takema, the West African focal point of
the Lassa fever epidemic, her shirt had stuck clammily to
her back and sweat rolled so relentlessly down her forehead, she'd given up attempts to wipe it away. Hope
Mkema's skin had been a vibrant brown. She had had huge
elfin eyes, high cheekbones in a heart-shaped face, and a
wide smile so engaging people smiled back before words
were spoken.

The first time Kiernan saw her was at the clearing that
served as an airport for the brave. Hope was laughing then.
"I understand you are here in spite of the Church. Perhaps
I will take your place in Catholic heaven."

"Not too soon, I hope," Kiernan had said.

"I'd better not. My country can't afford to lose one of
its women doctors. We're a rare, if not delicate commodity." Her cadence suggested schooling in England. It was
only later that Kiernan learned how much the village, her
family, and Hope herself had mortgaged for her to become
a doctor.

Still smiling, Hope had led her to a vehicle that had
been rebuilt so often, it was no longer recognizable as a
specific make of car. "I won't ask how many hours you've
been in transit from India. When you wake up, we'll talk
about that." She hadn't asked and Kiernan hadn't told her

why an American doctor who had been fired from the coroner's office in northern California had gone to India nearly two years earlier, or what she had done before she volunteered at a clinic run by nuns in Maharashta. Or why, when word came of the need for doctors in the Lassa fever epidemic, she had volunteered to fly to West Africa. That day she had been too tired to formulate any answers, and later was thankful not to have to corral her muddled emotions into a manageable line of thought. And even now, years later, she couldn't have said exactly what drove her toward a project on which three of the ten workers had died. Perhaps after two years of wandering in a strange country trying to banish memories of a life that was no longer possible, the idea of doing something vital, all-encompassing, was worth the chance of the small loss of herself.

When she woke, Hope Mkema had been working. The hospital, a pale brick rectangle filled with moaning patients on pallets on the floor with their families settled around them for the duration, reminded Kiernan of the railway stations in India in which families had lived for generations. The doctors had had to fight to keep even a curtain as a *cordon sanitaire* between the regular sick and those bleeding to death from Lassa fever. Inside the curtain of death, as the patients called it, the scene was different. No comforting relatives offering food and chatter. Here patients' throats were too sore for water, spiking fevers banished thought, words were replaced with uncontrollable moans. Faces swelled to grotesque masks. Blood oozed everywhere, from gums, noses, eyes.

That was where Kiernan had come across Jeff Tremaine. She hadn't realized he was on the project, hadn't heard of him since she finished medical school. It took her a minute to place him, not just because he was here on the other side of the world but because he looked different,

older, and strangely alive in a way he had never been in
San Francisco.

"As soon as we get the shipment of ribavirin, we'll be in
good shape," he'd said in lieu of greeting.

Kiernan had looked down at the patient moaning on the
bed and known that that shipment would be too late.

Two weeks later the shipment was still behind the lines
of guerrillas fighting a hundred miles away.

Two weeks later she had taken blood from hundreds of
patients, readying the samples to see which of the feverish,
pain-racked sufferers showed antibodies to Lassa and
which fortunate ones had similar but nonlethal viruses.
The heat was so intense that the fans scalded, and the
water, boiled of necessity, never cooled below lukewarm.
At dusk the regular twelve-hour day would end, and only
emergencies would be treated in the precious light of the
generator. Staff members would retreat behind thick mosquito netting, and revive themselves on dinners of barbe-
cued goat and beer, if the refrigerator was working, or a
local wine as potent as it was foul. No amount of additives
masked the taste. It was destined to survive when all else
died out, and they anointed it Cockroach Vineyards Last
Squeeze.

At the end of her third week there, dusk had settled as
Kiernan finished the frustrating process of taking a complete history of a patient through an interpreter with
spotty English, checking for headache, muscle pain, sore
throat, bloodshot eyes, bleeding gums, then taking urine
and blood samples. The heat was like a leaden robe, making every movement a struggle. She deposited the samples
and washed up. The hospital was already in night mode.
Her mind was suspended between the case she'd just finished and the cold beer behind the mosquito netting.

"Doctor!" One of the nurses led her past the moaning
patients to an elderly, frail woman lying deadly still just

inside the main door. There were no frightened, ministering relatives as with most patients. There was no chance of taking a history; that would come later, if the woman survived. In the meantime fluid samples would have to do. Kiernan found a vein on the bone-thin arm, pulled up the blood. Just then the woman went into spasm, flailing arms and legs. The blood-filled needle flew into Kiernan's arm.

Kiernan yanked it out and flung it to the floor, but of course that made no difference. They all knew what needle pricks meant. They had all seen the progress of Lassa fever—it took no longer than a week and a half to kill its victims. It was Jeff Tremaine who sprang into action. He had raised every hospital in the country on the phone lines. He had gotten the missionary phone-radio circuit humming, and finally tracked down the one batch of ribavirin inside the rebel lines, then spent nearly two days driving to get it.

"We don't know that the blood I got in that needle prick is Lassa," Kiernan had insisted when he got back with the vital cargo. She had mouthed the words carefully, sure then that she didn't have a fever, was merely suffering from the extreme heat. "The old woman is sick all right. But we can't use our only dose of ribavirin for me when we don't know—"

"Kiernan, we have no choice." Jeff was already filling the hypodermic. "We don't use this, you may die. We wait, you may die."

"There are people in these wards we *know* have Lassa—"

"Look, this isn't a political issue, it's a practical one. If we let our outside volunteer doctors die, we're not going to get more doctors. Then plenty of local people are going to die because there are no doctors to care for them, no epidemiologists to trace their viruses, no hope of stopping the next epidemic before it spreads all along the trade route."

"But—"

"It's not your decision, Kiernan. It's mine."

She remembered Jeff Tremaine's face, neither sympathetic nor angry, merely exhausted. It was Hope Mkema, beside him, who had offered her wide smile, a hand on Kiernan's arm that reminded her she was still part of the team. Hope administered the shot. Kiernan let her eyes close and relaxed her vigil against the repugnant thought she had kept at bay for forty-eight hours: Even if there was only one dose of ribavirin, she wanted it. She had thought she was willing to die. But death had wrapped itself closer than her skin for two days and now it was all she could do to keep her terror at bay. The next day she lay too feverish to speak, her throat so raw each breath rasped flesh against flesh. And a week later, when her fever broke and she recovered enough to recognize people, she learned she had had an extreme fever that could have killed her, but it had not been Lassa. What saved her she never knew, but it had not been the ribavirin.

She realized they had exhausted the entire supply of ribavirin for her when she saw Hope Mkema. Hope was dying in the next room.

A nurse helped her to the foot of Hope's bed. She stood staring in disbelief at the fever sweat that glistened on Hope's skin, the blood that oozed so thickly, it turned her eyes to red patches. The pervasive moaning cut through the lines of educated and illiterate, doctors and patients, and reduced all sufferers to one. Hope's wavering cry carried away the white coat of protection "Doctor" had promised. The sound flowed from her lips, and it took with it all that she was or had been.

"It is not safe for you here," the nurse had said, moving her away from Hope Mkema's bed. "You are still weak."

No one told her when Hope died. But she heard outside in the town, a dull tapping on metal and wood, thudding from a thousand hands, wood against rough metal.

Hope Mkema's family, her neighbors and friends, hadn't blamed Kiernan, nor had they objected when a plane arrived unscheduled, allowing her to be airlifted out. She was too weak to travel alone, and it was Jeff Tremaine who was assigned to accompany her, as it turned out not merely to the coast but on a connecting flight back to Bombay.

And it was Jeff who told her that the dreams and fortune of the area had died with Hope Mkema when she was denied the ribavirin Kiernan hadn't needed. Odd, she had thought when she woke from exhausted sleep at intervals during the days of travel, what a personal affront death is to Westerners. If Jeff Tremaine could have sued God, he would have. Instead he turned his own guilt on her, and she made no move to deflect it. By the time he left her in a bare-bones hotel in Bombay, she knew that it was time to leave India and go home.

She would have answered this call of his out of gratitude, but she was sure he wouldn't understand that. He had expected her to come out of repentance.

But she had come out of dread.

CHAPTER

8

DR. LOUISA LARSON had made only one faux pas: Grady Hummacher's boys.

She circled her forefinger around a clump of shoulder-length blond hair, around and around, pulling the hairs harder each time, as if yanking her skin away from her skull would create an escape route for her misjudgments. She stared at the empty examination room in her Las Vegas clinic. She no longer noticed the soft ambers and greens of the desert prints she had chosen to be every bit as nice as those in the clinic across town that supported this one in the barrio. Just a month ago the surprised smiles on her patients' faces when they entered her welcoming office had made the cost worthwhile. And she wouldn't have wasted half a month on some distant beach anyway, not when her patients needed her and she had a practice to build. And a community to make her mark in.

After med school a public health guy had talked up applying to a research project in Boston. "Vital, important work," he had insisted. "A lot of driven types get into it. But they could really use a woman like you, near the top of your class, but also diplomatic. You, Louisa, you sweep people off their feet"—she couldn't help smiling at that—"and right into your pocket where you wanted them all along." She had turned him down flat, said *You Bet Your Life* was not a game she chose to play. But the truth was the guy had made her feel as if he'd cracked her skull open and exposed her mind to the world. She was not about to go to work somewhere where people labeled what she did—focusing on her work and getting everyone else enthusiastic about it—manipulation. She'd worked her tail off in med school. She had no life outside her career. All those years had given her a good view of the failures of medicine, and she damn well planned to be in a position to make changes. You can climb to the top in spite of your competitors, but it's so much quicker if you can make them see the sense in giving you a leg up. If the research recruiter called that manipulation, then it was no wonder his establishment needed a woman everyone liked.

Manipulation was what Grady Hummacher had done to her. She had never meant him to be more than a diversion. With Grady all the doors were open and there was a prize behind every one. So what if it was all mirage; she didn't have time for more than that. A delicious diversion, to be dipped into totally, then shaken off, was exactly what she needed.

And then he'd shown up with the boys. "They're tabulae rasae," he'd said as if he'd known the perfect bait. "They've never heard a sound. They don't even have a concept of what language is. They'd be 'backroom boys,' if their tribe had lived in more than one-room huts." Grady had stood right here in this examining room, his wiry hair bleached almost white against his tanned face, his elbows barely bent to rest his hands on the boys' shoulders. Next to Grady's tough body, his let's-try-it expression, the boys looked like third-graders, scared, fascinated, exhausted, amazed. Carlos and Juan, Grady called them, though, of course, he could have called them anything. What he did know, Grady insisted, was that Juan and Carlos had no future in the Panamanian rain forest. Their only chance was with her help in the United States. With her standing in the medical community—everyone liked her—she could get the boys the best diagnosticians, surgeons, specialists, therapists. She could change their lives. She could *give* them lives.

She was intrigued by the challenge, the unlimited possibilities. She was hooked. What she hadn't factored in was coming to care about them. But it was impossible not to.

Juan was such a sparkler. His eyes were never still, always watching. Was he thinking like we do, she had wondered. Without words was there a mechanism to classify, speculate on experiences, on what other people did? When she got him a sign-language tutor, she would ask him. Could he really go from no concept of words as symbols of things, movements, feelings to philosophical inquiry? Some would say, "Impossible." But if you limit your goals, you get limited results, and she always looked to the top, for her practice, for herself, and for Juan. She noted Juan's delight at the refrigerator, and how he couldn't wait to bring Carlos there and let him play with the door within the door. His face had lit up when he saw the photos of Central America in the coffee table book that had pride of place in the little barrio apartment Grady had set them up in. Homesick, poor kid. Then she had remembered—the Breadfruit Park, as people had labeled the place. It had tropical foliage, as close to the feel of the Panamanian rain forest as they'd find in Nevada. She had gotten Grady a pass and was delighted that he took the boys there—and gave her a day free of them.

Grady had already flown back to Panama the first time when she realized that looking in on the boys, as she'd agreed to, meant more than the occasional ten-minute visit. It was shopping for them, cleaning for them, and cleaning up after them in the case of the first stove fire. After that it was either overseeing the cooking, cooking for them, or arranging for some kind of takeout that they might or might not find too foreign to eat.

And then they got sick! She ran every test. Checked every source. But she was flying blind with them. Poor kids couldn't even tell her where it hurt. In desperation she had brought them here to the clinic, where she never kept overnight patients, slept on the waiting-room couch, and watched over them like a mother. She had monitored their condition, kept records worthy of the CDC. Maybe she should have taken them to Children's, but what kind of care would they get there, on an overcrowded ward? Two boys who couldn't speak, couldn't understand? She would spend more time there answering questions than she'd spent caring for the two of them here. Why didn't you bring them sooner? Couldn't you see the danger of contagion in an impoverished, overcrowded neighborhood? What kind of doctor . . . ?

She'd never meant to leave them alone. Never would have for anything less than the call from Anne Barrington, already in labor. You don't tell the governor's niece to make do with an intern because you can't get a baby-sitter. The delivery should have taken an hour, not four. She was worried when she drove back here. But she never dreamed the boys would be gone. No way they could have walked out of the clinic with their killer fevers, and the bleeding through the skin. Grady, of course, had taken them. That became real clear when she picked up the police message about the break-in. She could have sicced the cops on Grady. But there'd be so many questions. What kind of doctor . . . ?

And if they were contagious . . .

And now at five-thirty in the morning they were gone. Grady Hummacher could have taken them anywhere. Beyond her help. Two-legged time bombs.

KIERNAN ADJUSTED HER mask, stepped back into the autopsy room, and pulled out the gurney. The woman's face and neck were swollen grotesquely, the edema almost obliterating her features. The skin had torn from the pressure in two places. Postmortem tearing, thank God.

"Kiernan?" a male voice asked.

Kiernan turned, shocked to realize she had been so engulfed in the procedure. Jeff Tremaine eyed her questioningly. She said, "I didn't hear you come in."

His pale lips twitched nervously, but he said nothing more. She remembered that about him, the silences. Physically, the last five years had been hard on him. The once athletically lanky torso now seemed gaunt and already past the flexibility of youth. His sandy hair was thinner, shorter, now. His face was weathered rather than lined, the blue eyes she recalled glistening in the African night now were dull, his shoulders stooped from years of bending over the sick. It struck her again, as it had on the plane out of Africa, that Jeff Tremaine seemed to be a different man each time she met him.

The bulky mask hung from his hand, but he made no move to put it on. He nodded toward the body. "It's overwhelming." He paused before turning his gaze toward her. "I knew *you* would understand."

Understand his fear? "Any doctor who's seen the effects of arenavirus would get it. You didn't have to drag me here."

"I had to know before I reported it. I needed a second opinion. If this is akin to Lassa fever, or Bolivian Junin, or Machupo from Panama, I need to know."

"No," she snapped, "you need to be on the horn to the health department and CDC in Atlanta. You should have done that before you called me. What's stopping you?"

"Look at her. What do you see? Not the effects of disease, but the person. She looks Hispanic. Maybe she's an immigrant, maybe illegal. Doesn't matter, though, does it? If word gets out that there's a threat of epidemic, from her, the government's going to be breathing down the neck of every immigrant, legal or not. You're from California, Kiernan, you should know that."

"I do know, Jeff," she said, just short of snapping at him. How could she have forgotten the righteous little whine to this voice? She'd heard it long enough on the plane to Bombay. "I've seen the results. When going to the clinic means you may be deported, people don't go. We—the government—are asking for disease to go untreated. The state is turning the barrios into petri dishes." She looked back at the swollen corpse. "Nevertheless, Jeff, I am not about to open up a body when I have no idea what's inside."

He grabbed her shoulder. "We have to know! If I could do the autopsy, I would. I need you."

She detached his hand. It was shaking. "If you could? We all did postmortems in Africa. You were there way longer than I. Surely you've done—"

"Not since Hope. Not on a body like this. I . . . couldn't." He turned to the sink and shoved the faucet full on. Water sprayed onto the wall, the floor, and she could see the fabric of his sleeves darkening with it.

"Okay," she said softly. "Let's do a visual. We've both seen enough cases of Lassa." She covered over the tray of clamps and scalpels, picked up the microphone, and handed it to him. "You start. And use your mask and gloves, unless you know something I don't."

Her gaze dropped to his hand, and it was clear from his startled expression he had forgotten he was holding the mask.

She watched as he settled the mask in place and fumbled with the gloves as if he hadn't pulled their like on and off a thousand times. Was it just nerves?

He said, "Well-nourished female adult, looks to be in her twenties. Olive skin, black hair, eyes—"

Kiernan leaned over the woman's face. Her mask was old and meant to be worn with a breathing tube. Already the visor was beginning to fog. She wouldn't have much time. Squinting into the face of the dead woman, she said, "Petechia evident in the eyes. There's so much blood, it's hard to see the color of the iris. The sclera is almost totally covered; barely a bit of white visible." She held a magnifying glass nearer to the skin. "Evidence of petechia in the skin too. Some cyanosis evident at the mouth."

She could hear Tremaine interspersing her observations with his own—"One hundred twenty pounds. Evidence of extreme edema in the face and neck. Facial features distorted by edema"—but his voice began to blend with the rumble of the ancient fan. She lifted the woman's arm. Stiff. The jaw, too, was locked. "Rigor still in effect. Jeff, when did you discover her?"

"Just before I called you."

"Here? In the morgue?"

"Yeah."

She braced her hands on the edge of the gurney and looked directly at Tremaine. "Are you telling me someone walked in off the street and dumped this corpse here and no one in town noticed?"

"Not off the street."

"What, then, through the roof? Come on, Jeff, stop beating around the bush."

He smacked down the tape recorder. "It's not a complicated concept. Out back"—he was speaking as if to a recalcitrant child—"there is an alley. The morgue has a back entry. That's where the deliveries are made . . . because . . . Kiernan . . . citizens on their way to the cafe don't find it appetizing to see dead bodies being carted across the sidewalk."

Her hand went to her mask, and she had to stop herself from pulling it off and striding out the door. "Hey, I'm here as a favor. You can answer my questions civilly or find yourself a more accommodating friend. Got it?"

He started to speak, reconsidered, and stood, pale lips quivering.

"Got it?" Her hand was still on the mask.

He grunted and she decided to accept that as a yes.

"How did this stranger get in?"

"Door's open. Morgue gets deliveries at odd times. Mortician doesn't want to be running back in the middle of lunch to unlock the door. Or be pulled away from a funeral to do it. It's easier to leave the door open." Before she could question that, he added, "This isn't San Francisco, you know. People don't steal everything that's not nailed down." He shot a glance at her face and added more conciliatorily, "The formaldehyde and the instruments and such are in locked cabinets."

"What did the mortician say?"

"Didn't know anything about it."

"And you believe him?"

"Yeah. He's too old to be involved in much more than getting out of bed in the morning."

Crime or no, it seemed like a slapdash system. "What was the deceased wearing?"

"Over there."

The pile was small. Navy blue walking shorts, white cotton cap-sleeved blouse embroidered with flowers, white cotton panties, runner's bra, white socks, and running shoes. "Jeez, what were you thinking? If she's an illegal immigrant, she's assimilated real quick."

"The blouse—"

"Sure, it's one you associate with Mexico, or with *vacations* in Mexico, or with import stores. But nylon hip-hugger underpants and a sports bra? And running shoes? This is a couple hundred dollars' of clothes. What's going on here?" She did a quick sweep of the body, her gaze coming to rest on the woman's feet. The leg was still stiff and she had to bend to see the heel. "This is not a woman used to walking barefoot, or probably even in sandals. Look at her heel; it's almost smooth. That's a heel that's been protected and cared for. And her toenails. See the pale peach nail polish? What you have here is a woman who cared about her appearance and had the time to—"

"What about her fingernails, though? They're a mess."

"Hmm. Same color polish, heavily chipped; encrusted with dirt or maybe blood. Chances are she had a bad couple of days."

"But the toes—"

"Jeff, if a woman wears shoes and stockings, toenail polish lasts forever. If nails were soldiers, toes would be the generals sipping bourbon in the Pentagon, and fingers the draftees in the trenches."

"Strange." He was looking at the corpse, but his focus was blurry.

Kiernan wished she had known him well enough to guess what was behind those eyes. Was he truly baffled or was he mixing her observation with data he had no intention of sharing? "So what brought this unknown woman in here dead?"

His mask had begun to fog, too, and Kiernan couldn't make out his expression as he said, "Maybe my past. Or because I'm the only one who would take a stand."

"But you didn't take a stand, did you?"

"I got you here."

KIERNAN STARED DOWN at the dead woman's grotesquely swollen face. Blood had seeped through her pores, out over her eyes. The neck was still stiff, and Kiernan had to bend to peer through the magnifying glass into the ears. "Looks like petechia there too."

"That's what I thought."

"Was rigor set when you examined her? Could you still get her mouth open?"

"Oh, yes." It was a moment before Tremaine continued, his voice shaky. "Throat's almost closed. You remember in Africa talking about raw hamburger, how the Africans were so fascinated by the picture of cellophaned package after package on the open freezer shelf that they lost the point?"

"The point that the patient's throat looked like hamburger? Are you saying this woman's throat's that bad?"

"All esophageal definition is gone."

Kiernan tilted her head so that she could see into the nose. "Oh, God, poor woman. The edema in the sides of the nose is so extreme, her nose is swollen shut." It all fit with hemorrhagic fever. If that conclusion held, beneath the skin every organ would be a wreck, jammed with platelets, fluids, dead cells, droplets of fat. Her heart would be clogged with platelets that the body had produced in one last desperate effort against the overwhelming forces of the virus. Platelets would be backed up into the arteries and veins. Lungs would be so jammed with fluid, death could have been from asphyxia. Liver, spleen, kidneys would look like plum aspic. "It's got all the markers of hemorrhagic fever. But the nose! I've never seen anything that bad. It's not a condition Lassa patients present."

"So, you think this is not Lassa?"

"I don't know what it is. It could be Lassa with a new symptom. Or, and here's the really frightening possibility, that the nasal sensitivity could be connected to airborne transmission."

Jeff swayed back against the cabinet, his buttocks coming to rest on the edge. He was staring at the dead woman, but Kiernan could tell his attention was within himself, asking the same questions she had after the needle prick in Africa: Am I coming down with this woman's fever or is it just hot in here? Or is it nerves? And that itch in my throat, is it the first indicator of my throat closing? By tomorrow will my eyes be bleeding and my face swollen beyond recognition? When I die—"Jeff, you treated hundreds of cases of Lassa and other fevers in Africa and you're still alive. In all your time there you must have let down your guard, been too tired to wash up properly, too rushed to bother with a mask, right? You may be one of the nonsusceptibles. Whatever, you don't look sick to me."

"I'm not!" Which could be translated as "Leave me alone."

"Surely you've thought where the dead woman might have come from—"

"Of course," he snapped. "My guess—it's not going to

do any good—there's a woman, up in the hills. She runs a safe house. Mostly for prostitutes on the run. They get stranded in brothels—trailers—in the middle of nowhere, and they're no more than slaves. Word is she takes gamblers, too, in over their heads. Guys on the run from the law or the mob. This close to Vegas she could do a booming business. Vegas is built on dreams, and there are plenty of nightmares to go around."

"So you think she was protecting this woman and dropped her off when she got too sick?"

"Yeah, I think. But, makes no difference. I've got no idea where that safe house is. No one does. She's been running it for twenty years. She wouldn't have lasted one minute if she let out word how to find her."

"How do the ones who need her find her, then?"

"Grapevine of need." Tremaine shrugged.

She straightened up. "Jeff, this is a waste of time. Without lab work we're not going to know whether this is Lassa, Junin, or some new virus, or something else."

"I don't want—"

"You're a doctor, you have to report this. You don't have a choice."

"I didn't have a choice with Hope. There was no choice left."

Kiernan's breath caught. She'd heard it before, but the words still cut through her mask, the protective clinical setting, her skin.

"I sat with her, Kiernan, every day as her fever soared, as her throat closed. I was there when her fever spiked, and no amount of ice made any difference. I dabbed a local on her throat, trying not to touch her flesh because it was so painful, trying to anesthetize her throat enough to let her swallow water. I held her hands when she couldn't stop the shaking. She was a doctor, Kiernan. She'd watched her people bleed out and die. She knew what was coming." He swallowed hard, but it didn't clear his thick voice. "I lied to her then, but I'm such a lousy liar. She wanted to believe me, but she couldn't." He swallowed again harder and turned directly toward Kiernan. "Do you know the last thing she said? She could barely get the words out. Each one was agony. I was so afraid I wouldn't understand, her voice was so thick. She said, 'Jeff, when I'm dead, don't kiss me.' "

She glanced around the makeshift morgue, through the window that led to nothing but an air shaft between buildings, at the door—looking anywhere but at Jeff Tremaine. She couldn't believe that sharp, lively Hope Mkema could have been involved with . . . him. On the plane ride back to India with her, he must have hinted at it; all those hours he had talked of nothing but Hope. But she'd never imagined them as lovers. What could Hope Mkema, whom she'd liked so much, have seen in Jeff Tremaine?

Or had Jeff dreamed the whole thing? She could imagine him settling into this drab life sparked only by hidden mourning for a dead love from the other side of the world.

Now, five years later, did the truth make any difference? To his wife, it would. "Does your wife know about Hope?"

"No. I never mentioned Hope to her at all. There was no point. I loved Hope so." The words gushed out. "Every moment with her was exciting. Everything was bright, fresh, alive, important, possible. She was a miracle that comes once in a lifetime. She came and was gone. It sounds trite to say, but when I was with her, I was alive in a way so different that it was like I had been dead before. And after." A shiver electrified his body. "What kind of jerk would come back and tell that to his wife? Since I left you in Bombay, I have never spoken Hope Mkema's name."

She reached toward him to put a comforting hand on

his arm but caught herself before she touched him with her gloves. Jeff gave no indication of noticing.

"I've 'seen' her every day. I've thought about what we might have had so often, it's as if that life exists." He snapped his head to the side. "It's a self-obsessed, maudlin, stupid indulgence. Easier out here where the highway is narrow and the side roads few, as they say. But that's no excuse. I'm sorry, really sorry, Kiernan."

Kiernan let a moment pass and then pulled open the freezer door and signaled Jeff to push the gurney in.

"Hey, what are you doing?" His hands were on the gurney, but he wasn't moving it. He was leaning on it, his eyes unfocused, mouth half opened but not speaking.

"Jeff, pull yourself together. What we've got here is possibly the beginning of an epidemic worse than anything either of us has seen. We won't know for sure till there are lab tests. This woman could be the index case of a hemor-rhagic fever that could wipe out half of Nevada."

"Take her to Vegas. You could leave her at the coroner's department there, and catch your flight. Kiernan, please."

She stared at him. "You want me to put a highly conta-gious corpse in a rental car with me and drive her through the desert for three hours? Should I strap her in the pas-senger's seat so the microbes don't have too far to travel to me?" Had Jeff Tremaine lost it entirely over this case? He had had spurts of irrationality in Africa, but this was way beyond that. "Jeff, don't dig yourself in any deeper than you already are. Nothing you can do about this anonymous woman is going to bring Hope Mkema back from the dead. And I'll tell you what you ought to know already: Nobody's going to thank you for finding this case.

"I'm taking off my gloves, then I'm calling the health department. They've got to get this woman in a Level Four room and—"

He turned back to the gurney and stood as he had been

before she spoke, hands braced on the rim. She couldn't tell from his blank gaze if he was staring at the corpse, the picture of Hope Mkema framed inside his head, or the awful possibilities in the near future. Finally he nodded toward the freezer door, waited for her to open it, and slid the gurney inside. "Of course you're right, Kiernan. I don't know what I was thinking. I've got a buddy in the health department—Wilson Brede, you know him? I'll call him."

"I'll use the bathroom while you call."

"Last door on the left."

She forced herself to wash with scrupulous care, begrudging each moment it kept her in the tiny gray room. The rental car, which had seemed tiny and slow, dull and awkward, compared with her Jeep Cherokee in her driveway and her TR-3 in the garage, now beckoned like a Maserati on the fast road to freedom.

"Did you get him?" she asked as she walked back into the morgue.

"Yeah. He's on his way." Tremaine rolled the gurney back into the freezer. "Kiernan, listen, I really appreciate your coming. I know this sent me over the edge, and I asked a lot of you. But listen, I did not mention your name to Wilson. No need for you to be held up."

Kiernan nodded. "Thanks. I have a five o'clock plane." She didn't offer her hand to shake, and Tremaine made no move toward her.

The rental car coughed. She should have warmed the engine. She let it cough its way to the highway. Better to call AAA from the side of the road than spend another minute in Gattozzi.

She tried her cell phone, but it was out of range. Radio stations grew and faded, and it wasn't till she'd been on the road an hour that she got a news magazine on a station out of Las Vegas, reporting on Las Vegas. She'd had enough of

Las Vegas and its surroundings. She put the radio on Scan, but nothing else came in. There was a time for the comfort of silence, but this wasn't it. Her consciousness was flooding with visions of people dying from symptoms worse than Lassa, more violently than from Ebola, and she needed the sounds of normality just so she could keep focusing on the road. She listened to the reports of phenomenal growth on the Las Vegas Strip, of large casino hotels being demolished to be replaced by even larger ones, of gaudy facades giving way to mini theme parks. The Hacienda's eleven hundred rooms had bitten the dust—literally—to be replaced by Circus Circus Enterprises's four thousand. The MGM Grand, Harrah's, and Circus Circus were metamorphosing into dreamscapes more unescapable. Thirty thousand rooms in all had been added. And more were planned. A whole new gambling city on a manmade lake was in the works. "Success here builds on itself. As long as the excitement keeps up, the city'll keep booming, and construction will keep constructing. Over seven billion dollars have been spent already. So, folks, keep those quarters dropping in the slots. The city's counting on you."

Kiernan pressed down on the accelerator. If Tchernak was here, she thought, he'd be seeing highway patrol cars behind every hillock, cocking his neck to check for traffic spotters in the sky. She smiled. And she'd be saying, "Do you really think the Nevada Highway Patrol is going to pull me over when I'm heading *to* Las Vegas? I don't think so. They're not going to settle for a fifty- or sixty-buck ticket and keep me from an hour's fleecing at the craps table."

Rounding a curve, she came into a wide plateau. Maybe the emptiness would save them here in Nevada. Maybe the dead woman had not been in contact with anyone, except the person who brought her to Jeff Tremaine. Maybe that person . . . Maybe. Maybe. Maybe whatever she had was not contagious at all. Maybe a hundred other Nevadans were just beginning to feel feverish. Maybe one of them was driving to Las Vegas, heading for a plane to L.A. or Chicago.

In the midst of awful possibilities she felt a rush of pity for Jeff Tremaine. He had loved Hope Mkema and she had died, and now this. The dead woman in Gattozzi could be the index case of an epidemic, and Jeff Tremaine would be the index doctor. Once the woman's body was dumped on Jeff Tremaine, he might as well have climbed onto the gurney with her. She knew that, and once he thought about it, Jeff would realize it too. Could she count on Jeff reporting the body?

She wouldn't of course. "Never count on anyone" was a rule she'd mastered early. And with this case she wouldn't have trusted Mother Teresa. As soon as she got to the airport, she'd call the health department herself.

BRAD TCHERNAK STOOD on the second-story landing outside Grady Hummacher's door. His first search. Every time Kiernan came bursting into the duplex at home, high from penetrating some guy's space, Tchernak felt like he'd been sidelined in a play-off game. Kiernan liked searches, but she loved breaking and entering. She was his quarter-back, she kept reminding him, and he was just waiting till she was thrown out of the game. Or carried off. And when she told him in indecent detail how she'd stood stock-still in the dark beside the door listening to voices outside, footsteps on the stairs, herself ready to bolt out the door if the intruder didn't spot her first, he remembered the time both safeties split the line and smacked his quarterback into the AstroTurf so hard, the guy was out cold for an eternity. He hated her being out there alone. With her it was a toss-up which were more of a threat—cops or crooks. Cops had some standards, but the woman had such an attitude and big mouth that she'd taunted them into locking her up more than once. "No taunting, no speed-ing, no defenestration!"—how many times had he told her that? Simple little aphorism that even the smallest detective could remember.

For all the good that did. Sometimes he wondered if all it did was goad her into hitting ninety miles an hour so she could get home quicker to thumb her nose at him.

One night, over a pitcher of margaritas, she had described the seductive allure of penetration. She'd detailed the foreplay, feeling the lock as she slipped in the celluloid strip. . . . And now Grady Hummacher's apartment stood in front of him, needing no foreplay at all, ready to open up like a flasher's raincoat and expose Grady's secrets.

Right, just what I need: ROOKIE DETECTIVE PICKED UP WET-DREAMING ON PORCH. But Tchernak couldn't restrain a grin as he grabbed the key Reston Adcock had given him and stuck it in the lock.

Grady Hummacher's place—four rooms over a double garage and storage area—was the smallest unit in this upscale suite for the upscale single moving in or out of the nation's fastest-growing city.

Tchernak's first reaction to the living room was that it didn't seem like Grady's place. Of course it wasn't, any more than it was Tom's place, or Dick's or Harry's, or whoever else had sprawled on the off-white leather couch or eaten cereal on the pale oak table. The rumpled newspapers on the floor, now that was more Grady's style. And the kitchen cabinet doors, none of them closed. That took some doing even for Grady. In the dorm twenty-one-year-old Grady had been a man of experience to the seventeen-year-old freshmen. Or a man of experiences. Before the first term was out, Grady had led his freshmen charges in a guerrilla war against Tasman Hall across the quad. He'd turned them on to underage bars, willing women, and a crazy car track with an amateur's night. To the frosh he'd been a god, to the administration a disaster. His room reflected his life.

Tchernak moved to the middle of the room and eyed the 360 degrees of beige. The place must cost a bundle, but that just showed that the furnishings of transience come in all economic levels. It would have been depressing to someone without Grady's skill in overlooking what he didn't want to see. In the dorm he'd ignored mail, shirts, slacks that needed a trip to the laundry room, and half-empty food wrappers that drove the guys next to him crazy, and finally the ants. Mere bland wouldn't have fazed Grady Hummacher. He would be in and out too fast to care. His mind would be on skiing, rock climbing, women, and getting back to where the action was.

That's what he knew about Grady Hummacher. He had assured Adcock that his insight into Grady would make up for being a babe-in-the-woods private eye. Well, that bit of knowledge was not going to make this no-thought apartment tell him Grady's secrets. You check the bedroom, the bathroom, the phone pad, the computer, Kiernan had once said when he'd asked about starting a search. See if you can tell when the subject was last here.

He moved quickly into the bedroom, the thick tan carpet nearly trampolining him. It had been over ten years since he'd seen Grady for more than a quick drink when he ran into him at McCarran Airport last month, but if the guy had changed, nothing of it manifested in this room. Grady was in his mid thirties now, but the room screamed "teenager." The bed was a whirl of sheets and blankets. It looked as if it had been made—this type of place had to have maid service—but Grady had managed to rumple and crunch the covers as much as a guy could without actually getting beneath them. Had he napped on top, stirred up the covers as he unloaded his gear, or had a lady on call as he deplaned?

Tchernak grinned. Grady was good, but he doubted he was that good. No, more likely Adcock's fear was right. Grady had picked up some bug in Panama and he'd grabbed a catnap before heading out to—wherever.

The dresser drawers were closed. Tchernak grinned as he pulled one open and confirmed his suspicion. Nothing in them. Closet: empty.

On the floor on the far side of the bed he found a backpack/suitcase half disemboweled. He could "see" Grady hunting for something on the bottom, yanking a yellow polo shirt half out, leaving it hanging like a pine-apple leaf as his hand dove in again. Tchernak nodded at the garment bag, unopened on a chair, the LAS tag for McCarran Airport still on the handle. Dated Friday, eight days ago.

Eight days, a long time to put off unpacking, even for Grady.

Tchernak moved into the bathroom. Towels were in a wad on the floor. So Grady'd come from the airport, taken a shower. His shaving kit was open, but his toothbrush wasn't visible. If he had used it, it would still be on the sink. Tchernak smiled again, recalling a guy on Grady's hall saying that Grady's gear—suitcases, shaving kit—were like archeological digs. You didn't need carbon dating for any one of Grady's belongings, you just needed to see how far down it was. The toothbrush was not part of most recent civilization.

But if he'd tossed around on the bed, dragged himself up, and taken a shower, he'd have brushed his teeth. Even Grady. And the maid would have straightened the bed. So—Logical Conclusion Number One—Grady was here since the maid was. Even if she came only once a week, that meant Grady had left here Monday night at the earliest.

Left with what? Did the guy have another set of suit-

cases standing ready for a second trip? Tchernak picked up
the duffel, emptied it onto the floor, and grunted in irritation. Nothing he couldn't have guessed. Clothes so wadded and dirty, they stank. Now he recalled the smell of
Grady Hummacher's college room. He dug around the
inside of the bag, feeling for a pocket that might hold
Grady's passport. Tchernak couldn't imagine Grady walking across the street without a passport, still. . . . But
there were no pockets, nothing left in the duffel but a
folded newspaper. A Spanish newspaper. The Ciudad de
Panama Something or Other. Damn, now he knew why he
should have taken a foreign language in school. There was
some reason Grady saved this paper. Tchernak stared at it
as if force of will would translate the words. City of Panama. Panama City. Something something. Novembre 12.
November twelfth. Twelfth? Today was the fifteenth.
Grady got home Friday, November seventh. What was he
doing with Wednesday the twelfth's newspaper from Panama City? Was there some Las Vegas outlet?

"Leave no trace," Kiernan had said. The hell to that.
Tchernak yanked out the bed-table drawers, the dresser
drawers, the desk drawers. Empty, empty, empty. Dammit,
the guy had to have left some hint of himself here.
Tchernak moved to the kitchen and attacked the drawers.
It was in the living room by the computer he found the
repository of scraps of paper, sales slips with the business
name too pale to read, note from the landlord about re-
roofing, and—*voilà*—a receipt from a Panama City hotel
dated November twelfth.

Suddenly the air seemed close, stale. Whatever Grady
was up to with this trip to Panama between his official U.S.
return Friday the seventh and whenever he got back the
last time, it left him too rushed or preoccupied to open any
windows here. Nevadans, trained on the desert heat of
summer, might leave their windows closed in November,

but Grady was an outdoor guy. Tchernak nodded to himself, recalling Grady on a flight to Phoenix one June (Grady'd gotten a deal on the flight and the use of a guy's grandmother's condo for five of them). Even back then before Grady got hooked on the wilds, he spent the whole flight griping about the canned aircraft air. And when he'd gotten to the condo in the middle of the desert, he'd shoved those windows open wide, let in the 100-plus-degree air, and laughed when the guy's grandmother screamed so loud long-distance she didn't need a phone.

Grady must have been in one big hurry to race past the closed windows here. Big hurry or big fog. Whichever, he'd moved out fast.

Out where? Tchernak checked the bedside table. No pad. Adcock said Grady had no messages at the service but the ones Adcock had left him himself.

Now what? If Kiernan were here, she'd check the computer. Adcock had given him Grady's business card with phone, fax, password, and e-mail address. He checked the computer. God, he loved this. He was doing it, checking out the apartment, grazing through Grady's files, all of it better than she'd do herself! He was doing it, all right, but he wasn't coming up with much. No personal files. He checked the icons on the toolbar, clicked on Grady's provider, and typed his password. The man had no e-mail. Shit, Grady probably never hit the Power button at all. The computer must be one of those "business conveniences" these types of places advertised.

But as long as he was on-line, why not get Persis, the woman-wonder at BakDat, started on the background check. Another thing Smug Woman who thought she could do without help was going to miss. Let her try and get Persis to drop everything. Picturing Kiernan glaring at the empty screen, grabbing the phone to chew out Persis, slamming down the phone and calling for him, he typed a request for background on Grady. The image of his frustrated former employer was still in his mind as he poised to push Send. "Trust no one" was Kiernan's aphorism. She wouldn't overlook Adcock, not as righteous as she had been about the guy. She'd see what Persis could turn up on Adcock Explorations. And airline flights from Panama City to Las Vegas, November twelfth. He typed and sent.

He checked the desk for notes. No notes. Not even a Grady-style mess there.

Damn, there had to be more. He didn't have anything! Kiernan would never let herself come away empty. He'd been through the whole place. What else would she do? "Think like he does," she would say. Well, that was one thing he should be able to do.

Tchernak sat on Grady's desk chair staring at the blank computer. He couldn't imagine Grady leashed to an indoor machine like this. Grady, always up for anything. Even last month, when he'd smacked into him at the airport here, he himself changing planes and Grady on his way back to Panama, Grady had seemed to have so many irons on the fire he couldn't get close enough to keep warm. Grady was so unchanged, it had taken Tchernak a while to realize that more than a decade had passed since their college year together. He was happy to see the guy, but mostly, he realized, he was relieved. He'd never have let himself think of a broken neck, a crushed back, unworking limbs when he was still in football. Then he was as untouchable as the guys who swore God was rooting for the team, and as a corollary protecting them. But when his disks ruptured, he understood that life was fragile and that no higher power was taking time off from running the universe to worry about his back. Then, when he thought of Grady Hummacher, who had already flipped his car, totaled a hog, and was talking skydiving, he pictured crutches, cervical collar, and back brace.

There had been time for only one drink in the sports
bar that afternoon. The place had been mobbed, the semi-
circular bar two-deep in sports fans frantic to see the last
possible play before racing for their gate. Carry-on luggage was crammed between their feet, duffel bags poked
out behind them, roll-aboards, held loosely by handles,
fanned out at oblique angles. Grady had sat at the tiny
table near the wall, pushing the plastic menu board around
the ashtray. What had he said about his job? Tchernak
squinted his eyes shut trying to bring up the film. Grady
sitting there, grinning, his pale eyes suddenly framed by a
myriad of tiny wrinkles and for the first time his years in
the sun and wind betraying his age. Grady put down his
beer, hands cupped around the glass, and leaned in toward
him. "Bet you figured I'd be walking with a cane now,
huh?"

Was Grady reading his mind? He'd shrugged away the
question. "What happened? When you left school, you
were all hot about skydiving."

"Broke my ankle on the first dive and had a few weeks
hobbling around to think. So, I took advice, my parents',
my doctor's, the minister's, my girlfriend-of-the-mo-
ment's—it was all the same."

"You were more careful?"

"Hell no. I went back to school. I'm a geologist now.
Hunting oil down in Darien Gap."

"Where the Pan-American Highway ends?"

"Ends going south. Begins again on the other side of
the rain forest," he'd said. And somehow he'd gotten onto
complaining about his latest girlfriend ragging him about
tearing up the rain forest. "Former girlfriend." Grady
grinned then shrugged it off. "She doesn't get it yet. It's
going to take a couple more of those miserable 'we have to
talks' before it gets through to her."

What was her name? Lesley? No. Linda? Lucille? No.

Damn. Grady'd said her name, but it was gone now. He couldn't remember it because, because . . . because he was thinking there was something odd about what Grady was saying. He remembered now, the staccato bursts of noise from the television kept breaking Grady's train of thought. Grady'd jerked toward it every time the announcer got excited or the crowd cheered. "You a Broncos fan?" Tchernak had asked.

"Nah. I'm gone too much to keep up with sports or much of anything here."

"Be glad to get back to Panama, then? Think you might just stay down there awhile?"

"Thought about it. Lots of things to like down there. Living's good if you're not in the camp. And the hunt, well . . ." He had leaned forward, and lowered his voice. Tchernak recalled biting back the urge to say, "Do you really think people are more interested in you than the game?" Grady had paused a moment, then grinned and said, "Oil exploration is ninety percent hype. I tell them I've got a sixth sense, a nose for oil, a rare ability to read the sediment. But here's the truth, Tchernak, what I read is the local people. I spot the guy who's nosed out the oil. Sometimes it takes me months, but I always find the real explorers. Then I follow them. It's that simple. Oh, my experience, my background in geology helps, but it's the locals who're key." He shrugged. "But now I've got responsibilities up here."

"Didn't you ask what those responsibilities were?" Kiernan would demand. Well, no. Grady didn't seem eager to talk about them, and God knows, he himself didn't want to hear about them. They'd sat, awkwardly silent, he suddenly swilling the watery beer, the familiar salt and grease of airport eateries smelling stronger, more cloying, till he could "feel" it on the glass and the table. And then the

Broncos scored and they could talk sports until it was time for Grady's plane.

What had struck him so strange, then? He squeezed his eyes tighter, trying to run the film back, to pause at that moment before he got caught up trying to avoid having to hear about Grady's problem with his girlfriend. The girlfriend. Footloose Grady signing on for three more maudlin evenings. Wasn't like the guy couldn't get laid somewhere else. Women loved Grady's little-boy bravado. Grady was only five-six, and still, when he went out with the football guys, it was little Grady who ended up with the girl. And here, hell, this was Nevada, any guy could get it here. So, why did Grady care about her? No, not the right question. Unless Grady had changed completely, the question was, What did he want from her?

Tchernak smiled. Grady had local responsibilities. And he was gone a lot. Bingo. He didn't have to have Grady here to ask who was looking after those local responsibilities in his absence. What *was* her name? But now that name might as well have been three civilizations down at the bottom of Grady's suitcase.

Dead end. For the time being.

He opened his eyes and stared at the dull gray screen. What else would Kiernan do? How would she find out what those responsibilities of Grady's were? Bills?

Three minutes later Brad Tchernak was smiling again, looking at a gas and electric bill from an address across town.

He checked the e-mail. But it was way too soon for Persis to get back, even if she pushed him to the front of the list. He could call her. He could e-mail and tell her to hold the data till he contacted her. No, as soon as she heard that, she'd figure there was no rush and go back to whatever she was doing when she got his message. Better to let things go, and check back in here after he tracked down Grady's local responsibilities at the utility-bill address. A man who makes a sudden foreign trip and comes home to disappear, what could he have stashed across town?

As Tchernak closed the apartment door behind him, he was thinking of Kiernan. Often enough he'd labeled her cold, distant, said it wasn't normal the way she could turn off emotions, but now he envied her self-control. Grady Hummacher weighed on him. He cared about the guy, and he was damned worried.

THE FIRST THING Kiernan noticed when she pulled off the highway was the line of dead birds, a thick black shadow of the power line above. Las Vegas. Was there any other major city so totally committed to winning the war against nature? She turned toward the McCarran Airport exit. The airport was in the middle of town. She'd almost taken the previous exit when she spotted the soaring tower. Only at the last minute did she realize that tower was not the airport control tower but part of the Stratosphere Casino. The whole city was so flat around the sudden bursts of cartoonlike casinos that she had the feeling of driving on a game board, looking out for oversized markers.

At the first stoplight she dialed Tchernak's message number. No message for her. The light turned green. She plunged ahead between the clumps of apartments, monuments to diversity in facade design. At the next light she called her own message number.

"You have one message."

"Dr. O'Shaughnessy? This is Sheriff Fox at the sheriff's department in Gattozzi. Please call me immediately."

She patted around for a pen. In her own Jeep there was a pad on the dash. Here, in this rental car, there was nothing extra. She wrote the sheriff's number on her hand.

So Jeff Tremaine did report the body. It made her think better of him. Jeff knew as much as, maybe more than she did about hemorrhagic fevers. What could she possibly tell the sheriff? Didn't matter. Before she'd started in the detecting business, she'd assumed second opinions were confined to medicine. Then she'd run into police departments, sheriff's departments, coroners, district attorneys, health departments, and discovered that the second opinion was the CHA opinion, as in Cover His Ass. Well, she'd have time at the airport to call and cover Jeff Tremaine's tail.

She turned right. She could see the Car Rental Return sign now. By tomorrow investigators from Public Health and the Centers for Disease Control would outnumber the residents in Gattozzi. Every assay would be begun, every lead would be followed. By the time she got home tonight, she'd be exhausted, but it would be from energy well spent. A day she could be proud of. She should be glad. . . . But she couldn't shake off the picture of the woman on the slab. She *might* have been an immigrant. But she could as easily have lived in Nevada all her life. Her family might have lived here for generations. Her hemorrhagic condition might not be contagious. The truth was, Kiernan admitted mentally, she knew next to nothing about the woman's death and truly nothing about her life. And yet the situation got to her in a way she didn't want to think about. Who had been so callous or so desperate as to dump her disfigured body in the morgue? The act resonated of the Black Plague, with terrified villagers throwing their sick sisters, brothers, parents outside the door to die. Of undertakers picking up bodies like litter in the gutters. Who was this woman who had died with a face too dis-

torted to recognize? These were questions too personal for
Public Health. The case cried out for a good investigator.

Was that why Jeff Tremaine really called her? She
turned right again, into the rental return area. Cars were
lined up at the return port. She pulled in behind a nonde-
script white car and began gathering her few belongings.
All around her, car doors were opening and slamming,
trunk lids being shoved up, suitcases smacked to the macadam. Voices were sharp with end-of-trip accusations and
instructions that referenced years of failures to please. To
her right a black cocker spaniel leaped excitedly. She pictured Ezra, alone in the flat, his big wiry face on crossed
paws, big brown eyes widening excitedly when he heard
her footsteps.

She registered the slap of shoes on pavement at the
same time a man said, "Dr. O'Shaughnessy?"

"Yes?"

"Deputy Potter." He emphasized the title in a way that
made her think he was new to it. The shield he flashed
looked shiny and his tan uniform was crisp and fit his
young thickset body well. "Sheriff Fox would like to speak
with you. My car is right over here."

"Fine," she said, walking the few steps to the blue-and-
gold patrol car. "I do have a five o'clock plane."

"We know that, ma'am." Without looking at her, he
opened the back door. "What airline are you flying?"

"Southwest."

"No problem. I'll give them a call for you and
reschedule your flight."

"Reschedule? I don't think so. Are you arresting me?"

"No, ma'am. We're just asking for your cooperation in
our investigation." His hand was still on the car door, and
he stepped back so that she could see the grating that divided front seat from back. To protect him from the likes
of her.

Her shoulders tightened. She took a step back.

"Are you carrying a weapon, ma'am?"

"What? No, goddammit, I am not carrying a weapon across the state line. I'm not planning to smuggle it onto the airplane. And I don't have time to stand here and discuss it. It's been a long day and I need to get home."

"Sheriff Fox is *asking* for your cooperation."

In a minute he'd be telling her to put her hands on the car while he patted her down. No, not telling, "asking" in an offer-you-can't-refuse manner. "Potter, what is this about? I know you've got an extremely dangerous situation in Gattozzi. But there's nothing you're going to find out from me that Jeff Tremaine can't tell you himself. The disease warrants immediate and serious attention, but I can't diagnose it for you. For that you're going to need a virologist, an epidemiologist, and a lab with Level Four capacity. I'm sure the sheriff has already been in touch with Public Health. What do you think I can possibly tell you?"

"It's not my place to say, ma'am. But Sheriff Fox in Gattozzi figured it was worth the expense of five deputies to find you."

CHAPTER

13

BRAD TCHERNAK WAS halfway down the steps when the idea of checking out Grady Hummacher with his neighbors occurred to him. Maybe Kiernan wasn't so fucking ingenious; he could spot the next move as well as she could. Detective work *was* all about instinct, just the way reading the defensive tackle was. There was no time on the line of scrimmage to scan a mental list of moves that meant the tackle was going to shift right and go underneath or shift left and spin behind you. You just had to *know* in your gut. Now his gut told him that the address across town would still be there in half an hour, and that the real question was here.

He turned back up the stairs and knocked on the door of the adjoining unit. It was an odd setup in these upscale condos. Grady's four-room unit was attached to this grander place as if it were the servant's quarters. The door to the "big house" was oak, half again as wide as Grady's. A Henry the Eighth kind of a door. Tchernak lifted the metal lion's head and let it swing back. Inside he could hear the bell ding through the foyer, a Henry kind of a foyer. He stepped back, glancing down the length of the long wooden porch. Unlike Grady's brown-shingle unit, the facade on this half was stone. Faux stone. He'd been an extra in a couple of movies in college and he'd seen enough breakaway walls to recognize the comforting, soft contours of "faux." But this was good faux—"faux of the highest quality," he could imagine the builder describing it. The windows were framed in hunter green, and the whole place gave the feeling of Henry's hunting lodge. Perfect for the wealthy or wishing-to-be-wealthy-appearing.

"It's open. I'll be with you in a min," a woman's voice called. Her accent was midwestern maybe, Tchernak couldn't tell. She wasn't shouting, but her deep tone cut through every other noise, and you couldn't miss it no matter how much you wanted to.

Tchernak smiled. Whoever she was expecting, it didn't matter. Kiernan had broken into houses; the cops had found her in at least one apartment after she'd loided the lock and let herself in, and she'd had to do some fast lying to get herself out of that. That was thinking on her feet; and she was as sharp as they come at pedal fabrication. He wasn't; he knew that. It worried him. But now he saw the truth; he simply wasn't going to get into that situation. Women would let him in, they always had. He didn't know why. He wasn't handsome. In truth—he knew it—he was an ugly guy. His nose was big and bony; his face long; his eyebrows were like moss; and when he'd seen snapshots, he'd noticed a certain haunted look around his eyes. And his hair, well, he didn't have to wonder about that. Every time he came home from college, his mother greeted him: "Vivien Bradley Tchernak, look at your hair. It's too long, too wiry. And that mustache!" He honestly didn't know what women saw in him. But *c'est la vie*, right? He let himself in the Henry door.

The room was huge, the walls dark oak (faux, of course), the arched ceiling two stories at its apex. Two overstuffed couches covered in some thick maroon flowered stuff faced each other in front of the giant stone hearth. And over the mantel where the moose head should have been, there was a publicity photo of a glitzy redhead, mike in hand.

"Hang on," she called. "You're early. If I had all of pharaoh's laborers I couldn't get myself put together in less than an hour. Go ahead and set up. I'll be there in a minute."

He followed her voice through an archway into a hall.

"I got these boots, real rhinestone cowboy boots. I'm thinking, maybe they'd work with the dress, you think?"

"Wow!" Tchernak stopped dead at the bathroom door. The bathroom was the size of a two-car garage, so big the sunken black tub, wall of mirrored cabinets, three sinks, and sauna left room for a sofa across from one of the two toilets. The woman standing in front of the mirror was the one over the mantel. In the picture she looked fresh, natural, eager, and just a bit naughty. Here he could see the faux that went into the picture. The woman looked like a fever victim—cheeks too red, eyes too wide, skin too slick. She had big hair, red, the kind that would draw a comment from his mother. And her hands never stopped moving, grabbing facial brushes, tiny ones, big ones, spreading brown on her cheeks, white over her eyes, stopping, looking, dabbing. Her green sequined dress came to the floor with a slit that sent his eyes right back up nearly to her crotch.

Now it all fell into place. "I wondered who you thought I was. Brad Tchernak here. You do look spectacular." Tchernak smiled.

She stopped an instant in her ministrations, started to

smile, then changed her mind. "What the hell are you doing in my bathroom?"

"You said come in." He grinned. "I'm a friend of your neighbor, Grady."

She considered, shrugged, and turned back to the makeup counter, fingering through four large shiny sacks as if he were a regular visitor to her bathroom.

Was it him? Tchernak wondered. Did he give off trustworthy "vibes"? Or was she too sure of her big-girl body and her tough-girl voice to worry? "I'm trying to track down your neighbor, Grady Hummacher. No one's seen him since he got back from Panama. People are worried. I knew him from college. He's a guy you worry about. Have you seen him in the last couple of days?"

"Brad, honey, you're asking the wrong woman." She had pushed three makeup cases out of the way and was rustling through the biggest one he'd ever seen. Soft brushes flew into the sink, pink disks, brown tubes, scattered. "And you're asking at the wrong time. With the Millennium opening in a week, I wouldn't see a neighbor if he moved onto my foot."

"The Millennium Casino?"

" 'The Only Place to Be at *le Fin de Siècle*.' "

"You're in the show there?"

"Honey, I *am* the show. I'm emceeing it all. There are five bedrooms in this house. Four of them we use just for dresses. There are fifty more outfits back there with enough sequins to pave the Strip."

"I should know your name, but I've been working out of town for the last few years."

"Cassie Marengo."

"The comedienne!"

"Yeah. You want to see me, come to the opening next week. I'll be there with a dynamite monologue I've been working on for a month. Whole new slant on Vegas. Stuff like you've never heard." She paused, looked at him as if seeing him for the first time. "Actually do come. I'd really like you there. It'd be nice to know I've got a friend in the audience the biggest night of my life and all."

He was staring at her the way he never could if she hadn't been a work in progress. Under the shades of brown and red he could make out a face that was too square, a chunky face on a body too spindly. The awkward kid who went for the laughs. Maybe she really did want a friend, even if that friend was a stranger in her bathroom. "Sure," he said. "But if you're emceeing the opening of a casino like the Millennium, you're not going to be needing anyone like me. Out of town or not, even I've heard about the Millennium. I mean, build a ten-thousand-room casino now and blow up the place a year later at the millennium! Boy, it shows me there's plenty I don't understand about economics."

"Yeah, well, I don't know how they'll balance the books on that either. I just figure I've got this year, this chance of a lifetime and I plan to work my ass off. I'll tell you, it's hard to come up with new material night after night. A singer, he can sing the same songs the same way, week in, week out, and the audiences hum along, like now it's their song, too, and that's all the better. But a comic, dang, you better be fresh, fresher, freshest every night or you are stale meat. I'll tell you I don't see anything without trying to twist the humor out of it. You can believe—Brad, right?—that the strange guy in the bathroom'll turn up somewhere in my monologue."

A muted sound, possibly a knock, came from the front of the house. The real photographer? If it wasn't, it would be in a minute. He didn't have time to ogle and dream. Jeez, he'd just about forgotten about Grady Hummacher. Some detective he was. "Cassie, do me a favor. Think.

Have you seen anything of Grady Hummacher in the last two days? Seen his car? Seen him going in or out?"

She shook her head unconvincingly.

Tchernak had gotten into the house here, into her bathroom, for Chrissakes, he couldn't come up empty! Think on your feet, Kiernan would say. Make up something that'll get her attention. Sickness? It had sure gotten Kiernan's attention when that doctor buddy of hers called. And Adcock did say Grady could have picked up something in Panama. "Look, Grady may be sick. He's been in Panama, in the rain forest. He could have caught a virus down there, he could be really out of it. He—"

"Virus? You mean like a contagious virus, like the Legionnaires' disease that wiped out whole hotels?" For the first time her hands stopped moving and she looked directly at him. Under her thick makeup her forehead wrinkled in horror.

He'd overdone it. He didn't even know if Kiernan's case of supposed hemorrhagic fever was really epidemic stuff, much less what was going on with Grady Hummacher. Kiernan wouldn't care, but he did. "I don't mean he's got anything that'll wipe out the city overnight—"

"Are you out of your mind? Plague? Do you know what that'd do to business?" Her face had gone clown white against her red hair. She shuddered, and for a moment he thought she was going to start throwing the bags of makeup at him.

"Really, I'm sure you're not in any danger. But the sooner I find Grady, the sooner I can get him checked. Did you see—"

She lurched forward. "I'm calling the cops. They can check the hotels."

Tchernak held up a hand. "Hey, wait. This may be nothing more than the flu. Don't create panic. I just need to find Grady." He took a breath, watching her body for charge-on or hesitate-back. She stayed put. Tchernak took that as hesitation. "Sorry if I upset you."

"Upset! Jeez, my whole damned career could be going down the toilet and you talk about upset!"

"Did you see Grady?"

"No, dammit, I didn't see him this week. Not him, not his damn car, not his damn spots or glow or whatever. You know that's one subject there's not a hook anywhere. No one no-how's going to get a laugh out of an epidemic."

"Did he ever mention a woman named Leah or Lindsay or Luanne?"

"Him? My neighbor? I think maybe I said hello to him once. Look, I've lived here only a couple months. The Millennium was going to use Ginger Staley until she got too big for her corset and they canned her, and *voilà*, me. So most of my two months here has been in and out of sequins. I wouldn't have had time to chat him up even if he weren't married."

"Married? He's married? You sure?"

"No, of course I'm not sure. Whadaya think, I asked? Nah, they just had that look, you know, like they'd been together long enough for the glow to be caput. She could have been his sister, but not quite, you know what I mean?"

"How about a girlfriend he wants to break up with?"

She cocked her head to one side, thinking. "Yeah, could be. But he said something. . . . What did he say? It was on the steps out front. He was— Oh yeah, he introduced her as Doctor."

"Doctor what?"

"See, that's why I didn't catch her name, I was so stunned with her being a doctor. I mean, doctors, they're serious people, and I've been around enough to know a good-time boy when I see one, and I'll tell you, my neighbor there, he's one. The two of them, Brad, they just didn't go together. I mean, I even wondered if he was sick and she was making a house call; that's how not-together those two were."

The doorbell rang.

"I need to find her. Did Grady ever say her last name or where she lived or—"

"Honey, I don't think so. But, you know, it's not on the top layer of my mind right now, what with the photographer at the door. You can answer that for me, let him in on your way out, right? See, some guys don't just barge in, Brad."

Tchernak summoned a grin. "Yeah, but I'm glad I did."

"Listen, you'll still come to my opening, right? If I leave you a ticket?"

He wanted to give her arm an encouraging squeeze; she seemed like such a bundle of desperation under all that makeup, up on those high heels. He almost said, "It'd be great if you'd make it two," but he caught himself. No *two* in Tchernak Investigations. "Sure, Cassie, I'll be there."

"You're sure about this plague stuff, right?"

"Sure."

She turned to him and stood stock-still.

It was like looking at the eye of a hurricane, he thought.

"Brad, I like you. You seem a little naive, but nice. So I'm going to give you a piece of advice. I don't make a habit of wasting my time on guys that know less than I do. I took my chances, so so can they, you know what I mean? But you I like, so listen. Don't go talking this plague stuff anywhere. You think I panicked, you ain't seen nothing till you see the chamber of commerce, the tourist bureau, the hotel industry, and that's not to mention the guys who're skimming off the tops of the casinos. Get it? You don't threaten to close the town twice."

Tchernak shut Cassie Marengo's door after the real photographer had entered. He hopped the railing, let himself back into Grady Hummacher's flat, picked up the phone. He just caught himself before he started punching in Adcock's number. Instead he hit Redial. Seven beeps greeted him. The phone rang; no one answered. He let it ring. Seven times. Eight. On the twelfth a small-sounding, scared-sounding female voice said, "Yes?"

"Is Grady there?"

"Who?" She was whispering.

"Grady Hummacher. He left this number for me to call."

"There's no one here by that name."

"Is this five two seven three three six eight?"

"No. It's nine six one—" The phone went dead.

Phone directory? He pulled open Grady's desk drawers. Zip. Closets? Zip. He dialed Reston Adcock.

"Adcock."

"Tchernak. Here's the thing, Adcock. I've got two leads. One's on a woman doctor friend of Grady's. Been here to the house. First name probably begins with an *L*. According to my source, she had the look of a friend rather than a lover, so she might be someone he listed in case of emergency on one of your employee forms. See what you've got, okay?"

"And?"

"Phone exchange of nine six one. It's the last number Grady called from here. I don't know the rest. And Grady doesn't have a phone book I can look that up in. Check that, huh, and I'll get back to you."

"What have *you* got, Tchernak?"

Tchernak grinned. No "Good work, Tchernak." What he had here was an employer who didn't like taking orders. Well, he should be used to that one. Adcock was going to have to go into a helluva pique to outdo Tchernak's former

employer. At least there was the sound of shuffling papers
on Adcock's end of the connection. Tchernak could have
let him stew, but why bother? He'd be big—he grinned—
and throw him a sop. "When I mentioned the possibility
of contagious fever, my source just about went ballistic.
You'd think I was talking death on contact. According to
her, once the word got out, I'd have half the civil service,
the health department, and the mob on my tail. Guess
that—"

"You mentioned disease? What kind of idiot are you,
Tchernak?"

"Hey, you're the one who—"

"Listen, idiot, you'll have a lot more than civil service
on your tail if the men who count think you're sheltering a
plague that could close the city down."

Tchernak forced a laugh.

"Yeah, laugh now. You see *The Ten Commandments*?"

"The old movie? Yeah."

"Remember the laborer who got in the way of the pyramid stone?"

"The guy who was crushed because—"

"Because, Tchernak, the momentum was bigger than
any one guy. And that was just a pyramid. A pyramid like
one casino in Vegas. Think about it. Here's the doctor:
Louisa Larson."

CHAPTER

14

RESTON ADCOCK PICKED up the phone and dialed. Sometimes you have to deal with guys you wouldn't take home to Sunday dinner. That's just the way business was. So what if O'Shaughnessy was perched too high on her principles to do business with him? And that was when he was above dealing with the Weasel.

So what? *What* was it left him with Tchernak who was coming up with zip. And it forced him to search out the Weasel.

"Yeah?" Cecil McGuire, the Weasel, yelled over the rattle of the washers and dryers on the other side of the wall. That was the trouble with having your office next to the washroom; it was fine till you wanted to be heard, or to hear. McGuire pressed the phone harder against his ear as if he could create a suction cup of silence there. When the speaker didn't continue, McGuire answered what he figured the question had been. He'd got good at guessing in the years he'd been in this basement. "Yeah, this is the

McGuire Investigative Agency." He could have asked "Who's calling?" but his clients weren't the type who took well to that kind of question. He wrote down the number he saw on the Caller I.D. display. "What can I do for you?"

"You good enough to find a man for me, Weasel?"

The guy gave no reference; it made McGuire nervous. He didn't like strangers. His clients didn't pay enough to get him out of the basement here, but they knew better than to hassle him. Strangers were amateurs, unreasonable, they screwed up, and they'd turn you in without blinking an eye. But they did pay. And if they were hell-bent on hiding their identities, they could end up paying a lot more than they planned. "Finding's my thing. He alone?"

"Unless he's hooked up with someone."

"Someone?"

How'd you even find me, he wanted to ask. It wasn't like he had an ad in the Yellow Pages: McGuire's Discreet Investigations, special attention to tracking down runaway hookers. Pimps welcome. His clients knew him, because he was into them too deep to say no, knew they had him because no one else would. He didn't have to spend the extra green he didn't have on the Yellow Pages. So how did this person know enough about him to call him the Weasel?

"What's your going rate, McGuire?"

"A—Two hundred a day, plus ex." Like he'd ever seen more than fifty a shot.

He was holding his breath until the voice said, "This is a flat-fee job. Find my guy. Five thou. You can set aside the time for this?"

He opened the reverse directory and began checking for the number he'd written down. If Mr. Important knew anything about him, he'd've known time was no problem; he wasn't ass-over-armpit in clients, and what clients he did have weren't asking for a lot of cerebral work. His type of work, pretty much he had his days free. His type of work he wasn't getting any five thou for. "What's the backside to this? You don't pay a fortune for a simple trace. He make off with drugs?"

"I'm offering you this 'fortune' so you don't ask questions."

No questions asked he did know about. "My life's worth more'n five thou that'll go to my estate." He almost laughed at that last word. *My estate*. He rolled his chair over the patch of indoor-outdoor carpet till he could see out the window. His portion of the Biggest Little City: sun setting behind the trash cans for the whole eight units. "Look, I'm not nosin' into your business, but I gotta know enough to do mine. Cops involved?"

"No."

"Drugs?"

"No."

"Hits?"

"No one's been touched. This is a missing person."

"Hookers, pimps, the Company?"

"Not if you work fast."

"He crazy?"

"Not any more so than the average."

The Weasel rolled back from the window, no longer concerned with his view. He had bigger things to worry about. The guy had started making impatient little tapping noises on the phone. He knew McGuire wasn't going to let five thou go. The tug-of-war wasn't about if he'd do the job, just about how much he'd have to lay on the line.

"You have accidents on those investigations of yours, McGuire?"

"Yeah, I get hurt."

"I don't mean you."

So that was it. It fit with the no-reference and no-name

shit. This was just what he hated about these damn amateurs. They needed the mud shoveled out of their way, but
they wanted their own hands clean. When they slapped
those scrubbed and manicured palms together and trotted
up the aisle to take the sacrament, they didn't want to be
tripping over corpses. "Yeah, but it'll run you more'n five."

"I'm looking for Grady Hummacher, a geologist just
back from the Panama/Colombia line. He may have two
deaf kids from Panama with him. If you can't get him back
here, bring them to me."

"Alive?"

"Yeah, alive. What do you think—I'm in the international memorial business?"

*No, I do not. I think you're Adcock Explorations. That would
make you Reston Adcock. And if you assumed I'm too lame to
have Caller I.D. and a reverse directory, why'd you bother hiring me?*

"Weasel, these kids may be sick, with some kind of foreign virus."

"You sure?"

"That's what Hummacher told me."

"Whew!" Disease, he knew what that meant. In 1994 a
hundred people got laid low from something in the Vegas
water. City went crazy. Tourists thought *Legionnaire's disease*, pictured their last breath disappearing up the air-
conditioning vents, and shunned the hotels like they were
coroners' slabs. City lost millions. Mob lost millions. And
that was over a bug that caused nothing worse than the
stomach flu. With this—"Whew! And you're asking me to
get next to these kids, these walking packages of foreign
germs? For five thou? I don't like taking risks normally,
and this, this is crazy."

"Ten thou. And you don't need to get downwind of
them. Just get me their location."

"Twenty."

"Ten. This job's big. I'll remember it."

McGuire hesitated. Disease freaked him. All those too-small-to-see things eating your insides out. He really didn't want this case. But he knew Adcock's reputation. It'd be easier dealing with the two little germ-bags than looking over his shoulder forever for Adcock. "Okay, but I need the ten now."

"Half'll be under your door when you get back."

"What're you, crazy? I don't work like—"

"It'll be there in half an hour. But you have to move now. You've got a date at a clinic run by Dr. Louisa Larson."

"There's a lead there to Hummacher?"

"What do you think?"

McGuire let out a wheezy puff of air and his lips curled upward. "You're hiring me for scorched earth. So this Hummacher character, you care if he's scorched?"

"I need Hummacher. Or I need the boys."

"Do you care what happens to anyone else?" McGuire waited, forcing the issue. At least make Adcock admit he'd be stepping over bodies on his way up the aisle.

"I need Hummacher. Or I need the boys."

LOUISA LARSON STARED at the spotless examination room. Her arms ached, her blond hair was plastered flat against her scalp with sweat. The room reeked of Clorox, enough to kill every virus in Nevada. She wouldn't be able to put a patient in this room for a week, even with the windows wide open.

She hadn't needed to clean that ferociously. One sensible scrub would have done it. As it was, she might as well have dunked Juan and Carlos into the vat.

Juan and Carlos. An icy shiver shot through her body at the thought of them. Why had she ever agreed to care for them? Because she was the one person who could make things happen for them. She could *give* them lives.

She should have realized how much time they would require. She had thought they'd be ripe for every virus in town, but until now they exhibited signs of no more than colds. But for the time they took, they might as well have had meningitis.

Oh, shit. Meningitis. Type-A meningococcal meningitis

erupted in fevers, headache, nausea, vomiting. But not hemorrhaging from the eyes. Not petechiae so dense that the bleeding through the skin turned it red. Not like Juan and Carlos. They had to have picked up something else. Somewhere else. Not here in her clinic. Surely.

Was she fooling herself? What was she going to do, tell the world they'd contracted an unnamed hemorrhagic fever while they were in her care? They had only been in their apartment, here with her, or off with Grady on the picnic to the Breadfruit Park. Oh God, they couldn't have gotten it from the research project. She wasn't a researcher by nature; she was a healer. But when you accept a college grant, you have to pay it off. So she'd worked on the project. It had only been for a year. Done nothing to advance her career. Less than nothing. All she had to show for it was the pass to the Breadfruit Park. That couldn't have had anything to do with the boys. Their condition had to be an anomaly. But two cases? It could torpedo her career.

She stepped into the hallway and walked slowly past the pediatrics room with the bunny decals on the wall, the adult rooms she had painted herself in cheery yellow or calming green. She stopped, gazing at the painting of the mountains that looked like you could walk into it and disappear. Too good for an examination room, her friends had said. "You don't need distraction in your living room," she'd shot back. "The exam room is where people need escape from the terror."

"First, do no harm." The primary tenet of the Hippocratic Oath. She hadn't meant harm. One rash decision in a week of crises, how could anyone—

But they would blame her. The guys with half-empty waiting rooms, the ones who called her a smarmy snake when they figured she could barely hear them, they'd elbow each other out of the way to cast the first stone. She couldn't let them, couldn't let anyone know.

She jerked her attention away from the painting, took a breath, and was almost in her waiting room when she heard the first knock.

"**WHY IS SHERIFF** Fox so desperate to see me?" Kiernan demanded as Deputy Potter pulled onto the highway.

Potter didn't answer.

"Where are you taking me?"

No response. Potter sat behind the steering wheel, hands at ten and two, eyes straight ahead. She couldn't tell whether his stiff posture was from fear, or just habit. She guessed him to be about twenty-one. The car was relatively new, but already the backseat smelled of stale sweat and the vinyl beneath the grating was streaked from being kicked.

"Look, when I agreed to this meeting, I assumed it would be here in Las Vegas, close enough for me to get back to the airport in time for my flight. If not, my agreement's off. Take me back to the airport. Now!"

Potter's hands didn't move; the car moved straight ahead. Finally he muttered, "Can't talk about it."

"Don't talk," Kiernan pleaded. "Let me out. This is kidnapping!"

Potter shrugged.

"Did Jeff Tremaine call the sheriff? What about the health department, are they in Gattozzi already?"

No comment from the front.

"Just tell me where we're going. It's not like you're letting the cat out of the bag; I'll find out when we get there anyway." She was aiming to make her tone conversational, but even she could tell she was failing. If he hadn't been protected by the grating between the seats, she would have thrust her hands around his neck and squeezed. It had been a long, frustrating day, and choking Deputy Potter would have made her feel better. *Control yourself, O'Shaughnessy!* Potter could be worked. And Sheriff Fox knew he could be worked, otherwise why give him this order of total silence?

As the patrol car passed beyond the flashy casinos of the Strip, she crossed out the question of destination. Potter was indeed taking her back to Gattozzi or at least to the county seat, which, as she recalled, was only about twenty miles closer.

Potter can be worked. A charming chatterer might lead him to a number of openings during the three-hour drive, but Kiernan knew better than to put herself in that category. One thing she'd learned in med school was that she had no bedside manner. And no interest in developing one. If she couldn't deal with patients with legitimate concerns, no way was she going to coddle Deputy Potter all the way to Gattozzi.

"Those birds under the power line, they're dead, right?"

Potter grunted. Taking the sheriff's injunction seriously.

"How come?"

"Poison and such."

"Poison from the covering, right? But what's the 'such'?"

Potter pointed out the window at a nonlinear scattering of corpses and feathers. "Buckshot."

"Little fun while they can't fly, huh?"

Sarcasm flowed from her voice. Potter's shoulders tensed. The man wanted to retort, but he kept his mouth shut.

"What happens when some local sharpshooter aims an inch too low and turns the lights off in half the county?"

A sound escaped before Potter slammed his teeth together. His neck and shoulders quivered, and Kiernan wondered how good a story he was keeping to himself.

She sighed. He had the radio so low, she could hear only static and the occasional mumble of sheriff talk, and see his jaw moving as he mouthed silent asides. Not a man comfortable in the great void of silence. Fine. The halls of no words, she knew well. If silence had been a craft, the O'Shaughnessys would have been purveyors to the Queen. The April after her sister's death she started counting back. Neither of her parents had spoken for eleven days. Potter, she thought, you are way out of your league. She leaned back, propped her feet against the front seat, and stared out at the desert shrubs. The light was beginning to fade and as she watched, the sand seemed to darken from tan to khaki.

Jeff Tremaine had lied to her. That was a no-brainer. But about what? Was there really a safe house up in the mountains to guard women like the one who had died? Surely that must be true; it was too elaborate a fantasy to create on the spur of the moment.

But it didn't have to be a sudden inspiration. Jeff Tremaine had had a whole day or more to concoct his story.

If you're lying, though, the simplest story is the best. Elaborate details are more likely to entrap the teller than entrance the hearer, she knew that from painful experience. Gaining entry to a suspicious San Francisco apartment with the story that she was a city earthquake inspector had garnered her no evidence, and she'd ended up having to check out every weight-bearing beam in the place. By the time she'd finished, the real stash, in the apartment below, was gone.

So what about Jeff Tremaine? What did she really know about him? The man had seemed so ordinary, so parochial. The biggest question she had had about him was why he chose San Francisco for medical school. But bedside manner or no, you couldn't say, "Why didn't you go somewhere duller where you would have fit in?"

But the change in him had not come after med school at all. There were plenty of dull, parochial cities with medical schools, but dull, parochial-seeming Jeff Tremaine had opted for San Francisco. And once there, he hadn't taken the safe road and limited himself to studies and spouse, he had come to the parties where he didn't fit in, had coffee with the students who found him parochial. He'd done it almost on principle.

Still, he was the last person she'd have expected to find in Africa five years later. By that time he should have been right up the interstate here, happily treating measles, chicken pox, and offering the occasional flu shot.

She shut her eyes and tried to recall him at those parties or in the rotations they had shared: ob-gyn, surgery, pathology. Try as she might, she could get no picture but the straight arrow, the guy with the naval scholarship who was pleased to be looking at four years' service in the navy.

Four years? Had he just been out of the service a year when he arrived in Africa? Why did she think not? It took dredging up six conversations in Africa before she recalled him saying it had been awkward to leave his practice after only three years.

So Jeff Tremaine had been in the navy only two years instead of the four he owed them? Why?

She stared out at the black power lines running in tandem against the darkening sky. The distant hills were charcoal shadows and the whole landscape had taken on the unreality of dusk, the time mystics called the doorway.

In the front seat Potter drove, hands still atop the wheel, shoulders tight.

Jeff? Did the navy discharge him for drugs, drink, incompetence? Maybe the dead woman in Gattozzi was a local who came to Jeff Tremaine ill, and he made the wrong diagnosis and prescribed the wrong treatment and when she died, he panicked and called for a second opinion. No. It would take more than wrong treatment to cause the woman to bleed out. And there had been no smell of alcohol on Jeff's breath, no dilated pupils or twitching hands.

But he certainly balked at performing the autopsy. And that, Kiernan realized was least like him. Because . . . because why? In Africa Jeff had been nowhere near the senior doctor, not even the senior American. But after her needle stab it was he who called everyone within five hundred miles of Takema to get her the ribavirin. *He* jumped in the truck and drove overnight and back to get it to her. *He* made the decision to use the only available dosage for her.

He had loved Hope Mkema. He hadn't even liked Kiernan. But it was the principle that had motivated him. Maybe he would have called more hospitals, driven twice as far for Hope, but by the time she was symptomatic, he knew there was no ribavirin left anywhere.

Potter jerked his head to the right. His mouth opened, froze open, then slowly closed as if he had realized the insubordination he was about to commit and caught himself just in the nick of time.

Kiernan smiled; the silence was getting to him. She decided to give it another few minutes. What other possibilities were there with the dead woman and Jeff Tremaine, her newly discovered man of principle? Did he know the woman who ran the safe house? He was the only doctor for miles. The keeper of the safe house had to have had medical emergencies before this one. The only reason for the safe-house keeper not to *know* Jeff Tremaine was if that keeper was Jeff himself. She smiled. That would fit the principled man.

And his wife, how would she feel about that? Kiernan nodded thoughtfully: Jeff would be the type not to tell her—on principle, of course.

She shifted restlessly in the backseat, and watched as Potter reached for the radio knob, then seemed to remember that there were no other stations from which a deputy might choose. She eyed him. "Do you have any water?" she asked, going for the most innocuous question in the desert.

"Yeah, but I can't give you the bottle back there. You're just going to have to dribble it down the wire mesh. You can hardly get enough that way to know you've drunk." The guy was positively garrulous.

"Let me try. Jeez, I keep thinking of that poor woman who died. You know what her throat looked like?"

He was tempted, she could tell. He wouldn't have seen the body. As soon as Jeff called him, the sheriff would have shoved it back in the freezer and locked the door. By now the dead woman would be the main topic in every bar and cafe in Gattozzi. A lurid detail or two would buy Potter drinks all night. As he poured water from a plastic bottle into a paper cup on the dashboard cupholder, she said, "Poor woman. I guess she was the type who'd go to Dr. Tremaine." She held the paper cup between her fingers on the driver's side of the mesh. The water spilled down her shirt, but she managed to drink half of it and realized that she was actually thirsty after all.

Potter cleared his throat. "Dr. Tremaine—"

His radio growled.

"Potter here."

"Potter, how soon'll you be back here?"

"Half an hour. Maybe less."

"Okay. I'm waiting. Ten four."

"Ten four."

Kiernan kicked the seat back ahead, but Potter was too absorbed with replacing the radio to notice. Her moment was gone. She ran the two words—Dr. Tremaine—back in her mind, but Potter was like a cold engine groaning and sputtering in a way that revealed nothing of the purr it would give off minutes later. Had Potter been about to disparage Dr. Tremaine? Or not?

Coming up on the right was the Doll's House. She considered demanding a bathroom stop but vetoed the idea. Even if she could shake Potter, where could she escape *to*?

Ten miles on, they passed a patch-paved road leading to the right. Spikes of gold from the setting sun touched the ground and were gone, supplanted by darker grays. In another mile she noted a macadam road paralleling the first. "What's back there, Potter?"

"Just—" He cut off the word as if suddenly recalling his personal no-fraternization rule. "It's . . . nothing."

"Two paved roads leading to nothing?" She waited a moment, then goaded, "The sheriff trusts you to talk about where roads go, doesn't he? Triple A can do that."

The back of his neck flushed. "It's one of those military places. State's chock-full of them. Half the state's off-limits."

"What's this one?"

"Navy."

"Navy? Here?"

"Yeah, Great Admiralty of the Sands. That's just our name for it, not the official one," he added quickly.

"Uh-huh. But what do they do there?"

"I don't know."

There was a sullen stubbornness to his voice, and she knew more questions would be useless. But she couldn't resist a final try. "I'll just ask Sheriff Fox. I'll tell him you pointed them out to me."

"Hey, don't do—" He caught himself, swallowed, and said in a more controlled voice, "Don't think you can trick Sheriff Fox. He's real sharp. He's way ahead of those criminals who think they're so smart."

"Oh yeah?" *Keep talking.*

"Yeah." He shot a glance out the right window and smiled. "Won't hurt to tell you—everyone knows. There was this high-profile guy, foreigner. Sheriff let him escape, let him *think* he escaped, and then followed him to his confederates. Big case. When he made the bust, it sure put Gattozzi on the map."

"Sheriff must have gotten a lot of publicity, huh?"

"No. Sheriff's not one for the limelight. Sheriff believes that law enforcement officers should keep quiet and . . ."

Kiernan sighed. The sheriff might as well have been sitting on Potter's shoulder.

By now the sky had darkened. Only the occasional headlights and reflective road signs illuminated the back-seat cage.

Potter turned off into Gattozzi, the rumble of the engine growing deeper as it pulled the car up First Street. There were no streetlights; the dark was broken only by headlights and by the light from windows of old miners' houses renovated a century after their creation, from the picture windows in the cafes, and from the dimmed saloon windows. And the round white light globe in a protective cage outside the county sheriff's department, Gattozzi Station.

She walked into the plain, serviceable, government-issue tan room that smelled of tobacco and Pine Sol. A bearlike man was sitting on a swivel chair behind the counter. There was no flag or state seal. The only decoration was a large photograph of a small, dank old slab building. In it cells and mattressless cots were visible through the doorway to the main room, and in that room she could make out the metal eyes to which leg irons were hooked. "The old county jail, behind the old courthouse in Pioche. Not a place you'd want to visit twice."

"Nor is this. I assume you're Sheriff Fox?" she said.

"Right, there, lady."

"And you need a second opinion about the body Dr. Tremaine called me here to view?"

"It's the truth we need. About the woman you brought here and dumped in the morgue before you sped out of town."

CHAPTER
17

THERE IS A "rule of living" in California: "Keep clear of windows in an earthquake." In New York it's "Don't make eye contact on the subway." Brad Tchernak added to himself, *In Las Vegas, "Never drive on the Strip when you're in a hurry."* Not at midnight, not at dawn, not at four on a Saturday afternoon. He idled in the number-four lane. The sun was already inching toward the calm cover of the mountains. But here on the Strip, life fizzed. Banks of utility lines transformed the power of Hoover Dam into millions of lights in the dozens of casinos crammed into these few blocks. Lights glowed, crackling, snapping on and off in wildly clashing colors, huge, soaring, screaming, trying vainly to shout down their neighbor. To his right sat a glowing green casino large enough to hold the entire Emerald City; to his left, King Arthur's Palace; and ahead on the left, a miniature New York City, Brooklyn Bridge nudging the Empire State Building. Coming up on the left, a huge pyramid gleamed the black of the Underworld. Ahead of him the Stratosphere tower soared more imposing than McCarran Airport's. All dazzled, beckoning, promising.

Tchernak loved it. The enchantment stopped at the casino door, and Kiernan hated the predictable disillusionment of it all. The City of Dependable Disappointment, she called it. But for Tchernak, Las Vegas was one great party with ever-new friends, endless diversions, beautiful women, and few inhibitions. It was the party of all parties, and the morning after, you were expected to have no memory of it.

After he found Grady Hummacher and collected his first fee, he'd treat himself to a night in New York, New York.

Eight, or was it ten, lanes of cars idled between the casinos. Good that it's me and not *her*, Tchernak thought, grinning at the picture of his employer—his *former* employer—fuming, muttering, opening the window to stick her head out and cause trouble. By now she'd have cut in and out of every one of the lanes, cell phone to mouth as she bitched to the highway patrol.

He, on the other hand, had used this lull to study the map. Louisa Larson's clinic looked to be a couple miles north. He shifted into second gear as the casinos thinned, and was in third by the time he passed through the civic center and on north. When the first barred window came into sight, he rechecked the address. Boarded windows led to broken windows, to a neighborhood of mom-and-pop stores struggling between deserted buildings like clover in sidewalk cracks. Horseshoe apartment complexes surrounded bare-dirt courtyards. Louisa Larson's address was on the next block.

Behind a macadam parking area the Larson Clinic sat crisp and white in the predusk haze. Browning cacti lined the sides of the long narrow building. The whole sad area looked like it had been sucked dry by the thirsty dice palaces to the south.

Tchernak pulled up next to a dark blue BMW and strode to the door, relieved that he'd made it before Louisa Larson packed in her black bag for the day.

Office Hours: Monday, Thursday 9:00–6:00, Saturday 8:00–12:00.

It was hours past noon already, but the car was here and the license said *MD*. Maybe she spent her Saturday afternoons cleaning up her files or whatever in her clinic. Tchernak knocked, waited, rang the buzzer, waited, rang again, holding his finger to the button. Tires squealed at the stop sign behind him, coughs of music burst from open car windows and were gone. He knocked again, harder.

"We're closed!"

"Doctor Larson?" he shouted.

"Closed!"

"Louisa, I'm a buddy of Grady Hummacher. Brad Tchernak. Give me a minute, huh?" The door was solid, the speaker shielded.

"Grady's not here."

"Right. And that's the problem. You know how Grady is."

A bus ground to a stop, brakes squeaking, engine belching, passengers calling back and forth as some disembarked.

"Louisa? Louisa, I can't hear you. There's too much going on in the street."

No answer.

"I flew in from San Diego to find Grady. I know Grady and I'll tell you, I'm worried about the guy."

Still no answer, and the traffic noises were too loud to allow him to guess what was happening inside the building. Why didn't she just open the door and get it over with? Tchernak's shoulder tightened and he caught himself an instant before pounding again. Brad Tchernak was not used to women ignoring him. If he could just get face-to-face, he'd be on the fast track. But what good was charm, or whatever it was he had with women, when the woman was behind a closed door? "Louisa, this'll only take a minute. Look, if you'd told me where to find Grady, you'd already be done with me."

Now he could make out something, feet moving but not away, voice muffled as if it were revving up its vocal cords.

"I'm staying right here on your doorstep. I'm a big guy; I'm going to be a real impediment to your business. Your patients'll have a hard time clambering over me."

"Really?"

She ought to have been grinning by now, but that voice didn't ring with smile tones. Still, it was as good as he was likely to get.

"Picture a casino on your stoop. Maybe Hercules with slot machines all up one arm."

"Okay." The woman's voice was tentative. "What do you want?"

This was one woman who'd never make a tourist-bureau ad. No endless party for her. She was the voice of the day after. "Grady," he said. "Where is he?"

"I don't know."

A bus harrumphed to a stop.

"Louisa, can we talk about this inside? I'm broadcasting to the whole neighborhood. Open the door. Five minutes. I'm too rushed to stay longer."

"No!" Louisa's voice. Panic.

"Okay. Then leave the door on the chain and just open it enough so we can talk." *And don't think how easy it'd be for me to snap that little chain.*

"There's nothing I can tell you." But the door opened an inch.

"Grady landed at McCarran yesterday, Friday. Have you seen him?"

"No."

"Talked to him?"

"No."

"You sure?"

"I'm not an idiot!"

It was the first sign of life that nervous squeak of a voice had shown. This was a woman used to barking orders. The Lady Napoleon tone. This voice was out of place in a woman hiding behind a closed door.

Tchernak narrowed his eyes, vainly trying to pierce the building's darkness. All he could see was a black strip, bisected by a silver linked chain. From Louisa's voice, Tchernak figured her to be about five eight. Two tones of voice, two personae. Kiernan would have chosen to deal with the snapper. Tchernak took the softer route. "Grady's in a lot of trouble."

"Look, I haven't heard from him. I don't know where he is. Got it?"

"He's somewhere. He landed here and vanished."

"It's a big empty state."

"Does he have another house? A hideaway? Friends he'd go off with, hide out with?"

The door shifted but didn't close.

"Look, Louisa, I'm a detective. Once I get ahold of Grady, he'll be out of your hair. Guys like me will stop looking for him. We won't be pounding on your door and bugging you. Point me in the right direction and you can eat your dinner in peace."

On the sidewalk a clutch of teenaged boys shouted at each other in Spanish. A car raced by, thumping bass smacking the air against her ears. Still, Louisa neither answered nor shut the door.

Tchernak grappled for a wedge question. "A week is a

long time to be missing. This is desperate, Louisa. Desperate enough for his boss to call me here from California. Grady could be lying off the road somewhere bleeding to death." He strained for any sound of acquiescence. "If you know Grady as well as I do, you can imagine him taking a shortcut that leads him fifty miles from the main road and getting stranded there. Without food or water." Still no response. He was sweating. Why didn't the woman trust him? What proof— "Grady and me, we were in college together. Maybe he mentioned me? Did he ever mention the raid on Tasman Hall across campus when ten of us pushed a VW bug up the stairs to the fourth floor? Not easy around the corners. Took all ten guys. And then—this is the Gradyism of it—we get to the top and there's only a little person-sized door. Not even a landing for the car. No place for us to leave it. So, we have to lower the thing down again, all four flights. That's real work when you've gone all out pushing the damned thing up. And of course when we got down to street level, the campus cops were waiting."

Behind the door Louisa sounded like she was choking.

"Any lead, Louisa."

"*Street News!*" a man called from the parking lot. "Hey, man, you got your issue of *Street News*? Just off the presses." He ambled toward him.

Tchernak waved him off. "Louisa, *any lead*!"

"Grady had two deaf teenaged boys he brought back from Yaviza."

"Were they here?" Tchernak asked.

"They were until Grady broke in and took them. He got them an apartment three blocks north, half a block to the right. Number One."

"THAT TRUE?" CECIL McGuire kept the point of the knife against Louisa Larson's throat. Damned woman was bigger than he was. But he'd taken her by surprise. They called him the Weasel, and he was good at finding holes and passages, but when it came to springing like a cat, dead quiet with fangs ready to slash, hell, there was no one better.

This lady doc, she thought she was street-smart. Lot to learn for this one. She didn't open the door right up wide like a hooker looking for trade. She figured she was smart just cracking it an inch.

Smart? Yeah. Open's open. She put up a helluva fight, but the stupid broad broke half the pictures and beakers and glass gizmos herself. And then she told him where the tape was, like he was going to do like he said and not tie her up. Stupid broad. Then the dick's banging at the door. His pulse is banging at his skin. All the doc needs to do is scream. But she don't. She plays it smart. If she'd been that smart to begin with . . . But she was too scared then. "I said: Was it true, what you told him?"

She didn't answer.

He pricked her skin. Scare her some more.

She didn't even gasp. He ached to do another, dig the knife in deeper, but good sense stopped him. He hadn't made it all these years in Vegas, when big guys were going down all around him, by being stupid. "Don't fool with me, lady. You don't give me the truth, I won't be giving you just a scar. Get it?" He levered her around so that she was looking into the upended chairs, smashed pictures, broken glass. "What you told the dick, that true?"

"Yes!" He could feel her body lurch forward as she let out the word. He yanked her back by the wrists. His free hand was ready to slap over her mouth, but she didn't scream.

"These kids, they know where he is?"

"I don't know."

He hesitated. "Maybe I better take you with me. Let you get them to tell me."

She turned her head toward him. And then the damned bitch laughed. "By the time you do that, they'll be gone. That private eye'll have them halfway to L.A. by then."

He gave her a good cut for that, a slash right beside the eye where she'd remember it. She gasped at that one.

Then he ran for his car.

THE GATTOZZI SHERIFF'S Department was not much bigger—or better—than the picture of the century-old Pioche lockup on the sheriff's office wall. The whole affair was one storefront wide, with a counter blocking entry to two cells, bathroom, and the twelve-foot-square office in which Kiernan sat. The cells in the old Pioche jail were tiny windowless rooms with metal bed slabs and low openings barely large enough for a meal tray. The other half of the dank slab building was the "exercise room," whose main features were the drain in the floor and the big metal eye for shackling prisoners. Lest the rustlers and card cheats conjure thoughts of unhooking themselves and escaping the garrote that hung in their future, the cellblock was surrounded by another building as if the two were Russian nesting dolls.

The sepia-toned photograph hung on the side wall of Sheriff Fox's office where the present-day interrogee could study it in horror and the sheriff could ponder better days gone by. "Gives you pause, doesn't it?" he said. "What it tells you is, in the state of Nevada we don't lose prisoners. In Nevada we've had a century of practice keeping them."

Fox nodded toward the photograph, vibrating his lower chin in the process. There was nothing of the fast, lithe fox in his bearlike build, his wide nose, brush of a mustache, his round red cheeks. It was as if the fox were in costume and visible only in the tight hazel eyes that peered out beneath his fluffy red-blond eyebrows. At a distance, Kiernan thought, Sheriff Fox's big, soft body, his round face, could have lulled the unwary onto his lap to present their Christmas wishes. "We don't," he repeated, "lose our prisoners."

"Congratulations."

He might have mumbled something in response, but Kiernan couldn't hear it. The voice that shouted in her head was Tchernak's, repeating his oft-repeated maxim to her: "No taunting, no speeding, no defenestration!" Well, she'd already blown the first one. If she didn't watch it, she'd have to count on the last two—in reverse order.

Fox leaned forward, his red-blond brows scrunched angrily. "Look, lady, you don't dump a dead body, not in my district."

"You want to talk law, let's talk about kidnapping. I'm willing to discuss Jeff Tremaine's dead woman with you, but if you continue to threaten me, you'll be talking to my lawyer."

"You better think carefully before you make your one and only phone call."

She took a deep breath and then another. No way was she going to let Fox find out, but she wanted to know his take on the dead woman as much as he did hers. She breathed more slowly, until her skin no longer vibrated in anger. "The policeman is your friend," Tchernak had teased her the last time he'd launched into his lecture on dealing maturely with authority figures. She hated authority, and the authority she hated most was this kind of ass-hole made omnipotent by his isolation.

She had ended up in jail three times before. This jail in Gattozzi was not one she wished to make number four. She took a deep breath and said, "Dr. Tremaine called me to confirm his findings on the cause of death of the deceased. I am a pathologist. We worked together in Africa and we had both seen Lassa fever deaths. This woman's condition appeared to be similar. But there's no way to tell until your pathologist does a complete postmortem and gets the results of toxicology reports. Doctor Tremaine would have told you all that if you had bothered to ask him instead of dragging me back here."

"I interviewed him, all right. Know what he told me? He told me you dumped this body and ran."

For an instant the room seemed to swirl. She gave her head a sharp shake. "Why would he say that?" She put up a hand to forestall his retort. "I mean, what reason would I have? I'm a licensed—" This was not the place to mention being a PI; she didn't need Tchernak to remind her of that—"physician in San Diego. I flew in this morning, rented a car, and drove up here. The only place I stopped—the only place *to* stop—was the Doll's House Cafe. Are you suggesting I came all the way from California to transport a dead body from there to here?"

Fox jerked back as if she'd punched him. Then he hunched forward, as if protecting that bruise. "I don't know you flew in. The airline will tell me someone with your name came in."

She held up one finger. "Someone who had to show a photo ID."

Fox laughed. "Someone who's got their picture on the ID that says Kiernan O'Shaughnessy."

She lifted a second finger. "So pull up my motor vehicle file from California."

Slowly, deliberately, Fox glanced around the room. "Darn, I guess the big fancy computer the taxpayers out here bought us just up and disappeared."

Her fingers crushed into a fist. "What kind of lawman are you? You're so determined to believe I'm a fraud, you won't check the evidence. You're wedded to the idea of me crossing a state line to relocate a corpse I have no connection with. Do you have psychedelics in the water out here?"

"Lady, I don't put up with—"

"What're you going to do? Arrest me? Take me back to Vegas and kidnap me again?"

"Lady!"—His face was all red now. He was yelling—"I am damned well going to make you tell me the truth about this."

"Fine." She leaned back on her chair, propped her feet against his desk, and said, "You've decided what the truth is. Tell me about it."

His arm came down hard, stopping an inch from her shins. She forced herself to maintain the rhythm of her breath, to give no indication that his muscular control was more frightening than the hit would have been. "Am I under arrest? Or is police brutality a gift to every citizen?" Her voice was too loud for her languid pose, but she needed the volume to cover the quiver that was threatening to expose her. Fox was twice her size, but she wasn't about to lose.

"You brought the body here because you figured you'd dump it out in the country where we wouldn't be smart enough to know it was contagious."

"Did I bring it from California? Flying in coach? I flew Southwest; maybe I got a 'friends fly free' fare."

The cords in his neck sprang out, but he didn't speak. He fingered a small picture on his desk, staring at it as if for control. "You're a private eye. You got hired out of Vegas."

So he'd already done a background search on her, a background search that he'd had to get the sheriff in the county seat to do on his computer, then dispatched five deputies to pick her up. This guy had a lot riding on her guilt. A sensible woman would choose each word with caution. "So I'm disposing of someone else's dead body, huh? Why would one of your fine citizens hire an out-of-state detective to get rid of a corpse? Surely in Las Vegas you've got enough thugs who are expert at that?"

"You've got no local connections. Word's not going to be all over town before the body's cold."

"But why would I bring it here? This state is ninety percent desert. I could have driven ten miles out of Las Vegas, dumped the body, and made my flight back to San Diego with an hour to spare for the slots. Why would I go to all the trouble of bringing her up here and foisting her on a guy I haven't seen in years?" She dropped her feet to the floor with a thud. "Just tell me that."

Fox's pudgy face broadened into a smile. It was clear from the strained lines across his jaw that this wasn't an expression he employed often. "You brought the body here, Doctor, so that you'd have a reason to see Jeff Tremaine again."

"So you're changing your story? I didn't just drop the body and run, then?"

His hard-held smile dropped, and for the first time he seemed flustered. The picture frame slid from his fingers, landing facedown on the desk.

"You know, Sheriff, if I'd wanted to see Jeff, I could have met him and his wife in Vegas for dinner. It would have been easier."

"Ah, but that's just what you couldn't do. Mrs. Tremaine is a fine woman, much too fine a woman to eat with you. She knows what happened in Africa."

Kiernan stared, the game gone flat. The air felt thicker, filled with the stale odor of dust like the dry earth that swept around every door and through the windows in Africa. How could Jeff Tremaine's wife know about Hope Mkema? Jeff had said just today that he hadn't mentioned Hope's name since he left India. There were no other Americans on the project. Surely Mrs. Tremaine in Gattozzi, Nevada, hadn't been in contact with the British or African doctors from the Lassa fever project. And yet, if Jeff didn't tell her . . . She herself certainly hadn't. And Hope Mkema was dead.

"Gotcha there, Doctor. Crime always catches up with you. You should have just left Jeff Tremaine alone."

Her eyes shot open. "What! Are you crazy? You think that I—"

"There's no point in lying now."

"I'm telling you—"

He started to reach for her arm, then seemed to think better of it. "You come in here, dump a body, lie to the sheriff, and now you figure I'm going to believe your word over that of one of the most respected citizens in town?"

"Sheriff," she said through tightly clenched jaw, "there's a lot of accusation without the presence of the accuser going on here. Get Jeff Tremaine and his wife over here and let them speak for themselves."

"Out of town."

"What?"

"They're out of town."

"Jeff was just here this afternoon."

"And you were in Las Vegas this afternoon."

"Fine, then let me speak to the person who says he saw me dumping that body off."

"Maybe you weren't paying attention. I just told you, he's out of town."

She opened her mouth, but there were too many questions to ask, and, she knew, no answers forthcoming. She let her mouth close, and she sat staring from the back of the fallen frame on Fox's desk to the photograph of the dank and cruel nineteenth-century jail built in the era when accusation and guilt were one and the same.

Her silence seemed to stump Fox as no previous assault had.

After a moment she stood up. "Sheriff, I know nothing of this dead woman. I didn't bring her here. You've got no evidence to merit charging me. So call your deputy and have him drive me back to Las Vegas."

"The bus comes at seven A.M. Hotel's two doors down."

She took her time poking her arms into her coat sleeves, hooking her pack onto her belt, glancing at the jail. What had she been thinking to let herself be stranded in a desert village with not even a bus out till morning? She was as trapped as the photo in the overturned frame.

Idly she reached for the frame, tacitly daring Fox to make a territorial fuss.

"Sheriff, maybe you don't realize the potential danger this dead woman puts you in. You and everyone in Gattozzi and beyond. We don't know what she has, but it could be contagious enough to wipe out anyone downwind. Jeff and I didn't go near her without protective gear. We're talking epidemic, bleeding out—"

"That's going to be your defense, huh?"

She bit back her normal retort. This was too important. She leaned her hands on the edge of his desk. "What can I tell you to convince you?"

"You can confess."

She took a final look at Sheriff Fox. The man was no fool. Behind his pudgy face was the mind of a fox, she was sure of it. A fox used to big empty fields where the hens had nowhere to hide. He'd be a fox who didn't have to scheme any too often. Was he just plain bored enough to break the law for the hell of it? Was the idea of epidemic too awful to consider? That didn't follow the law of reason, but when you're the law, the law's however you want it to be.

Before she stood, she righted the frame and looked at the photo. "Oh, shit!"

"Excuse me?" Fox exclaimed with smarmy righteousness.

In the picture Fox stood smiling in a boozy way, each arm around a plumed and bikini'd chorus girl. In the background was a banner for the Nevada Casino Board. "Sheriff, you can believe me or not, but don't fool around with this. If you're thinking of covering up an epidemic so it doesn't ruin your tourist trade in Nevada, you're crazy. It's way too great a risk to take."

"For billions of dollars?" he asked.

"What's your life worth?"

"Like I said, bus leaves at seven."

CHAPTER

20

OF COURSE JEFF Tremaine's office was closed, Kiernan thought as she stood banging on his door. It was after dark Saturday night. Even if he hadn't been avoiding her, he'd be gone. He and his too-fine wife, who'd figured Kiernan had seduced him. She glared through the glass door into the reception area. Rats.

The wind whipped down the mountain snapping her inadequate jacket against her ribs. She couldn't even figure how cold it was. Snow weather. Nothing was open but a cafe, the saloon where Fox had so generously directed her for the night, and a bar up the street with only the *AR* lighted in the window. She ran across the street to the saloon. She'd use the phone, get a drink, and get out of here. Spending the night was something she definitely was not doing. If Jeff Tremaine had lied to the sheriff about her, she could hardly count on his veracity about calling Public Health. So far she had met three people in this isolated town, and they'd been ruthless, suspicious, and treated truth like something from an alien dimension. Were they joined in a conspiracy to hide the possible danger from the town? Or was there more to it, more people involved? She needed to get a hold of her own connections in the Centers for Disease Control. Those numbers were at home.

She tried her cell phone and got an earful of static. "Phone?" she called to the bartender over the jukebox. The bar could have been lifted from a back lot at Paramount—a Western set. Long, wooden, with a brass foot rail, it curved to an end halfway into the long, narrow room. Heads of wolves and cougars, deer—animals who'd been cornered—looked down at her through their blank glass eyes. All it needed was a jukebox whining "Red River Valley."

Two men in jeans, plaid shirts (one red, one blue), and work boots huddled over beer glasses at the bar, and an elderly couple with the look of regulars nursed highball glasses at a table across from the music. The rear was taken up by a pool table and, thank the gods, the phone.

As long as she had to call Tchernak and listen to him crow about his indispensability, after he'd given her the CDC numbers, he could pull up Nevada car-rental agencies on the computer. He could get one in Las Vegas that delivered. It would cost a fortune, but he was no longer in her employ to remind her of that. She dialed; the phone rang. The answering machine picked up. "Tchernak?" How could he be out, now of all times? "Tchernak, pick up!" Was he truly off somewhere or just sitting back enjoying her discomfort? She took a breath and sounded light-years more businesslike than she felt as she said, "I may be late. Would you take care of Ezra for another day? You can reach me at"—she read off the phone number. "I'll be home in the afternoon."

She hung up and dialed information and took down five Las Vegas car-service numbers. It took her the better part of half an hour to survey the laughter from the five representatives when she asked for a pickup in Gattozzi on Saturday night. Money was not the issue, the last guy assured her. It would take them six hours to do a round trip to Gattozzi. In that time in Vegas they could make enough to buy Gattozzi.

She dialed Tchernak again, got his machine again, and replaced the receiver slowly. Bad enough her instructions to the message tape were about to alert the entire bar, but hearing an exchange with Tchernak would provide them amusement all winter. "You'll be taking the bus?" Tchernak would have howled. "For you a bus is just a slow-moving blockade in your lane." If she protested, he'd add, "It's Pavlov's road law; it pulls out, you honk." Then he would remind her of the before-today worst day in her life, when she had taken scenic Route 1 going south along the cliff above the Pacific—two lanes, sharp curves, no passing lanes for a hundred miles—and found herself behind a double-wide motor home piloted by an acrophobe.

Suddenly the saloon seemed louder. In the few minutes she had been on the phone, the patronage had doubled. In a country town like this, 8:30 P.M. was late for regulars to be happening by. These were folks dropping in for the show—herself. Did they know they might have the index case of an epidemic across the street? She wanted to warn them, but who would believe her over their own doctor and sheriff?

As she moved toward the bar, she scanned them. Which piercing eyes might have spotted the dead woman on her clandestine trip into the morgue? Somebody had to know where she came from. Who had the skinny on Jeff Tremaine? Was the word out that she herself was suspect? Two women in their forties had taken a table across the room. The elderly couple sat silently at a round table, obviously too long married to bother with the pretense of conversation. In a town of limited events, running out of discussion was no shame.

Kiernan stood a moment longer, listening to the waves and valleys of conversation, again aware how loud it had become. How loud since she had stopped talking.

Since they had stopped listening.

She moved to the bar. It was still guarded by the two middle-aged flannel-shirted men, now joined by a woman with short gray hair, jeans, and leather jacket, and a lanky guy in his twenties, swaggering as he held up the chip on his shoulder. The woman stood eighteen inches away from the others, and when the stocky guy moved, she adjusted to keep the distance.

The shelves behind the bar were surprisingly well stocked. "Dickel and water," Kiernan ordered. "Is the Dickel the twelve?"

"Just got the eight. Sorry."

She smiled. "I'll rough it."

The bartender nodded and she could tell from his expression that he had slotted her onto a higher shelf. "Over or up?"

"After today? Up." She asked without hope, "Is there a car-rental place in town? Or a limo service?"

"Ma'am, I'm afraid the Dickel is giving you a more cosmopolitan image than Gattozzi deserves. We got the Greyhound in the morning and we're glad of it. Other'n that, if you're going to Vegas, there's the senior bus, runs Tuesdays, and from the look of you, you'd have to wait years to get on that." He grinned and passed her the drink. He was big enough to have played offensive line with Tchernak, broad-shouldered, but now, at about fifty, broad-gutted too. His fair hair was short, his brush mustache trimmed a mite too short over his surprisingly pink lips, and the eager look on his square face belied his closed-end comments.

"How about a used-car lot?"

"I'll tell you what we do when we want to buy a car. We go to Vegas."

"Right." The gray-haired woman pushed her spiky bangs away from her eyes. The cut might have been thought of as a pixie had it not been for her decidedly unpixielike jaw, a jaw that said, "Any Peter Pan in front of me better be swinging pretty damned fast." Kiernan liked that. She watched as the woman lifted a brandy snifter that would have better suited the bar in the Del Coronado Hotel. It was about the last thing she'd have expected in her rough, veined hand. But the woman took no notice of her observer. Her caramel eyes were almost shut amid squinty lines, lines from looking long, not peering into the eyes of the person across the glass. "Or, Milo, we get a truck from a friend."

"Ah, Connie, how often does that come up?"

Kiernan had guessed her to be mid fifties, but then realized she'd been using urban markers to judge: creases in skin from years of wind and sun without the emollients city women take for granted, and gray hair that always adds a decade. This woman was closer to forty than fifty.

Connie straightened her shoulders. "Guys get sudden needs for cash. It happens. You remember Artie Mayeno, the time he 'sold' the cafe twice in one day . . ."

"The cafe Mayeno didn't own," Milo put in.

"—and he had to disappear for a month. He cashed in everything he had before he headed for the hills. That old truck of his was the last thing he sold."

Kiernan put a hand on her arm. "If you know some-one—"

"You're real anxious to leave our little town." The indictment was Milo's, but it could have come from anyone in the room. The two women had moved to one end of the bar, the elderly couple to the other.

"No aspersion on the town, but all I've seen is the inside of the sheriff's department." She wished she could cut through all he already knew, but this, like all games, had its rules. "I was here earlier today as a guest of Jeff Tremaine. We were in medical school together." She almost added "in San Francisco," but caught herself in time to avert the danger of a detour into travel talk.

"Oh, you're a friend of Jeff's?" Connie set down her glass. She didn't add, "and his wife?" but that question hung in the air.

The room had gone silent. All ears were cocked for her response to "and his wife?" Were they waiting because the answer had so often been no? Was Hope Mkema not the love of Jeff's life, but merely his first extramarital fling, or not even the first? Kiernan could see Hope again, sweat sparkling on her dark, delicate face, sweat mixed with blood, her hands quivering beyond control. Hope would have died, Jeff Tremaine or no, but it didn't make Kiernan think any better of Jeffrey Tremaine, as a habitual user of women.

She had had her own share of lovers, but consecutively. Being straight with them mattered; she liked crisp edges in her life. More than one lover on the way out had called her cold, labeled her unfeminine in her apparent ease of dismissal. Maybe.

But Jeff Tremaine, he was one guy she had not seen through. Her hand tightened on the shot glass and she pressed the edge of her palm into the bar to keep from jerking the glass to her mouth. "Yes," she said, *just a friend of Jeff's, not a friend of Jeff's wife*. She took a swallow of mash, not as much as she wanted, but she didn't know how long this scenario would go on. If she ended up here overnight, three hours on the Greyhound tomorrow would be bad enough without bouncing along hung over.

She glanced over the Saturday-night crowd, so seemingly safe here in their isolated town, in their friendly saloon. There was no way to alert them, she knew that. Her head throbbed and her hands were tingling from the tension. If she could find out the truth about Jeff, maybe with that leverage she could make him talk. *If* she could find him.

Or maybe the dead body was not contagious at all.

She couldn't say, "Has your doctor lost his senses? Is your sheriff a megalomaniac?" She'd have to ease into it. Schmooze. Tchernak would have them eating out of his hand in a minute. But schmoozing was definitely not her strong suit.

She shifted to her right to open the conversation to the two flannels and the elderly couple on her left. They each gave a nod, a hint of a shrug, but asked no questions. Clearly Connie and Milo, the bartender, spoke for them all.

"Tell me about the Admiralty of the Sands."

"The Vanished Armada?" Milo said laughing. "Boy, you don't let any grass grow under your feet."

"Even if the navy does?"

"Yeah, right."

"But what do they do there?"

He shrugged. "Big secret. They *say* they use it to store classified records. But I'll tell you, you come up to the gate, there's a guard staring in your window before you can roll it down."

"So, Milo, what do you think is in there?"

"My guess, and it's just a guess, you understand, is radioactive waste."

"Makes sense," the blue flannel agreed. "Only time the feds think of Nevada is when they're looking for a dump."

"Or bitching about the Mafia," his pal added.

Connie let out a long sigh, loud enough to stifle half-hearted conversation. "So, I take it you haven't been in town before?"

"No. I haven't seen Jeff since med school."

Kiernan couldn't read the woman's face. Disappointment or disbelief?

"Well, at least not since Africa. We were both there during one of the Lassa fever epidemics." Quickly she glanced around, hoping for a revealing nod. But no one reacted to *Lassa*.

"Africa," the red-flanneled guy said. "Boy, that's some place. I had a cousin back east who went on a safari—pictures, not shooting—had her own tent put up by the bearers. Had its own shower right in it. Servant washed her clothes every night. Only problem was he was a Muslim and he couldn't wash women's underwear—his religion and all—so Susan, my cousin, she's no fool, you know what she did?" He didn't wait for guesses. "She got herself some boxer shorts and wore 'em." He guffawed, overpowering the modest laughs of his companions. Connie shrugged and walked off.

"If her Muslim was just doing her laundry, didn't he catch on?" the old man asked.

"Guess not."

"Maybe it really is just women's unmentionables he can't handle," the other flannel shirt offered.

"So where'd he think the boxers came from?"

"Maybe he figured she had a boyfriend who slipped in at night."

"Every night?"

"And forgot his underwear every time. Boy, Herb, your cousin must be some hot number."

"Jeff Tremaine," Kiernan said slowly, as if she had drifted in thought rather than seen the conversation drifting away. "He was great in Africa. Patients really warmed up to him." She fingered her glass thoughtfully. "Maybe they'd never had a man listen to their problems like that."

Milo bent down and came up with a can of spicy tomato. Both the flannels occupied themselves with their drinks. The couple, who had never made eye contact with her, just sat. Kiernan sipped her drink. The topic of Jeff Tremaine and women had probably enlivened many a Gattozzi weekend, but no one was going to open up in public.

Openings could be forced. Warnings could be dribbled out. "I remember when we were in Africa, standing over a dead body like that woman in Jeff's office. The only difference was then we didn't question whether she'd died of hemorrhagic fever, we knew she had. But this woman . . ."

It was one of the flannels who took the bait. "Hemorrhagic fever? You mean like Ebola, where your organs turn to mush?"

She shook her head. "Organs don't turn to mush. Organs get too congested with dead cells to work. Blood cells and platelets fill up the arteries and veins. Fat dropules clog the liver. The heart gets too congested to pump. The cell walls fail, and blood seeps through the skin. So it looks like the organs have all melted into red goo—"

"Jeez!" The other flannel held out his palm. "Stop!"

But the elderly woman wasn't deterred. "But is it like Ebola? I mean contagious?"

"There's no way to tell without cutting into the body, sending specimens to a good lab. It wasn't anything Jeff or I could do here. You need someone from Public Health and the CDC. But, yes, it could be very contagious. It may be nothing; it could be deadly."

The woman edged back on her stool. "Well, where did she get it?"

Thank you! Kiernan thought. "What did Jeff say?"

"Not word one." The blue flannel stamped his glass on

the bar. Beer splashed over the side. The others ignored
the gush as if it was not the first such episode.

"Jeff can be pretty closed-mouthed for a guy who grew
up here." The red flannel lifted his glass slowly, the movement announcing he was readying himself for the rest of
his pronouncement. "Suppose that's a good thing in a doctor."

"Not if we're talking epidemic," the woman put in.

"Jeff had no business—" Suddenly the blue flannel was
staring at his glass.

No business what? The words were almost out of
Kiernan's mouth when she caught herself. Dammit, this
was the first promising thing any of them had said. And
now the flannel had gone silent and the rest of them were
studying their glasses like the amber liquids might hold
arenaviruses. She was leaning an elbow on the bar, sitting
facing them. Now she shifted, following the line of their
vision in the mirror behind the bar.

She turned to face the room and saw the problem. Jeez,
this certainly was her bad-luck day.

"AH, SHERIFF FOX!" Kiernan flashed him a smile. "Can I buy you a drink?"

Fox's round *Bürgermeister* face froze. Had he not recognized her from the back, or had she derailed a plan of attack of his own? He hesitated only a moment—she suspected no one else would have caught even that—and started toward her.

"What'll you have, Sheriff?" she asked. Not taunting, not quite.

Fox nodded to the bartender—clearly the signal for a standing order—and pulled out his wallet.

Money or not, she'd staked her ground here. And now to force his hand and make him alert his citizens. "We were just talking about the body in the morgue. You probably figured that, right?"

Fox extricated a five and held it between his fingers.

"Is she really the start of an epidemic, Sheriff?" the elderly woman asked.

So Fox was not local or sociable enough to be called by first name. Less so than Jeff Tremaine, who kept his own counsel. The two flannels had edged back as if there were outstanding warrants for them. Even Connie was silent. Fleetingly Kiernan wondered what had brought Fox to this isolated little town.

Fox took his glass—Scotch with a splash—paid and waited for his change. She wondered if he was considering his answer or waiting for someone else to jump in. No one spoke. The entire room was silent. "There's no epidemic."

The silence resumed. Kiernan leaned back against the bar, ready to nudge Fox if she had to. But much better if questions came from the townspeople, who would have knowledge she didn't.

Finally the red flannel asked, "Did Jeff say that?"

"What's he say she died of?" his emboldened friend added.

"Jeff'll be sending the body down to Vegas tomorrow for autopsy."

"Then he doesn't have any idea what's wrong with her, right?" the woman demanded.

Fox occupied himself with his drink.

Connie slipped back in between the flannels and nodded at Milo, who about-faced to the bottles behind him. He moved slowly, slipping the glass into the ice bucket, pouring the liquor, all the time watching the show behind him in the mirror.

Kiernan eyed Fox. Time for a nudge. "You must have some idea who the deceased is."

"Not yet."

"Are you circulating her picture? Someone must have seen her?"

"Not necessarily," he snapped. He was glaring at her as if they were alone; as if the room full of his constituents didn't matter. Perhaps sheriff was not an elected office in this county.

Connie was not about to be ignored. "Well, Sheriff, what does this woman look like? Maybe we've seen her."

Fox shot her a scowl. Her compatriots flinched, but Connie held her ground. Still, the tension between them was so sharp and formal, it was clear even to Kiernan that this was not their first skirmish. The flannels, the elderlies, Milo, and the rest of the drinkers leaned in from their safe distance like prizefight fans at ringside.

"Well, Connie, she's small, thin, could be Mexican . . ."

"How old?"

"Hard to say once she's been sick enough to die. Ages you."

"Twenty? Sixty?" Without taking her eyes from the sheriff's face, Connie accepted her glass from Milo. She was enjoying this.

Fox was not. "Mid twenties, but that's just a guess. I'm surprised you don't have an opinion."

That, Connie just shrugged off.

Fox leaned in toward her like a boxer readying the knockout punch. Milo put down his rag. The room was so silent, Kiernan could hear the clock ticking. The door opened and an icy draft smacked the drinkers, but none of them shifted their gaze to see who had left. They watched and waited.

Then Fox pulled back. No communal gasp followed, but every face in the bar looked as if it had just seen him throw the fight.

Don't think you're just going to walk away! "Sheriff," Kiernan said, "didn't the dead woman have an ID? It's odd to have absolutely nothing."

"Not if you're dropped off. Not if someone's taken it." As soon as the words were out, his face tightened in irritation as if this was the punch he'd just avoided. He tossed back his drink, too fast, leaving a spray on his lips. Despite the feverish move, the process seemed to calm him. He set the glass down, leaned against the bar, and studied Kiernan. "What are you, some kind of high-paid smuggler? I don't know where this woman's from—Mexico, El Salvador, Guatemala. Did you pick up just her in Vegas, or was your car full of illegals? Were you dumping them on us here, or taking them to Ely or Reno? Were you—"

"Just a minute! Because a woman looks Hispanic, you're labeling her an alien, illegal at that? Show me proof."

"You looked at her body. You saw the tattoo on the back of her shoulder."

"What tattoo?"

"Don't try to bluff me. Capital *L*, for Luis Vargas, the smuggler. Vargas is violent, unscrupulous, and doesn't ask twice. I don't want Vargas or his people here in my territory. Get it?" He hadn't moved, but his whole body had stiffened with the challenge.

Kiernan met his gaze and for a moment was suffused with the foolishness of the public staring contest. Foolish, but so much of life was. She was willing to bet he truly didn't know the woman's identity and it was driving him crazy. But did he have any idea how serious a danger she might be? Could anyone here in safe up-country Nevada, who hadn't seen fever-dead bodies lined up in makeshift morgues? It would be almost impossible to believe—until it was too late. "Rigor was still in force this afternoon," she said. "You couldn't have lifted the dead woman's arm to look for tattoos. Are you saying you turned the whole rigid body?"

The room had seemed silent before, but now not even breath moved. Every eye was on Fox, every ear waiting for his answer.

"That's exactly what I'm saying, and if you take it as a warning, all the better." He picked up his drink and strode determinedly to a table, marked possession with his glass, and headed into the men's room.

The room was dead silent. There was not even a communal exhalation when Fox disappeared. She could tell by the uneasy way they leaned against the bar or held their arms just off the tables, that a vote in this room would go for Undecided. Much as they obviously distrusted Fox, that didn't speak well for her. No one here was going to go out on a limb for her.

Finally she shrugged. "Guess I won't be asking the sheriff to borrow his car."

They laughed, all of them, in ragged waves as those farther away got the relay. Nervous laughter. The morning Greyhound was beginning to look real good.

Connie slipped in beside her at the bar. Softly she said, "My friend with the vehicle'll be here in an hour. Whether he'll sell is another issue." She glanced in the direction of Fox. "Keep it quiet till then."

"No question about that. And thanks," Kiernan said, taking ridiculous comfort from this minor effort at goodwill. She turned to face Connie, effectively shutting out the rest of the listeners. "You sure didn't hesitate to tackle Fox," she said approvingly.

She expected Connie to shrug off the compliment. Connie downed the rest of her drink and said, "My family's mined land around here for over a hundred years. You saw that picture he's got displayed like the flag in his office, the one of the old Pioche lockup?"

Kiernan nodded.

"Two of the first men to die outside it were my ancestors—probably not my brightest ancestors," she added, shifting to face Kiernan. "I'm not about to let some guy come out of nowhere get himself appointed as our sheriff and carry on like he's the CIA."

"Has he hassled you?"

It was a moment before she said, "Not yet."

"What about Jeff Tremaine?"

Connie started, reached for her glass, realized it was empty, and signaled Milo. "Jeff? You mean does Fox hassle him?"

"I mean, what's their relationship?"

"Jeff's a closed-mouth kind of guy. Knows everyone. Hell, the guy's a member of the Carson Club—"

"Carson Club?"

"Big Men in the State and junior Big Men. Not the first thing you'd guess for a small-town doctor, is it? But he's a fifth-generation Nevadan." She accepted her fresh drink and sipped slowly, staring into the glass. When she put it down, she glanced at Fox, who was still sitting by the juke-box, back to the wall, gazing straight ahead. For the first time she lowered her voice. "Jeff's gone. No one knows where. But he didn't go to Vegas for the weekend."

"And you think—"

"No one . . . knows." Without a glance at her nearly full glass, Connie turned and walked out.

Kiernan took a long swallow of her Dickel, her gaze on Connie's departing figure. She liked this no-shit woman who was clearly worried about Jeff Tremaine. She turned to Milo. "If Fox's likely to be in here for a while, I'll go somewhere else and grab dinner. Anything open?"

"Bar on the far side of the morgue's got burgers. Better than going hungry."

Kiernan handed him a twenty. "For my friends." To them she said, "See you in an hour." As she hurried to the door, she gave a last look at Sheriff Fox, now sitting by the jukebox sipping his Scotch. He looked as if he was settling in for the night.

Jeff Tremaine was gone. Sheriff Fox was lying about the body. And she had only an hour to find out why.

22

TCHERNAK SQUEALED TO a stop in front of Villas de las Palmas. He forced himself to sit in the Jeep Grand Cherokee Laredo he had rented and get a sense of what he was about to charge into. Two-story cement slabs sat around a hard-dirt courtyard with a hole where a palm tree might have been. Twenty units were divided between two facing rows of five up, five down. Tchernak had banged on doors like these the summer between his sophomore and junior years in college, before he'd made his splash on the field and got enough of a scholarship to live on. Encyclopedias were what he'd been supposed to be selling then, the gift of knowledge, fast lane to the better life for your kids. Just a few hundred dollars, a few hundred more than any of those, or these, people had. He knew what he would find inside: twelve-foot-square living rooms with a wall heater for decoration, ten-by-twelve kitchens with dinette sets by windows overlooking the walkway. In the back there would be bathrooms and bedrooms with high aluminum windows over the parking lot. Tenements laid on end, the Sun Belt's answer to poverty.

Some building owners tried to buck the tide with court-yard swimming pools, colored lights, landscaped gardens. Not here. Cement-slab stairs to the second-floor balcony were chipped and the bottom one was gone entirely. In the front upstairs apartment a broken window had been boarded on the inside.

He was wrong, this wasn't encyclopedia turf; this was one of the places the sales manager would have gone right by. These tenants were not savvy enough to know well-managed property from bad. Or maybe they were too desperate.

In the courtyard, plants in plastic buckets pushed out fragile blooms. Yellow, purple, green, and red streamers wove around a pole that might once have sported a flag. A row of school-painted shoe boxes stood under the broken mail slots, like boxes on a rural route. The tenants were doing what they could. Even so, windows and doors were shut tight, and the only sound came from the televisions. Apartment 1 was dark. Apartments 2 and 3 showed lights only from their televisions. Number 4 was dark, 5 lighted.

The boys' apartment was the corner unit nearest him. Unlike their neighbors', their shades were up, their dark rooms bare to the courtyard. They weren't there! Damn! This was his only lead; they had to be here. Tchernak forced himself to ease out of the Jeep and walk, not run, to their door. A big Anglo like him, he'd seem threatening even if he were wearing a Bozo nose, much less stalking over like a repo man. He stared through the window into a kitchen that screamed, "Teenagers home alone." There couldn't have been a plate, glass, or cup left in the cabinets. He knocked. They could be asleep in the back. But of course they wouldn't hear him.

Loiding the lock would be a snap. If he hadn't been so desperate to get inside, he would have been grinning at the prospect, picturing Kiernan left at home this time missing all the fun of defenestration, or whatever they call it with a door. He took out his wallet and extricated the plastic strip.

He reached for the door, but caught himself before slipping plastic between wood. Would the neighbors call the cops? Bet on it. Someone in those nineteen units would be on the horn before he could pass the threshold.

He would have to make one of the neighbors his ally. All he'd need to do was tell them the truth, that these kids were missing, and that any way you looked at it, they were in a heap of danger.

Five steps and he was at Apartment 2. No sound came from inside; no light shone from the television that had been on minutes earlier. He knocked gently. *Needn't have knocked at all*, he thought. *Not like they don't know I'm here*.

The light had gone out in Number 3 too. Number 4, he recalled, was already black, and the tenant in 5 chose to ignore him with more flair, leaving the television going and the lights on while he didn't answer the door. There was no way to tell them he understood fear of authority in a strange country, not when he looked exactly like their picture of an enforcer of that authority.

There was a whole floor above to try, and the units on the other side of the courtyard to tackle. He could either spend another forty minutes or leave now, the only difference would be that the tenants got a better look at him. He was fingering the 'loid when he spotted the girl on the sidewalk.

Cecil McGuire spotted it a block away: Big gold Jeep Grand Cherokee Laredo was a real sore thumb in this place. Park wheels like that in this neighborhood, sheesh, you might as well drive it to the border yourself. And the thing was clean. He pulled up behind. A rent-a-car, sure.

God, this guy of Adcock's was some kind of novice. Why didn't he just get a sign made: Know nothing Dick, for hire cheap.

McGuire slid out of his own Barracuda, glancing with a certain pride at the fender. Rumpled, just a bit, but not with dents big enough or deep enough for anyone to remember. Parking-lot fenders. And he had a nice coat of dust on it. He'd spent a lot of time finding this ride. But for the engine, it was worth not a cent more than the few hundred he'd paid for it. With that, a good thou more. But he was no fool; the way he drove, no one would guess there was anything but rust under the hood. No one was going to bother stealing it. He'd be fine till the damn thing became a collector's car. He shrugged; so he'd get a few more dents.

Even in the 'Cuda there was no decent cover here. That was the problem with Vegas. No trees, no bushes, none of those little bus-shelter places to protect you from the cold like there were in the East. They were clear plastic, hardly the best for concealment, but if there'd been one of them here, it'd be so thick with graffiti that it'd do just fine. But there wasn't. The only cover this neighborhood provided was suspicion of the police. Nobody was going to chance the cops coming to their place, or the neighbors seeing the cops there, not just to report a guy sitting in a car. Still he slunk lower in the seat, leaned his head against the side window, and watched Villas de Las Palmas as if it were a floor show.

He didn't have to keep an eye on it long. Nothing moved in the dirt courtyard, no doors opened, no window shades shot up. For five minutes the place could have been a still photo. Then he spotted the guy coming out of the last unit in the row. McGuire snorted. Guy coulda been a redwood. Adcock, the bum, hadn't mentioned this dick of his was seven feet tall and built like a bear. Sheesh, the guy must weigh twice what he did!

The giant baby dick was in the courtyard now, just standing there. All he needed was a neon sign saying, "What do I do next?"

McGuire snorted again. He was, well, insulted. It wasn't like he had a license himself or anything, but, sheesh, any idiot could come along and call himself a PI. No wonder the pay was so bad. The guy was lucky this was just a poor neighborhood, not a really rough block, or he'd a been picked off from three sides by now. Didn't he even know enough to do his thinking in his car?

The Weasel relaxed. This baby dick was going to be no problem. Twice his size, sure, but the Weasel hadn't survived all these years on the Marquis of Queensbury. Blockhead like this, he'd be around behind him and have his big face in the dust before he could say Weasel.

Then McGuire spotted what the blockhead was puzzling over. Girl. Looked to be seven or eight. Walking toward the apartments. Blockhead was coming toward her, like a chiquita like that was going to do anything but run when she spotted him.

One chance was all he'd get, and Tchernak knew it as he eyed the girl on the sidewalk. Kids liked him in the same way they liked Ezra. In some way they felt like they'd tamed this big creature. But there had to be trust to begin with, and here in this neighborhood he might not get a chance to show he was okay.

The little girl was half hidden behind her brown paper bag. She glanced toward Villas de Las Palmas, kicked something on the sidewalk, glanced back at the building, moving slower with each step. With a final glance toward her destination, she swung her foot hard and lobbed the lump toward the street.

Tchernak sprinted into the street, scooped up the deflated ball before it splatted to the macadam, and sailed it back to the haphazardly lit sidewalk.

The girl hesitated, then grinned and kicked it back.

Three plays later Tchernak said to her, "You're good."

Again she hesitated. "Never talk to strangers"—she had to be weighing that injunction against the seduction of praise. "I'm on the Blessed Virgin soccer team."

"Well, then, you guys must be champions."

"Not yet. But we're in the play-offs."

"Betcha win."

She couldn't restrain a grin.

"You ever play with the boys in the corner apartment?"

"I used to, a little," she said, shifting the bag to her left arm. "They could kick good, but they didn't know the rules. They were dumb."

"They didn't speak English?"

She shrugged. "They never said anything. I told them the rules, but they didn't listen; they just did what they wanted."

"Where are they now?"

"Gone. They got sick and the blond lady came and took them away." She shifted the bag again and looked toward the apartment. "I have to go."

"The blond lady, did she come with a man like me? Like me, but a lot smaller?" he added, grinning.

The girl smiled, then looked nervously toward the apartments.

Had she spotted a shade moving? A big gringo hulking over one of their children, that was something they'd call the police about, pronto. Or worse. Tchernak stiffened, keeping back from the girl. "Was the blond lady with a man?"

"No, not her. The nice señora came with him. I have to go."

"Your mother doesn't usually let you out after dark?"

"No. I always have to be home before the streetlights are on."

"But she's sick, huh? So she broke her rule and sent you out for groceries."

"Yes. The blond lady won't come and take her away, will she? You won't tell?" She was edging back now, the desperation clear in her high melodic voice.

"Thank you." He was tempted to stay and watch till she was safely in the apartment, but good sense told him it would be better for both of them if he did his watching from the car.

He hurried to the car, suddenly awash with guilt. What was this sickness the boys had and who was the "blond lady" who had taken the boys? Maybe his next move should be calling hospitals.

He climbed into the Jeep.

He didn't note the old sedan across the street, or hear the soft steps crossing the macadam, didn't see the Weasel making his way around the building.

Louisa Larson was parked so far away, she couldn't make out facial expressions. But she could read body language, and she guessed the girl gave Tchernak more than was good. Sarita was a chatty little girl. But Louisa froze around children. It always surprised her; she was so good with adults. But kids didn't take to her the way adults did, and it bothered her every time she came up against them. Now that she needed information from Sarita, each time she had asked, she knew there was something the girl wasn't telling her. Something, it looked like, she'd blurted right out to the big detective.

She shifted her shoulder and braced her legs, ready to slide out.

Before Tchernak started his engine, the door to an old car she had barely noticed banged, and there was that little thug shooting across the street. If she'd blinked, she would have missed him. Who'd have thought he could move that fast. The guy wasn't young. The big guy, Brad, missed him entirely.

For a moment she lost sight of the thug in the shadows of the building, then he moved and she couldn't so much see him as make out a darker black that could have been anything. She had to keep looking back at it to remember which shadow was his.

Tchernak was pulling out. She tensed, started her engine.

Still camouflaged by shadows, the thug eased toward the courtyard. It didn't take a Nobel researcher to figure out his next move. He was just waiting till Brad cleared out. Her he hadn't even noticed.

She hoped Sarita's mother could get to a phone fast. Or bang on the wall. The complex was full of people. She could scream and have neighbors pouring in from both directions. Living in a place like this, she'd know how to take care of herself and her child.

Brad pulled out.

She had to follow him. He didn't know where the boys were, but he knew *something*. He was the only lead she had. There wasn't time to wait here. Besides, what did she think she was going to do to stop the thug? If she could have handled him, she wouldn't have ended up trussed like Sunday dinner in her own office. She started the engine, stepped on the gas, then eased her foot off, picked up her cell phone, dialed 911, and gave them the address. "Man threatening a child in Unit Four." She hung up before they could question her. The police would have her phone number on the screen. Could they pull up the make and license of her car too? She couldn't wait around to find out.

She gave a last look at Sarita's door. She liked the little girl, she realized with a start. But the boys were her first priority. She had to find them. She couldn't let Brad's Jeep out of sight. She had to get to the boys. She stepped hard on the gas and shot through the intersection. Brad was barely doing the speed limit. It wasn't till she had settled in half a block behind that she realized she hadn't heard any police siren.

CHAPTER

23

THE WOMAN IN the morgue was no farm laborer, no illegal immigrant beholden to Luis Vargas. Well-cared-for hands and feet like hers wouldn't have survived a day of hard labor in the fields. So why had Sheriff Fox latched on to that explanation? Kiernan wondered. To foist blame on her? Or was it a sidebar to something else?

When she walked out of the saloon, Kiernan wasn't prepared for the utter black, broken only to her right by a lone set of headlights mounting First Street from the highway and, to her left, by a blinking red neon *AR*. Doubtless the place that served the mediocre *'amburgers* that she was not going to get a chance to eat. The windows of the other shops were dark as a ghost town. And the silence . . . In the city there was the hum of streetlights, the roar and grind of acceleration and braking, bursts of music, conversation, dogs barking, doors shutting—always something. But here the only sound was the night wind scratching the sidewalk and her rubber-soled shoes slapping it. She felt as if the scene were not quite real, governed by rules she didn't know. In the city there was safety in numbers. She knew how to work those numbers, to find the ally, the distraction, the group to use as a shield. Here there was nothing.

She hurried up the sidewalk and crossed to the covered walk by the morgue. Wind smacked her collar against her neck as if taunting her with the inadequacy of her cotton jacket. She had forgotten how cold nights were in the dry and treeless desert. Her arms were already pressed against her sides, but the attempt at warmth was useless, one cold body part wedged against another.

The mortuary was dark, boasting no viewing-room light to outline a burglar. For a place with an unlocked back door, keeping a front-room light on all night would be an uncalled-for extravagance. She hurried on, wishing she had used the daylight to note how far the end of the block was and if an alley looped back. In autopsies she had uncovered bodies layer by layer, first observing clothing, then scrutinizing the skin, and finally peeling back the skin and snipping the ribs. Often, by then, her exterior examinations prepared her for findings inside. Building searches should be the same. And tonight was like being led blindfolded, handed a scalpel, and told to find the liver. Or in this case the *L* tattoo. *If* Fox's tale about the *L* tattoo was not just bait, not just a setup.

Two storefronts were dark, and even the *AR* window was dim. A gust of voices blew out of the doorway as she went by, but it was quieter in there than she would have guessed.

Next to the bar was a walkway. She moved in, immediately thankful for the shelter of the buildings. Anyone looking at her progress up the street would assume she had done as she said and headed into the bar for dinner. Anyone not invested in a setup. Now, if only the walkway went all the way through to the back of the businesses. She hurried on, moving flat-footed. The light from the bar was gone, and she squinted against the black, moved carefully up a wooden staircase, and found herself on a narrow street. Dim squares of light shone from houses on the far side, marking the windows but adding no light to the street. On the near side an overgrown bank led down to the row of businesses. She counted three storefronts to the mortuary.

Scrambling down an incline through underbrush she couldn't see, for the purpose of breaking into the funeral home to eyeball a dead body—good she wouldn't be telling Tchernak about this. She heel-skied down the incline, her feet smacking into hard protrusions, sharp things grabbing at her pant legs, accompanied by scurrying noises she chose not to think about. Closer now, she could make out an unpaved alley one lane wide running from the corner as far as the funeral home. The bar owners, with their more-socially-acceptable street-side deliveries, hadn't bothered to clear ground another fifty feet.

She stopped beside the alley, checked around her, but in the dark she couldn't tell if a car had parked there recently, only that the brush had not been smoothed by regular parking.

No light illumined the wood-paneled double door, but she could make out the sign next to it: Constant Mortuary. It was a door she was *not* going through. Slowly she walked along the track back toward the hotel, looking for nooks between storefronts, sheriff's deputies huddled in them. In this little valley between hillside and buildings the wind was weaker, but the cold from the ground held her feet and calves like icy metal clamps. After fifty yards she turned and started back, this time eyeing the roofline. There had to be a window well midway to the street.

Was she walking wide-eyed into a trap? The don't-try-this-at-home-kids of investigators' training? "Couldn't re-

sist, could you?" Tchernak would be saying. "Just couldn't
wait and see."

For once the man would be right. Fox had made his
reputation by letting a suspect assume he was free. If she
walked—or morgue-broke—into a trap she'd not only be
in jail, she'd be a fool. But if she did the prudent thing, the
woman's body would disappear into the bureaucracy or the
crematorium, and Fox's statement about her would become accepted fact. There would be no proof Fox was
lying. She would never know if this was the index case of
an epidemic barely dodged. And the dead woman would be
a faceless, nameless addendum to a blip in history, hidden
forever.

Besides, she could move fast. She took the stairs to a
porch, two units down from the mortuary, swung herself
up over the porch, and stepped onto the tar-paper roof. In
the starless dark the wind snapped her pant legs. Scraping
noises came from behind her. She jerked around. Roof
rats, she told herself. Frightened little creatures running
away. But suddenly her running shoes felt paper thin.

The window well was close to the back alley, an octago-
nal hole three feet across, a one-story-high air vent. It was
hardly large enough to funnel in sunlight at noon, but for
her purposes the narrow space was ideal. She ran a foot
along the edge of the roof, knocking pebbles and other
detritus into the well. She froze, alert for reactions to the
telltale noise. Whisperings, feet moving closer. All she
could make out was the wind playing with an edge of tar
paper.

Kneeling, she stuck her head over the edge and peered
down into utter black. The smell of rot was nauseating.
Creatures had died down there for a hundred years.

She tested the gutter, swung herself over, and walked
her feet down the wall till she could feel the top of the
window. The air was so thick with dust, rodent hairs, and

decayed organic matter, she felt like she was inhaling mulch. With sudden foreboding she slid her feet along the top of the window frame. She had been assuming the mortician opened this window, this lone source of natural light, but now, as she tried to shift the window down with her feet, she realized the truth. This window never was opened.

Her arms were tiring. She didn't have time to ponder. Kicking in the glass would be so simple. And so stupid.

She swung her feet to the far wall and, splayed out flat, she inched her way down toward the window. Her shoulders burned, her hamstrings cramped, and she had to jam her legs to keep from dropping facefirst into the pit. The stink of decay filled her nose, and she had to breathe through her clenched teeth. She felt the top of the window, grasped it so hard her fingers throbbed, and swung her feet down to the window ledge.

The putty on the top window crumbled at her touch. The pane moved. She wedged her fingers around it, gripping the glass between fingers and palm, vibrating the pane till it came loose.

Her arm was shaking. She couldn't feel her feet. Gripping the glass harder, she lowered it as far as she could and dropped it into the carpet of decay at the well bottom. She slid through the window and into the mortuary, and stood, ignoring her screaming wrists and ankles, listening for the sheriff's voice, for doors opening softly, for muffled footsteps. But the only sound was her own constricted breathing.

The reek of formaldehyde confirmed that it was the embalming room she was in. Even in the dark she could make out the table on which the dead woman had lain hours earlier. It was empty now. The woman's body would be stored in the fridge at the far end of the room.

She scanned the countertops, but of course there was

nothing like a flashlight. She stood still once more, holding her breath. No telltale breathing or hiss of official whispers outside. That was as good a sign as she was likely to get, and it meant nothing. She switched on the ceiling light and waited.

The switch was red. Her hands, she saw, were covered in blood and soot. Her scraped palms stung. Oh, God, an open wound. She grabbed the antiseptic she'd used earlier and poured it on her hands straight. Her skin was still burning as she yanked open a drawer and pulled on latex gloves.

The fridge door was heavy; she braced her feet and pulled.

The gurney was empty. The body was gone. The freezer air wafted out and wrapped the icy smell of death around her.

A door creaked. She eased the freezer shut and stood still, listening. Above were noises she hadn't heard before—crunching, swishing. Feet? Or was it just the wind? She couldn't tell over the drumming of her heart.

She gave her head another sharp shake. She couldn't come up empty here; she had to have some proof of the woman she saw, the carefully groomed woman. She pulled open drawers, eyed boxes of insurance forms, boxes of pens.

The creaking of boards stopped her. It was coming from the back of the building. She stiffened. Wind? More like feet, cold feet on the back porch. Waiting for the go-ahead to charge inside.

She yanked open cabinets and saw brown bottles, white bottles, clear and opaque bottles, syringes. Nothing unexpected.

The back porch creaked. No gust of wind would do that. If there was a sheriff at the back, there'd be a deputy at the front. She emptied the wastebasket onto the counter. Nothing there but slightly stained cotton swabs and a bottle of nail polish remover. The bottle was almost full. The stains were the same unusual color of pale peach as the dead woman had been wearing. That didn't prove anything, never would. But it made her wonder why someone had gone to the trouble of removing nail polish from a dead woman's toes.

A loud snap came from the back of the building.

She eyed the window. Too late.

24

THE WEASEL PRESSED himself into the wall. He could stand a long time without moving. He watched the gold Jeep charge down the street and the doc's BMW take off after him. He hadn't figured the doc for being in this deep. But her he could deal with later. He moved out of the shadows and strode around to the door and gave it three hard bangs. "Housing Authority! Open up!"

Feet scuffled inside.

"Lady, I'm already working on my own time. It doesn't put me in a good mood. Don't make me madder than I am already. Open the door!"

He heard the chain rattle before the door eased open an inch, then he pushed hard and was inside. The woman looked like a rag. But not bleached out. No. Hot, feverish, blotchy red. Hair stringy, damp, clumped to her head. Eyes wild. Touch her on the arm and he could push her over. Her nightgown hung half open down her breasts. Good pair of mangoes. Odd, a woman like this not covering herself. Oh, shit, how sick was she? Did she have the same thing as the boys? "Some kind of foreign virus," as

Adcock put it. Was this stuff one of those flus that knocks you out for weeks? He shoulda made Adcock cough up the facts on this plague business. Not that he was likely to *make* a guy like Adcock do anything.

Ignoring the woman's cries of "I pay rent, I pay already," he pushed past her into the bedroom looking for the girl. "Where is she, your daughter?"

"Señor?"

He heard the girl before he saw her, squeezed between the dresser and the door. Her face was blotched red; the kid was shaking.

"What'd you tell the big guy?"

"I don't know."

He had to strain to hear her.

"You talked to him five minutes ago. You know. Tell me and I'm gone, understand?"

"I don't know."

He started to reach for her, caught himself, and let his hand threaten her. The mother'd be a problem if he touched the kid. He didn't have time for that. Turning to her, he said, "You tell her not to talk to strange men?"

"*Sí.* Yes."

He turned back to the shaking child. "This is what happens when you talk to strange men. You can make it okay by telling me what you said." He shot another look at the mother.

"Tell him, Sarita."

"He just wanted to know about the boys and the blond lady who took them, and the man and the nice lady they went with one day and came back."

The blond lady, the doc. The man'd be Grady. "The nice lady, what did he call her?"

"Irene."

A siren ripped the air, so close he could barely hear her.

"Last name, did he say her last name?" He was moving toward the door.

Sarita shook her head.

"Come on, think!" The siren shrieked and cut off. The cops were here. The Weasel slid out the door and ran.

"YOU READY?" A whisper. It came from the back.
How many deputies did the sheriff have here?

Kiernan pulled her latex gloves off, tossed them in front
of the freezer door, and hit the light switch. The room
turned black as she slipped out into the hall. Hand to the
wall, she hurried forward, past other doors to other rooms.
There was no time to check them out. She couldn't chance
a dead end. She had to go with the one place she knew, the
viewing parlor in front.

A key scraped in the back-door lock. The lock that Jeff
Tremaine said kept no one out.

The viewing-parlor door swung easily, silently, and the
room let in a dim glow from the street-side windows.

Metal jangled outside on the sidewalk. Keys. Fox's men
would be coming in both doors.

Desperately she looked around the room, squinting to
pull the dark forms into recognizable shapes. Dais, po-
dium, rolling wooden platform ready to hold a coffin, twin
bookcases that reached nearly to the ceiling, twin cabinets

in the back. The cabinets she crossed off immediately—too obvious. Under the dais? Dicey.

Metal scraped metal as keys moved into locks.

The bookcases. In California they would be bolted to the wall. Here? She had to hope. The shelves were too small to hold an adult; that's what Fox would assume. No adult would think to climb on top, he'd think. If she got out of this, she'd never again complain about petite-sized pants being too long. She grabbed a high shelf and climbed. The few books shimmied. A stack fell on its side.

Across the room the dead bolt gave.

The bookcase shimmied but held. Silently she swung herself onto the top, knelt, and scrunched over chin on knees. The dust flew up her nose. She rammed her hand over her mouth, pinched her nose. The fallen books, could she reach them, right them? Her nose tickled. It took all her concentration not to sneeze.

The door opened, banging back into the bookcase. The light came on. Sheriff Fox stood in the doorway, a thick angry figure turned black by the backlighting.

If he spotted the fallen books; if he questioned them at all, he need only look twelve inches up. She was in clear sight. She swallowed hard against the tickling dust. She could hear the back door banging open, feet clopping in.

Fox took a step into the room. He looked left and right. "Come on out. We know you're in here!" He strode across the room, yanked open the cabinet doors. "Shit!" He peered under the dais.

Deliberately Kiernan didn't hold her breath. She breathed through her mouth, so softly air barely moved.

Pushing his meaty body up, he stalked to the hallway door and wedged it open. "We've got both doors covered. There's no way out. Make it easy on yourself. Step out, hands up." He waited. "Jeez," he muttered, and started forward.

She didn't move.

He turned, surveyed the viewing room, eyeing the open cabinets, the dais, the windows, the bookcase. His gaze stopped—

Forget those fallen books, every cell of her body screamed.

His gaze moved to the door, on around. With a satisfied shrug he headed down the hall, flinging open doors, dismissing the rooms behind them. Outside the embalming-room door, he stopped. "We know you're in there. Open the door."

The viewing room was clear. She counted to five before Fox said, "Okay," and pushed open the door.

Light flooded the hall. The deputies followed him in. "Hey, look at this! Gloves! She must be in the freezer!"

"Maybe we should let her sweat it out, huh, Sheriff?" a deputy cackled.

Kiernan resisted the urge to leap to the floor and race outside. There were at least two deputies in here with the sheriff. That had to be the whole force. There couldn't be anyone else watching the front.

"Go ahead, Potter, open 'er up."

She lowered a foot to a shelf, swung herself around, and stepped quietly to the floor. Moving as silently as she could, she crossed the room and let herself out the door into the street.

"**NOW THEY'RE TELLING** Dad he needs chemo. Yeah, I know. Government sets off a bomb, sprays radiation all the hell over the grasses, the streams, the cattle, so the kids downwind get cancer from drinking the milk, ferhevvin-sake, and now fifty-some years later they're still saying it's not their fault when Dad come up with cancer. Life east of the proving ground, eh?"

Tchernak sighed as he leaned against the wall between the Gents and the Ladies and eyed the guy jabbering away on the phone—the only phone in this greasy spoon where conversation was the tastiest thing you could buy. He could understand why there was no phone book here, what with the pages and pages of escort services, with their full-page colored pictures of ladies you wouldn't escort home to Mom. Probably fourteen-year-old boys ripped them off as fast as Nevada Bell sent them out. When he finished this case his first project would be to get himself a cell phone.

He had dawdled over the miserable dinner trying to use the time to figure out what the hell was going on with Grady Hummacher. Truth was he didn't know Hum-

macher at all anymore. Much less the blonde and the bru-
nette the little girl had seen with him. The blonde would
be Louisa Larson. But the other?

"Government swore there was no danger. Where did
they think the radiation was going, straight up to heaven?
Dust went halfway through Utah.

"So I says to my sister, Milly, you know her, right? The
one in Connecticut that just broke with that loser of a
husband?"

Tchernak glanced at the two women behind him in line,
then turned his gaze back at the man on the phone and
loudly shifted his feet. The strawberry pie had been a mistake. At home he didn't deal with chain restaurants, period, much less a joint like this. Half the hotels he wouldn't
waste his money in. Even with the best chefs he spotted
flavors too strong, sauces too thick, fish breaded and fried
when it should have been poached. If salmon wasn't flown
in fresh from the Northwest, he didn't deal with it. He had
a standing order for Dungeness crab the minute the season
opened in San Francisco, and organic garlic from Wat-
sonville for his garlic-pepper marinade. And there were the
Maine lobsters, and the Jersey bluefish.

He shoved the memories away. He'd never get another
chance to cook like that, with a boss who never stinted.
He'd known that when he quit. But dammit, it didn't have
to be this way. If Kiernan hadn't been so pigheaded—"I
don't like to share." What kind of reason is that?—they
could be halfway to wherever the phone number in
Grady's apartment led him. They'd be eating sun-dried-
tomato focaccia with black olives, capers, and wild fennel
and hashing back and forth what Grady could be up to.
She'd be sitting with her knees to her chest like a teenager,
bitching like a special-teams coach, egging him on to everything on the far side of the law.

"No, the old man did not sue. He was a good citizen.

Prided himself on being such a damned good citizen that now he's near dead.

"Come to Vegas, Milly, I says. I mean, what's to lose, right? That loser husband of hers lost everything they had before she lost him. But here she could get a union job and do good, you know?"

Tchernak cleared his throat. The women behind him paused long enough to look him over. The man, the only one he cared about, reacted not at all.

Tchernak tapped his shoulder. Guy's head came up to his armpit. He almost had to bend to reach his shoulder. "Your time's up."

"Hey, who're you to—"

"Time's up."

"I'm not done."

Tchernak glared down at him. "Go to the back of the line."

Tchernak couldn't make out the guy's reply as he stalked off because the two women were laughing too loud.

He checked his watch and dialed Adcock.

"Adcock."

"Tchernak," he snapped. Did Nevada Bell charge by the syllable? "Where the hell are you?"

Tchernak told him.

"Okay. The phone exchange Grady called is somewhere around Gattozzi."

"Gattozzi? Where's that?"

Tchernak listened to the directions, then had Adcock spend a lot of syllables repeating them as he wrote them down.

"You shouldn't have any trouble, Tchernak. There's only one way up there. There's a cafe called the Doll's House on the highway. You can't miss it, it's the only thing there. Meet me there in two hours."

"Right. Two hungry kids, good chance Grady stopped

there." Tchernak put down the receiver, checked his watch again, and tapped the sour-faced little guy glowering behind the women. "Fifteen seconds. See?"

Half the strawberry pie was still on his table. He pushed it away and signaled the waitress. Gattozzi had to be some little town in the middle of nowhere. Why would Grady fly in from Central America and head straight into the back country? If he was up to the kind of double-crossing Adcock was tied in knots about, couldn't he do that crossing right here in Vegas? Maybe he had a cabin or something up there? Yeah, but you don't fly in and out of Panama twice in a week and then take a few days for R and R before you screw your boss. The whole thing just didn't make sense.

What would Kiernan do? First thing she'd kick up a fuss about how slow the service is. He laughed to himself. "Never know when you'll need a new enemy," he'd told her the last time. That hadn't struck her as funny as it did him. For a woman with a good sense of humor she did have her dead spots.

Food. She'd stock up like she was going camping. Well, he'd already stoked his fires on a couple burgers and shakes. Still, a dozen Hersheys couldn't hurt. And some bottled water. Six-pack of Coke. Crackers. You never know.

He collected his larder, paid the bill, and got in the Jeep. One thing about Las Vegas, you didn't have to wonder where you were. Billions of kilowatts marked the Strip. And next to the Strip was the freeway.

There was still the question of how to get to the freeway entrance. He got the car door open and swung into the seat, twisting to get the map. First, where was he now? Here? No, a couple of squares to the right. Two squares beneath Grady's place.

Grady's place? Something about it pulled at him. He couldn't think why. Maybe he should be keeping notes.

"Stupid! Jeez, maybe Kiernan's right!" That's what Kiernan would do, get the e-mail from BakDat! Grady's place would be the easier venue for that. With Persis's backgrounds and the lead to Gattozzi, he'd be onto Grady in a snap.

The Weasel eased out of the parking lot, stick of beef jerky in hand. If he'd known the giant baby dick was going to lounge over his food like he was dining at the captain's table, he'd have had time to get something decent himself. He could use a good relaxing meal after the run from the kid's house. Cops were in front before he could get the car moving. He'd had to slide down to the floorboards and hope the cops weren't too thorough. Which they weren't.

Coming up with a working phone in that neighborhood was just about as hard. He prided himself on always knowing the nearest pay phones, but he'd really crapped out on that one. Had to go a mile and a half before the neighborhood changed and he spotted one outside a fast food grocery.

And then he didn't have time to get on Adcock about all the bastard wasn't telling him. All he could do was get the location where the Jeep was and race over here before the baby dick drove off.

What was with Adcock? He knew the guy's reputation, and now word was the guy was desperate. Maybe the truth was Adcock was just wacko. This time he says the baby dick's headed up 93, but the guy wasn't even going toward the freeway.

Wacko or not, Adcock had paid pronto. The Weasel closed the space between the 'Cuda and the Jeep.

CHAPTER

27

OUTSIDE THE FUNERAL home Kiernan turned uphill and ran, cutting into the alley, up the covered stairs. Her rubber-soled shoes were quiet but not silent. At the landing she looked around. No deputies in sight. Probably still in the mortuary, checking more carefully behind all the doors she had rejected. She followed the path to the street and turned left, uphill. It wasn't till the street ended two blocks farther on that she found herself in open field and felt momentarily safer.

There was no real safety, she knew that. She could hide out all night and Fox would be at the bus stop in the morning. If by some sleight of hand she managed to get on the bus, he'd be waiting in Las Vegas. If she got on the plane, he'd be on her doorstep. The dead woman hadn't been her case, but it definitely was her case now.

What she needed was that car Connie's friend might be willing to part with. He was one guy about to make an easy sale.

The wind was stronger now, spraying her with sand. The dusty smell of the arid street was stronger. The air had to be colder, but she no longer felt it. Inside her thin jacket she was roasting. Below her the commercial portion of First Street ended and it veered left, becoming residential. She made a wide loop, crossed First, and cut down the narrow street behind it. First Street lay between two hills, and from her position she could see headlights coming from both directions, the cars moving fast. Otherwise the street was empty. She waited till both vehicles had passed, then clambered down a slide-and-jerk path to the back of the saloon.

It was the most dangerous place. But she had no choice. She took a breath and walked in.

The heat of the saloon seemed equatorial, the crowd triple the size it was an hour ago. Now Waylon Jennings's notes of remorse were almost lost beneath the buzz of conversations flowing over one another. As she walked in, conversation stopped for a second, then picked right up. They'd all have heard about her of course. Even without the break-in, she'd be front-page gossip for a month. She tried to read the eyes of the one or two who glanced around now, but no one indicated a sheriff's warning.

She made straight for the bar. More carefully now she surveyed the room. No sheriff, no deputies. Also no Connie. Connie said she'd be here; where was she? Time to wait was something she did not have.

"Hey there, lady." Milo smiled a welcome. "Another Dickel and water?"

"Easy on the water, Milo. Connie here?"

He nodded to his left.

Kiernan heard herself sigh out loud. Connie was there all right, half shielded by a paper fern. She was sitting at a table alone. Kiernan started to slide in next to her, but Connie pointed to a chair across the table instead. "Where's the guy with the car?" Kiernan asked.

Connie cocked her head toward the next table, where

five men in jeans sat, four drinking beer, one a Coke. "Jesse," she called to the Coke drinker.

The short, sallow man's shoulder rose protectively, lifting a faded shirt that hung loose on narrow ribs. He glared at his glass, at Connie, and finally at Kiernan. He looked, Kiernan thought, like the poster boy for Losers. This far out in the country, with the bus a once-a-day event, selling a car was a drastic step, and from Jesse's face he understood that only too well. He made no effort to shift out of his chair. At his table, conversation had stopped.

"Jesse," Connie repeated. There was no edge to her voice, but this time Jesse hoisted his thin frame and moved to the empty seat between Connie and Kiernan.

"What's your car and what are you asking?" Kiernan said.

"No hello, how are you, nice to meet you, Jesse? What am I, too low-life for that?"

Milo put down the Dickel. She handed him a bill and took a grateful swallow of the bourbon. At the best of times she was no diplomat. Tchernak would have no problem with Jesse. Tchernak wouldn't be downing bourbon and impatience, he'd be chatting up all five guys at the table, them and Connie and Milo too. A couple of straight-from-the-gridiron stories and they'd be ready to sell him Jesse's car, and Jesse in the bargain.

If she'd had Tchernak here, there would be no problem, all right, because Tchernak would have made such a stink about entering the mortuary that she'd still be in here arguing with him.

She glanced past Jesse out the window. No movement yet. She'd better be able to mend this fence fast. "Jesse, you've caught me at a bad moment. Can I buy you a drink?"

His sallow face twisted downward. A high whine cut

through his words as he muttered, "I don't drink any-more."

"Oh, right." The edge to her voice was sharp. No one was going to mistake that for charm. She didn't have time to coddle a whiner. "So, Jesse, about the car?"

"Ford pickup. Five hundred, but I've changed my mind."

She jammed her teeth together. It was a moment before she could trust her voice. "So you don't need the money anymore?"

"Yeah, right."

"It's great not to have debts."

Jesse's friends guffawed. Jesse glared. "Hey, what's that supposed to mean? You think I don't pay my debts?"

"Hell, we *know* you don't!" The guys laughed louder. From the bar two couples eased closer.

Ignoring them, Jesse glowered at Kiernan.

"You could sell her the car and your house and you'd still be in the red, man." A guy at the table nudged an elbow toward him, sending all the friends off on another round of guffaws.

"Yeah, right," Jesse growled to her. "No point. I get zilch."

Kiernan inhaled slowly through clenched nostrils. Con-nie leaned forward. Before she could speak, Kiernan said, "You get to pay off your debts, and not be known as a loser. You get integrity." She let a moment pass before adding, "I assume that's why you decided to sell your car."

"Integrity, yeah, you could use some of that, Jess."

Jesse flushed.

Kiernan looked at his wavering gaze. He was damned if he did and damned if he didn't. And his type of whiner could sit here till dawn making up his damn mind. Across the street something was moving, she couldn't make out what.

Tchernak, of course . . . No, Tchernak would be boxed in now. There'd be no goad that a guy twice Jesse's size could use. But she, on the other hand, had a chance. "If I were a guy, Jesse, I'd say we arm-wrestle for it."

"Yeah, well, if you were a guy, I'd take you on and have you flat on the table before you knew you'd lost."

"Hey, man, you can't turn that down."

"I'll put ten bucks on . . . on her."

Jesse's "Oh yeah?" was almost lost in the howls of his buddies.

"Yeah." Kiernan sat back, brow wrinkled to show thought. "You serious?"

" 'Course I'm serious. I mean, if you were a guy."

"Okay," she said slowly. "But how about we make it more even. How're you on sit-ups? You think you can take me? I've got to be straight with you, I did gymnastics when I was a kid. I've got good muscles."

His gaze dropped to her stomach. He didn't answer.

She put her wallet on the table. "Five hundred. If I lose, it's yours. If I win, I get the car and the cash is still yours. You can't beat that."

Murmurs of agreement came from the table behind.

Jesse tapped his teeth together.

She checked the window again. Definitely movement, definitely men. Still across the street.

It was Connie who broke the deadlock. "Jesse?"

"Yeah, okay. Where's your money?"

"Five says Jesse takes the little lady."

"Covered, man. You know what Jess had for dinner?"

Neither man across the street was Fox, but they had the look of deputies. Who else could they be? Maybe Fox figured the saloon was the last place she'd go. Even so, he'd be in here to tell citizens to keep an eye out. At the rate things were going here, by the time side bets were made and drinks poured and more bets laid, the Las Vegas bus would be sitting at the curb. She lowered her voice under the growing buzz from the other table.

She counted out the five hundred dollars. "Let me see the truck."

"It's out back, around the corner."

"Okay—"

The two men, definitely deputies, were crossing the street, headed for the saloon door.

RESTON ADCOCK STOOD, staring at the receiver he had just put down. *Put*, not slammed, he was not a slammer. There had been plenty of times while he was working for Amoco or Texaco, Betaco, or one of the other Ocos, when his muscles had ached to slam the phone not just down but into some guy's head. Even then, with the company snatching his ideas and giving him shit in return, he knew the value of keeping cool. If you get into a pissing contest, when a real chance comes on the horizon, you can't grab it because you've got your hands full.

If there's one thing you've got to make in the oil-exploration business, it's quick decisions. You screw around and a couple hundred million gushes into some other guy's pocket. He'd told that to Maida before she took the kids and left, but she was too timid to see. It was now or never, all or nothing with Adcock Explorations. He'd played it right; it was now, it was all. Until Grady Hummacher.

Grady in Gattozzi, that sounded like the guy. He could remember Grady saying something offhand about Gattozzi. Over drinks. What? Some girl had taken him up

there, shown him some park or something. Or had he
taken some girl—the same one, or another one? Adcock
had been only half listening. He sighed irritably—well,
how could he have known that Grady Hummacher's social
life would become a multi-million-dollar issue? He tried to
picture Hummacher, sitting in his office, leaning back on
his leather couch, drinking a beer, saying he'd been late
getting here because he'd taken some girl—some chorus
girl?—up there for . . . what? But Hummacher hadn't
been specific. He'd delivered the girl. He'd done her a
favor. Took her someplace safe.

The kind of place he'd choose for a meeting to sell out
Adcock Explorations? What'd he do, sell out and keep going till he hit the ski slopes?

Adcock didn't need to read Grady Hummacher's reports. By now he could just about recite the damn things.
Could he do without Hummacher? If he had those boys,
just maybe he could.

And he wouldn't be giving them a cut the size of Hummacher's.

Adcock reached for the phone. This Tchernak guy, he'd
served his function. Why not cut him loose right now?

Because he was out of phone contact. And maybe he'd
be useful, big guy like that.

Or maybe he'd get in the way.

For once Adcock did hesitate, but only a moment. Then
he dialed a friend up near the Naval Proving Grounds half
an hour east of Gattozzi. He was calling Simkin at home,
of course, a good five miles from the Grounds. The
damned naval experiments were so secret, the President
probably needed a pass, and the governor up there in Carson City probably thought the place was one of those na-
tional reserves the feds got cheap because no one wanted
the land.

"Hello?"

"Hey, Simkin, Resty Adcock here. Listen, I'm flying up your way now. I need to use your landing strip, and I'm going to need a car."

Simkin didn't answer.

"I *said*—"

"I don't know, Resty. Car's fine. But this close to the proving ground, I don't like putting the strip lights on. They can lean on you hard if you get in their way."

"I'm not getting in their way. Just get the damned lights on in an hour."

"BOY, THAT BROAD'S had one too many!" The assessment and accompanying laughter followed Kiernan as she ran for the saloon bathroom. Inside, two women stood talking. They looked to be women used to taking care of themselves on the harsh, lonely roads. The sink and mirror were beside them, but neither was paying them much mind.

"First right, hon," one said, pointing to the two stalls.

Behind them the single small, high window was open only an inch. The pink paint on it was scratched and thick, and one glance told Kiernan she wasn't going to shove it up eight inches. "How far is the drop from the window?"

"Whew! Guy trouble?"

"Believe it! The window—"

The taller woman grinned. "Step aside." As she pushed the window up, her companion turned over the garbage can to make a stair. "It's a good ten-foot drop, but the landing's soft. Be prepared to roll."

"You're not from around here are you, hon?" the shorter woman asked.

"Just passing through—fast."

"Word of warning, then. Don't wander off the road. This area's full of old mine holes. Some of them, the roof hasn't caved in yet. No one knows how many people have gone up-country and never come back."

As tacit thanks, Kiernan stepped on the garbage can she didn't need and slid her legs out the window. "If you could keep them out of here for a few minutes . . ."

"Don't worry, honey, you're not the first to use 'the emergency exit.' "

Kiernan slid, hit the dirt with a soft thud, and rolled. She dusted herself as she ran for the lot behind the saloon.

"Not here," she said to the group gathered around the truck. "Give me a test drive."

Before Jesse could object, Connie said, "Gallows frame," and headed for a big Chevy pickup.

The gallows frame held the huge bucket that had carried ore from the mountain down to the road. During World War II, Jesse told her, there had been a cable, and every few minutes a brimming bucket with manganese passed over First Street. Over half a century later the bucket was gone and the wood so dry and feathery she was surprised the vibrations of the truck hadn't toppled it. But at least it provided a shield between them and First Street.

Until she stepped out of the truck, Kiernan hadn't realized how protected First Street was. Up here—two streets higher than the saloon—wind slapped branches of scrub pines against the building and iced her sweaty back. The Chevy pulled up and Jesse's gang piled out of the back. So far so good—no procession of vehicles here. Still, noise carries.

The dim light illuminated the defects of the truck for which Kiernan was about to pay five hundred dollars. It was old, with hood and fenders pocked and blotched with rust. Daubs of orange paint attested more to Jesse's good intentions than to actual bodywork done on the truck. The engine had turned over on the third try, and even now it idled with an erratic grumble.

"You're getting a good deal, Jesse," she said as he turned off the engine.

"I don't know. I just don't see how I can be without wheels. I can't—"

"Jeez, man, stop the bellyaching, will you?" Glasses in hands, Jesse's buddies stood around the engine as if unsure whether they were there for the christening of a new owner or the wake of the vehicle. Now they moved to the back, re-forming their arc around the bed. Behind them headlights seemed to wink, then darken, and Connie got out of a sturdier-looking truck.

"You ready?" Kiernan asked before the momentum could falter and Jesse try a new stalling tack. The change of venue had bought her five minutes, no more. "Truck bed's as good a spot as any for sit-ups. Right or left side, your choice?"

"I don't know. I got stuff back there."

"Your friends will clear it for you. It's going to have to come out anyway."

"Not if I win, it won't."

"Right," she said, hoisting herself onto the bed. It hadn't crossed his mind that he might lose this macho contest to a woman who weighed not a hundred pounds. It hadn't crossed hers otherwise. If she lost, well, there was no Plan B.

Jesse clambered onto the tailgate and stepped beside her. Wind flattened his plaid shirt against his chest. Standing there shoulder to shoulder, or more accurately the top of her head to his shoulder, she could see the definition of his pectoral muscles. She couldn't make out his abdominals, but it was a rare man who worked his pecs and let his gut go to pot.

She took off her jacket and handed it to Connie. "Feet against the cab, Jesse?"

He plopped down mid bed, feet to the flat tailgate. "Hell, I don't need that kind of wimping out."

"Fine." Better, she told herself as she sat down next to him. Just like in gymnastic warm-ups, crunching scissor lift after scissor lift, her abdominals aching to get shoulders eighteen inches off the ground, feet higher—all that before the four-hour practice proper began. Of course, she was fourteen years old back then. So what? she assured herself. This'll be a snap.

"Okay," Connie said. "A lift means your head goes higher than the truck sides. You two will probably pace together, but just in case, Craig, you count for Jesse. I'll take Kiernan. Ready? Go."

Jesse was already moving. Kiernan inhaled fully. Jesse was on his second lift. The man was fast. Exhaling, she lifted her arms and chest. Her stomach knotted. Her breath caught and she forced herself to keep it flowing out. She shouldn't have had that second drink.

Jesse was moving up again as she lowered down. That had to be three to her one. Don't look! Just do your own warm-up! The coach had screamed that at her day after day. She exhaled, lifted, inhaled, lowered down. Exhaled, lifted. Jesse was lifting, speeding past her. How could the little whiner be in such good shape? She inhaled and lowered, exhaled, lifted.

"Way to go, Jess!"

"Keep 'em coming, man!"

She exhaled, lifted. Her breaths were shorter. By the time she was upright, she was holding her breath. That hadn't happened in the gym, not till the end of warm-ups, not at all when she was really in shape. Inhale, lower. God, how long had it been?

There was no sound but their panting breaths, the

slither of fabric against truck bed. And the grumble of distant shouting.

Don't worry about the sheriff! She exhaled, and came up alongside Jesse. He was slowing down. But so was she. And he was way ahead of her in count.

"Hey, man, you're doing great. Ready for that second wind!"

He breezed past her on the way down. But when she started up, he was even with her. As she inhaled down, he flopped to the bed, shaking the truck. She lost control, came smacking down, banging her head against the metal bed.

"Exhale up!" she told herself. Head aching, she lifted. Beside her, Jesse was moving. She inhaled and lowered down. In the distance car doors slammed.

"Come on, man, another inch. Just an inch, man! Great, you did it."

She tensed against his flop down. Her abdominals screamed. Jesse groaned.

"Hey, man, you got ten to her six. Don't give up. Give us eleven."

He groaned, but started up. She lifted. Sweat coated her face. Her heart smacked her ribs. She lowered. Seven.

Jesse collapsed down with a groan. The truck shook.

"Okay, man, ten's your tally."

"I . . . can . . . rest. . . . No . . . rule . . . against . . . that. . . . I've . . . got . . . time."

"I don't!" She lifted again. Her abdominals cramped. That had happened once in the gym when she had drunk a milk shake before practice. The coach had sent her home in disgrace. No point in staying, he'd said, you can't do anything. She could taste the bourbon coming back up her throat.

She pushed the memory away, swallowed hard, and lowered down. Eight.

Car engines started below. How long would it take them to drive two blocks?

Scrapping her rhythm, she lifted on the inhale. Her stomach screamed. She lowered. Nine. Lifted. Her head barely cleared the side panel of the truck. Lowered. Her head banged down, out of control. She needed to get her rhythm back.

Wheels squealed in a fast turn.

"Come on, Jess. One more."

Jesse groaned. "She's not close, right?"

She lifted, let herself flop down. Ten. Sweat poured off her. She lifted again. "Eleven," she squeaked out.

"Ten," Connie said.

It was eleven. It had to be. Why had Connie—? No time. She flopped down, scrunched her chin to her navel and lifted. Out of the corner of her eye she could see the side panel looming far above her head. Her legs were shaking, her heels were drumming against the truck bed. She gasped for breath, struggled to keep from crashing down. Her stomach ached. Any moment she'd be hanging over the side retching—if she could sit up that high.

"Hey, she's done," one of the guys proclaimed. "It's a draw."

"Like hell!" She let out a huge groan and shot up. Her nose barely passed the top of the side panel, and if holding the position there had been life or death, she'd have been shopping for a shroud, but none of that mattered. She let herself down as slowly as possible, still clanking her head against the truck bed.

A car door clattered. The sheriff?

Ignoring the pain, she rolled to the side and pushed up. Jesse was already signing the pink slip.

"Anything I should know about the truck?" she asked.

"Leaks oil."

"And?"

"That's it. She's been a good ride."

She shot a glance at First Street. No action there now; the sheriff had moved out. To Jesse she said, "How do I get to the highway south?"

He was still telling her as she climbed in, started the engine.

Connie slid in front of Jesse but kept her head well outside the open window. "Be careful. Fox is a loose cannon. There's no one here can tell him not to fire."

She grabbed Connie's arm before she could move back. "You've helped me all the way tonight. Why? Why do you want me out of town?"

Connie's shoulders rose. She braced her free hand against the cab as if to push.

"We're talking possible epidemic here. If the dead woman's contagious and nothing's done, everyone in this town could be dead. So what's your agenda with me?"

Connie leaned in till her face was inches from Kiernan's. "You know things about Jeff. I'm not chancing them getting back to the sheriff. Jeff's in deep enough."

"Is he running the safe house?"

"How safe . . ." Connie's laugh cut the night silence. Kiernan hadn't noted the rumble of talk by the Chevy until it stopped.

"What about you, Connie? Are you the safe house?"

"No, not me."

"But you know who is, don't you?"

"I can guess."

"And you guess who?"

She laughed, this time softly, dismissively.

"What's Jeff so involved in he'd call me here and hand me to the sheriff?"

"Just take your good fortune and get out of here. The highway's to your left." Connie pulled free, loped to the Chevy, and climbed into the cab.

Kiernan watched the Chevy take the sharp curves down the hill. From her vantage point she could see First Street, Jeff's office, and the mortuary on the far side, and on her side the back of the saloon.

It didn't surprise her that Connie knew who ran the safe house. Nor that she knew a lot more about Jeff than she had admitted.

Kiernan expected to lose sight of the Chevy as it pulled up in front of the saloon and the gang headed inside to help Jesse spend his five hundred. But it stopped in the same spot it had left from—in back—and only the passengers got out. Connie, the driver, headed east. She drove two blocks and made a right.

Kiernan started the engine of her new vehicle and followed.

CHAPTER

30

TCHERNAK TURNED ON Grady Hummacher's computer and sat in his chair. Was his machine at home this slow, flashing self-congratulatory graphics on the screen and all these numbers no one gave a shit about? He didn't have time for this. Should have been out of Vegas an hour ago. Should have thought to check the e-mail when he was here before. At least Grady's password was easy—Grady—or it would be taking weeks.

Ah, but there was one message. He pulled it up. From BakDat Information Services. Bless Persis. "Your request filled, cher. Unwise to leave at unauthorized address. Call me."

A bolt of fear shot through Tchernak. Was she right? Had he been too green to see the danger? But this was Persis. He shook his head and grinned. Then he called her.

"Tchernak, honey, you know I love talking to you, but collect? From out of state? This is going to go on the harridan's bill." She laughed, a little trill.

Tchernak had never seen Persis McEvoy, creator, owner, and by herself, the entire staff of Kiernan

O'Shaughnessy's preferred background service, but he pictured her as a tiny, voluptuous blonde, with bouncy blond curls and baby blue eyes. Just a bit plump all over. Pleasingly plump. He liked that. He pictured her in bed, in a teddy. He didn't figure she conducted the rest of her business that way, and when he made the mistake of describing this scene to Kiernan once, on a drive back from L.A., he found himself scrambling to defend the illogic of Persis hearing the phone, sensing it was him, tossing off her businesslike beige jacket and slacks, her one-size-fits-all running bra and cotton boxers, and slithering into the lacy black teddy before the third ring.

"Right," Kiernan had said, "this nubile charmer would choose to spend her days home alone with her computer."

"She's self-employed like you are. She can go out."

"You've called her, day and night; when hasn't she been there?"

He hadn't bothered answering that one.

"Tchernak, here's what she really looks like. She's—"

"Stop! I get whatever data you need from Persis, and I get it *tout de suite*, right?"

"Sure, because she thinks you're such hot stuff."

He had nodded seriously in the face of her sarcasm. "Persis comes on to me because I'm a sexy guy. No, wait! The reason I'm such a turn-on on the phone is because I'm picturing her stretching her plump white legs on her rumpled sheets while she takes down the data *you* need. If suddenly I'm picturing Mrs. Khrushchev, we're not going to get our order bumped to the front of the line."

Kiernan had groaned.

He had called Persis from the office only a couple times after that, but more gratifying than Persis's come-hither voice, or his own double entendres had been the joy of watching Kiernan biting her tongue.

Of course she hadn't bitten it hard enough or soon

enough, and among the terms Persis used for her, *harridan* was relatively kind.

"Bill the call to me, Persis. I'm on my own now."

"Super, Tchernak. Every case you take, you call me right away and I'll get you every little thing you need, you hear?"

He gave a low laugh, picturing those golden-blond curls bouncing, her plump white breasts jiggling with enthusiasm. "So what you got for me now? My first case, this is really important."

Suddenly she was the woman in the beige suit with cotton underwear. "What do you want first, Grady Hummacher or Adcock Explorations?"

"Adcock."

"Hocked to the gills. You want figures?"

"No. Gills are enough. And Grady Hummacher?"

"Okay. There isn't much on him. Not surprising. He's kept an address in Las Vegas for two years. Only membership is the Carson Club."

"The Carson Club?"

"It's more legit than it sounds. Lots more. Association of young movers and shakers throughout the state. Speaks well of Hummacher to get accepted. As for work history, a couple of movie companies—"

"Fifteen years ago? I know that."

"Got a graduate degree in geology. Then signed on with Exxon for two years, then Aramco, then Nihonco—"

"Never heard of that one."

"Japanese exploration company. You know how desperate the Japanese are for oil. They're hot for a good find in a country that will give them sole export."

"Countries like?"

"Central America, for one area. That's where any data on Hummacher comes out of. So then he quit Nihonco and signed on with Adcock Explorations."

"Quit? Not fired?"

"Nope. Nothing to suggest anything but normal job movement. That's not the interesting area with Hummacher."

She paused long enough to make Tchernak antsy. He didn't exactly beg, but was starting to picture himself as a Chihuahua, panting a little.

"What's interesting, Tchernak, is that Hummacher was detained—not arrested—but questioned about the company employees whose visas he'd arranged."

"I thought people arranged for their own visas."

She let a beat pass before saying, "That's the normal way. But the two essential workers he brought into the country last month were never seen at the embassy in Panama or the INS in Las Vegas. Two seismic aides."

So that was how Grady Hummacher got two deaf teenagers into the country. He knew the answer before he asked, "Names?"

"Juan Gomez, Carlos Rios. And here's the thing you're really going to find interesting, the source of the INS complaint. You can guess, right?"

He didn't have to picture her at all to sound desperate now. "Persis!"

"The INS was notified by Reston Adcock."

"But didn't these two come in as seismic aides to Adcock Explorations? You mean he called the INS and said he had nothing to do with them?"

"You got it."

"Whew!"

"Well, Adcock Explorations is not exactly a blue-chip stock. Adcock was a senior vice president of explorations for Exxon before they split off a number of their operations four years ago."

"Was he fired?"

"No. You'd think being a big shot in a new offshoot

company would be a good deal, but here's the thing, Tchernak. Big oil cuts these operations loose, so if there's a disaster, like the big Alaskan spill, it's not big oil with deep pockets that's liable anymore, it's the little offshoot with wee little pockets. One spill and it's history, and the public's left paying for the rest of the cleanup. But if there's no spill and the offshoot does find oil, they've got to sell it to big oil."

"So they're damned if they don't, and if they do, they don't get much cash for it?"

"You got it, my man."

"And so, Adcock figured rather than head an offshoot, he'd do better on his own."

"Safe guess."

Normally Tchernak liked these little guessing games, but this one was beginning to irk him. "So, then, why is Adcock Explorations mortgaged up to its derricks?"

"He's a little guy now, competing with the deep pockets of multinationals. He needs a big strike quick before they bury him. The geologist he had before Hummacher . . . in Yaviza . . . ?"

"Yes?"

"Shot."

"Really?"

"Really. Six months ago. No suspects. But the last person seen having a drink with that guy, Ross Estes, was a representative of Nihonco."

Tchernak leaned back in Grady Hummacher's chair. "Would Grady have known that?"

"It was in the papers down there."

"Not here?"

"No. But—"

"Yeah, sure, it would have buzzed around the grapevine down there and made a new circuit every time someone arrived from the States—"

"Especially Estes's replacement. And Tchernak, no one would be more anxious to meet that replacement than the guys from Nihonco. Too bad Estes was shot, but that doesn't help ninety million Japanese with tanks to fill."

"Are there any data to indicate Grady was negotiating with the Japanese?"

"Nope. But there was nothing on Estes till the bullet."

Tchernak fingered his beard, pondering Hummacher's trips back and forth to Panama. As far as he could see, frequent travel indicated nothing perfidious. "If it had been Tokyo Grady'd been heading to, that'd be one thing, but coming home to Adcock headquarters isn't the first thing a turncoat would do. And he definitely wouldn't go to all the trouble of getting 'seismic aide' visas for two deaf teenaged boys from Panama so they could have a better life in this country, not if he was going to be moving right away."

Persis was laughing, not the sexy little blond-curl giggle he'd come to expect from her, but a series of sharp hoots. "Tchernak, who do you think those boys are?"

"A couple of deaf kids who weren't getting adequate medical care down there."

"You must think Grady's quite the decent guy, huh?"

"When I saw him, he was real concerned about his responsibility for them."

"Well, it does make a good story, and I guess there's no reason not to believe it if you don't know better."

"Better is?"

"I did some research on oil-exploration methods down there. South of Yaviza it's rain forest. What they call impenetrable rain forest, which means you can't drive through it and you're not going to walk any too fast if you're not a tribesman born under the banana trees. The oil companies are trying to get the Pan-American Highway cut through. This is the last link they'd need and you'd be able to drive from Canada to Chile. They're not going to all this trouble to add a couple of gas stations and fill up a few more VW vans. The reason they want the road through is so they get the infrastructure to get into that rain forest and explore for oil."

"But they don't have it yet, right, Persis?"

"Right. But they're still after the oil, so who do you think they count on to lead them into that rain forest?"

"Ah, the indigenous tribesmen. So, okay, Grady's boys are not street urchins but tribesmen or tribe boys. Still, why bring them to Las Vegas where they are useless, and helpless?"

"No research is going to answer that one. Maybe tribesmen were murdered down there, but that wouldn't be likely to make an English-language newspaper."

Tchernak sighed. He liked his banter with Persis, and no one touched her when it came to research. But she had her limits. And now when he wanted to speculate back and forth, it was clear that Persis had hit those limits and stopped dead. If Kiernan were here . . . But she wasn't.

"You need anything else, Tchernak, you know where to call."

"You got it, Persis. You're going to hear from me lots." He hung up, but stayed in Grady Hummacher's chair. The Grady Hummacher he remembered was a college kid, a good-time guy, fun to have around if you wanted to blow off steam. Was he really the kind of guy who would make the commitment to care for two teenaged boys? Tchernak could picture Grady fuming that no one was bothering to test the kids' hearing, much less teach them to communicate. He could see Grady in one burst of energy getting them visas and shepherding them onto the company plane. And he could imagine only too well how those boys had ended up alone in a rented apartment among people with whom they could no more communicate than if they had lived next to Cassie Marengo. Grady was like the kid who got bunnies for Easter, and lost interest when he discovered they didn't retrieve or roll over.

But Grady hadn't forgotten the boys. When he got off the plane from Yaviza, he hadn't even slid between the sheets in his own apartment before going to the boys' place and spiriting them out of the city. Maybe Grady had done the sensible thing and taken them back to Yaviza.

Tchernak hit Redial. "Persis, can you check airline rosters this last week? Grady flew in from Panama a week ago Friday. Then he made another quick trip and got back Wednesday morning—"

"Wednesday morning, you sure?"

"He checked out of his hotel down there at four A.M. Where would he go besides the airport?"

"I can't answer that, Tchernak, but I've done enough eyeballing of airline schedules from that part of the world to know there are no flights from Panama to Las Vegas at five A.M. No commercial flights. What leaves at that hour are corporate jets, angling to get their execs stateside while there's still time for meetings."

"Adcock Explorations—"

"They could have leased a jet, but they don't own one."

"Grady wouldn't have leased one without Adcock's knowledge. He must have made that quick flight south with some other company, like Nihonco. No wonder Adcock's going crazy." Again, Tchernak paused for input, and again he was reminded that with data, Persis gave, she didn't ponder.

If Kiernan were here . . . But he didn't need Kiernan to realize that if Grady had used the boys to find oil, then they were the only ones who knew where that find was. If Grady was selling out to Nihonco, he wouldn't want to leave the boys in Yaviza for Reston Adcock to follow.

Tchernak jumped up and raced for the door.

CHAPTER

31

THE CHEVY WAS newer, bigger, and Connie knew where she was going. Kiernan pressed on the gas and narrowed the distance between them. She was off First Street in a dark land of small buildings set far back on lots. Connie picked up speed; her taillights were dots in the distance. Kiernan stepped harder on the gas. The truck sounded like a mariachi band. She thought of the auto club warnings about driving into the desert. Know your route. Did she even have a route? Have adequate food and water. Not. Have your vehicle checked by a mechanic before embarking on the trip. Ha! She didn't even have a full tank of gas. But Connie was her only lead.

Suddenly the taillights were gone. In front was blackness. She was heading into a wall of dirt. A hillside grew out of nowhere. The street evaporated. She spotted taillights up the hill to her right before she made out the narrow corkscrewing road. Pulling the wheel hard, she took the hill in third gear. The old truck sputtered. She jammed in the clutch and slammed the gear stick back and to the left till it found its niche and the engine took a thankful breath and pulled itself uphill. Connie's taillights flashed and were gone as she whipped around curves she had probably known since childhood. The black of the night was blacker here, devoid of even lamp glow muted by curtains. Sand and scrub pine walled in the winding road.

The engine coughed. Kiernan shifted the truck to first gear. Christ, she might as well be walking. She had to keep Connie in view. Connie'd know someone was following. In such a small town, could she recognize her friends' trucks from their headlights? Probably some, and one as old and battered as this would be a good candidate for uneven lights. Without slowing, she leaned into a curve and then pressed harder on the gas. If she ever needed her own fine Jeep from home, this was the time.

The road leveled off, dipped, and climbed again. Surprisingly the taillights were larger. Connie hadn't whipped through the curves like a teenaged boy. Lucky thing—unless the sheriff had spotted two sets of taillights. There was not one side road. And the road itself was getting narrower. Even if Fox was on Route 93, he would be back soon and then he'd be eyeing alternate roads. Was this one of many options leaving Gattozzi, or the only road out of town?

She crested a hill, and a sudden swatch of moonlight showed a road to the left, angling up a higher peak, then down. Connie's taillights blinked in and out of her range of vision. Depressions could have been turnoffs, but Kiernan couldn't spare her gaze from the taillights ahead to check. She didn't know how long she'd been driving when the lights disappeared altogether. She floored the gas; the truck bounced and shrieked into a curve. She swung her gaze from it to the road ahead, desperately searching for the red lights.

Connie had turned. Kiernan followed before she realized the road was gravel. The truck rattled so loudly, she couldn't tell if the engine was coughing. Irritably she slowed the truck, checking for four-wheel drive, finding none. Pebbles spit at the sides. She was hanging on as much as steering. To her right, pine trees not much taller than the cab grew close to the road. To her left she could see the outlines of small, rough-looking plants, the type that would spike you if you fell on them.

Maybe Jeff was hiding out back here. "If I get ahold of him," Kiernan muttered. The man wasn't just a liar. What he'd done made no sense. Why was he so desperate to cover up the woman's death? Why not just bury her?

A gust of wind sent the truck half off the road. Kiernan braced her elbows against her chest and held steady.

Jeff had called her here. Connie had gotten her out. And Fox? No question why the locals were edgy around Fox. But what had encouraged the man to this desolate area? There was beauty here, all right, and the wild openness appealed to Kiernan. But Fox was not the kind of guy to choose a small town like Gattozzi. Fox, Jeff Tremaine, Connie, and the dead woman—what had drawn them together?

The road shifted back and forth, never cutting through a hummock if there was the possibility of a wide loop around it. Connie's lights were blinked by the land. If she had a homestead ahead, no building was visible. There was no turning back, no possible place to turn. It was like driving into a sock. She crested a summit. Wind broadsided the truck. She wedged her hands harder on the wheel— would a little regular auto maintenance have killed Jesse?

Irrationally she had expected something at the summit—what? The Top of the Mark, with maybe a revolving bar?—but the road was the mirror image of what she'd just traversed, now headed down. Trees clumped closer to the road, the surface smoothed out, and as if she realized Kiernan had hit the good road, Connie shot ahead.

Feeling back in her own element for the first time to-day, Kiernan pressed on the gas pedal. The old truck lurched forward, gasping for a moment until the wheels caught up with the engine.

A clearing materialized before her. She couldn't tell where the road was. She needed to slow down, but she couldn't chance losing Connie. The truck lurched to the right. She yanked the wheel. Too late. The hood was going down. She smashed the brake pedal to the floor as the wheels spun. Then the truck stopped dead.

Kiernan sat, still gripping the wheel. In front of her was a hole that hadn't existed a minute earlier. Bracing her feet against the floorboard against the angle of the cab, she peered down the line of the headlights into the ground. Was it ten feet deep? Fifteen? Twenty? She turned off the headlights and peered into the dark. The hole had to be forty feet wide. It wasn't a sinkhole, the kind that erode at a gentlemanly pace. This had to be an abandoned mine. The roof had caved in leaving a huge underground hole. The truck's front wheels were poised on the edge.

CHAPTER
32

CECIL McGUIRE WANTED to pinch himself. The whole thing was like one of those dreams you can't get out of. He'd never had the college dream his educated friends laughed about, but chasers, he'd had plenty of them at night, like the one where he went to meet a new client and opened his door and found himself in an alley that smelled of shit, with rats big as rottweilers, and he kept running around the alley trying to find the door he came in, but all he could see was plain brick wall a million feet high. This case, following the baby dick Tchernak, was getting like that. When Adcock told him they were headed north on 93, it was like the door out of the alley. Action, instead of this pussyfooting around here. And now, Tchernak ignores the freeway like he's a city bus or something and here he is pulling into Grady Hummacher's driveway again.

Was the guy such a novice he was knocking off for the night? Did he think this was a nine-to-fiver, with maybe an hour off in the afternoon to go to the dentist?

More to the point—the Weasel groaned—did this mean he was in for another night slumped behind the 'Cuda's

steering wheel? Tourists pictured Vegas as sun and sand
and air-conditioning and tropical strolls between the casinos and maybe a moonlight swim in the palm-rimmed
pool. Here in November he'd have been better off sitting
over a subway grate.

Inside Hummacher's house the living-room lights were
on. Tchernak was probably settling in with a beer from
Hummacher's fridge and the late movie on the tube.

The Weasel shifted. He could use a beer, a movie, a
burger, a leak. He eased out of the car, not letting the door
close completely so that there'd be no sound. Tchernak
was watching out for him. Keeping the car and the house
door in sight, McGuire slipped into the bushes and took
his leak.

As he zipped up, he made a decision. The phone was
three blocks away, but what the hell, he knew where the
baby dick was supposed to be going. He slid into his car
and started the engine. The blue BMW across the street,
was it the same one? He hesitated, then drove off. If he
spotted it again, he'd worry.

He checked again when he pulled into the 7-Eleven lot,
and once more as his call went through. "Adcock," he
shouted over the recorded message, "I'm calling you from
a pay phone. It's three blocks away from where the action
is. I can't hang around here waiting for you. Pick up,
man."

Louisa Larson was not cut out for this cloak-and-dagger
stuff. Bad enough she'd had to run two red lights following
the thug across town, all to end up at Grady's place, but
then the thug ups and leaves. And leaves her to guess what it
is that he knows so well that he can dismiss the whole
business and go make a phone call. She had to guess and
guess fast. She'd learned that when she'd worked the ER.

There you don't get a second chance. She'd learned to make her move and not look back. And if it was the wrong move, she figured she'd do it differently the next time. That's how it had been when she saw the boys last week. The symptoms they'd presented were consistent with hepatitis. She had given them the standard treatment, and mostly to calm the neighbors she'd brought them into the office.

When had she realized she'd guessed wrong?

It was a serious mistake, one that could be devastating. But not if she took charge. She had good judgment; she had to trust it. Stay at Grady's with the new gold Cherokee like the one at Las Palmas? Follow the thug? Which way would get her to the boys? She went with the thug. Now she was sitting down the street eyeing him at a pay phone. Should she stay in the car? Try to get closer to him and not get beaten to a pulp for the effort?

Who was it who said you should never avoid taking the chance because you're afraid? Eleanor Roosevelt? Well, Eleanor'd be proud of her now. Was Eleanor the one who talked about turning lemons into lemonade?

The thug's back was to her as she made her way around the corner. He was leaning his grungy little body into the phone cubby, his head almost enclosed, like a terrier barking down a hole. She reached the apartment next door and kept watch on him—he could put down the phone anytime, turn around, and be staring her in the face. She was out of cover. There was nothing to do but head for the shrubs. Forcing herself to take long, silent steps, she moved across the dry, prickly grass till she was five feet from the guy.

"Pick up, man," he was yelling.

"McGuire, what the hell are you calling about? I don't have time—"

"Then don't waste it complaining, Adcock. Do you want me to sit and watch your bab—Tchernak—relax in Grady's flat all night?"

"What's Tchernak doing there?"

"You don't know?"

"Hell, no. Listen, McGuire, forget Tchernak and whatever he's screwing around doing. He found Grady's contact up Ninety-three, and that's where the action's going to be. I'm flying up there now. Meet me."

"Where?"

"There's only one place open up there this time of night. Called the Doll's House. Then we'll go on to Gattozzi."

"Gattozzi?"

"Little town beyond the Doll's House."

McGuire nodded. He knew the Doll's House. "Two and a half hours up Ninety-three."

"Make it two hours. Grady's already had time to move on."

"Word I got is those boys of his are sick, Adcock. Maybe they slowed him down."

"Or maybe he dumped them."

"Is that what he's like?"

It was a moment before Adcock admitted, "No. The guy's got a soft spot. Me he'd screw, no question. But those kids . . ."

Reston Adcock had turned off the phone before he said, "Jerk." He could have had the Weasel take care of Tchernak before he left. Tchernak was a disaster. And now what was the guy doing at Hummacher's? Was Tchernak onto something there he needed to know about? Maybe it was just as well he hadn't sicced the Weasel on him. He'd need to cover that base and make sure Tchernak had left no thread hanging before he made a final decision.

Louisa Larson pressed herself so hard against the apartment building, she was sure the stucco pattern was imprinted on her back. She watched as the thug strolled to his jalopy and rolled off like a guy who'd picked up a six-pack and was heading home for the night. She watched till he was out of sight, then pulled herself off the wall and hurried into the 7-Eleven. She hit the bathroom, grabbed food, considered coffee, and realized caffeine was something she was definitely not going to need. She knew where she was going. She'd been up that way often enough to know where Gattozzi was. Now the question was where in Gattozzi the *thug* was headed.

CHAPTER
33

KIERNAN CONTROLLED THE desperate urge to leap out of the sinking truck. In the black of night she couldn't tell how far into the mine hole the front wheels were. Too far. She eased out onto the step. Icy wind slapped her face. As the truck swayed, the temptation to leap to safety was almost overwhelming. But that could be the added force that would send the vehicle careening into the hole, and her with it. She turned from the hole and looked toward solid ground. Holding on to the side wall of the bed, she stretched till her right foot was on the tire, slid her hand along the truck, brought her left foot back, shifted her hands to the tailgate, swung herself behind it, and leaped onto the ground.

The truck rocked forward and then back. She exhaled so hard she thought for a moment it was the force of her breath that had moved it. Despite the cold wind she was sweating. She stared at the miserable truck. She was stranded.

As many unfenced, unmarked deserted mines as there

were in this area, wouldn't you think a decent driver—even Jesse—would have a winch? Did he? Nooooo.

The mines were supposed to be off the road, not where the road would have been if it hadn't curved abruptly to the left. The front wheels were definitely over the edge of the hole. She looked down into the hole and gasped. It was as big as the Gattozzi bar and twice as deep. It was just dumb luck that she wasn't lying at the bottom with a broken neck. She was shaking hard as she stepped back away from the hole and dropped to the ground. She sat there, shivering with cold and fear, her mind devoid of thought.

Slowly her fear shifted to anger. What kind of government leaves a hole this size right by a curve in the road? How was she to know the road cut right? Only locals would know. . . . Connie would know.

By now Connie would have realized the headlights following her were gone. She hadn't circled back to see why.

Kiernan's breath caught. Had Connie intentionally led her into the hole? Was she willing to kill her? Why?

But there was no time for speculation. She pushed herself up and assessed the truck. The front wheels hung over the crumbling edge of the mine hole. It was a situation meant for a tow truck, a huge one. But even if she could roust one in the middle of the night, she wouldn't know where to tell it to come. It was a moot point anyway. Her cell phone was in the cab.

She bent down by the rear of the truck and stared at the ground. The right wheel was solid, but under the left there was nothing but loose dirt. Two front wheels nearly into the hole didn't matter. The truck would have rear-wheel drive. But would someone like Jesse have plunked down extra for limited slip differential? Or would a guy with limited cash figure he'd be lucky enough never to be in a spot like this?

She stood staring down into the mine hole. If the truck

went careening down there, it would end upside down, like a broken bottle on the barroom floor. It would be crazy to get back in that truck.

And if she didn't try? She had done a postmortem once on a hiker who had died of exposure. The clothes she'd cut off him had been way warmer than hers were now. Taking a breath, she climbed onto the side of the truck, moving carefully until she was standing on the tire. Then she eased her foot forward. The toe of her shoe caught at the door-frame. Slowly she moved her hands forward. The truck lurched; she swung her weight back. She froze, trying to feel whether the truck had stopped moving. Gusts of wind smacked her and there was no way to tell whether the movement she felt came from the truck or the wind. No way to know if her next move forward would jerk the al-ready loosened vehicle into the shaft. No way—

She blanked her mind as she had done those days years ago in gymnastics, and moved forward, bracing her feet, reaching for the door handle.

Again she felt the truck shimmy. Too late to go back. She wedged open the door, and when no lurch followed, slid her foot inch by inch along the side of the truck until it was in the door opening.

Then the truck lurched. She froze. It wasn't the wind this time. The truck was moving. Kiernan forced herself to stay still, to wait till the movement stopped.

The back wheels are on the ground, she reminded herself. She swung herself carefully forward and into the cab, slipped the gearshift into reverse.

In her mind she saw the engine starting, feeding power to the back wheels evenly, the back wheels taking hold, and the truck rolling gracefully back onto the road.

She turned on the engine and eased up on the clutch. The truck groaned.

"Goddamn you, Jesse, you cheap bastard!"

The truck lurched again. She could hear the shriek of the wheels as they spun backward, the dull groan as they dug into the ground. The truck jolted back hard. The engine stalled.

The last jolt had brought all four wheels onto firm ground.

The fear and panic she had pushed aside engulfed her. She sat, heart pounding against her chest wall, chest wall banging into air that felt like cement. She reached for the handle to roll down the window and cool herself off and almost had the pane lowered before good sense returned. She wasn't going to die in a desert mine shaft, but on the other hand she was still in the middle of the desert on a road that was leading nowhere. She had almost forgotten about Sheriff Fox and her escape from him at the mortuary. This was still his territory and he'd still be looking for her. In the open, empty land the sound of her engine would reverberate for miles.

Jeff Tremaine had vanished. "Jeff's in deep enough," Connie had said. Deep in something connected to the dead woman? Connie wanted her out of town to protect him. Were the stakes high enough for Connie to kill her? She would find that out face-to-face, or die trying.

She turned on the engine and headed in the direction Connie had taken.

CHAPTER

34

"IT'S LIKE LOOKING for a pebble on the track while you're sprinting to the finish line," Reston Adcock grumbled. He could barely hear himself over the noise of the Cessna's engine. Any other time he'd be so caught up in flying, he'd feel the roar flowing over him like air over a wing. He loved the whole gestalt of soaring over mountains small as the ridges on his knuckles and men too tiny to see, the cool, round feel of the throttle giving way to his hand, the instruments responding to attitude and altitude. Takeoffs posed the most danger, but landings were the real challenge, and that first notch of the flaps was when he really came alive. Oil exploration used to be like that. But now the big challenges were financial. He wasn't driving through the forests gauging the spot to set the explosives, he was driving to the visa office greasing the palm to get his operatives into the country. He wasn't watching for poisonous snakes ready to drop from branches, he was looking over his shoulder for spies from Sunoco, BP, Phillips, Nihonco. Now if he flew the Cessna at all, it was likely to be over the flats to Oklahoma City or Houston, as exciting as driving an empty freeway with cruise control.

Even this flight would have been a no-brainer if it weren't for Simkin.

He keyed the mike to activate Simkin's runway lights. As soon as he spotted the two strips of light, he pulled back on power and when his air speed was within flap range, put on the first notch. All thoughts of Simkin were gone now as he focused on the sequence of bringing the plane down on the dim, rough dirt.

But as soon as he had shut down the engine and pushed open the door, it was Simkin who was on his mind. And there he was, running like a bullmastiff toward the plane. Adcock had barely lowered himself to the ground when Simkin clapped a thick arm around his shoulder. Simkin's breath was coming in huffs. "Come on, we've got to move fast. There's been a problem. Car's over there."

Adcock looked around. The strip lights had run their time limit and gone out. There was no light in any direction, and he knew he could spot one miles away. "Problem, how could there be any—"

"Navy. I told you this was their land, right?"

"*Near* their land, you said."

"Well, see, normally they don't care. They've got close to a million acres here. Don't need more than a city block for their office and barracks. Not like they can dock a destroyer or a nuclear sub here."

Simkin was wandering. Adcock had forgotten that infuriating habit of his. The guy lived alone. He could talk to himself all day, as much as he loved hearing the sound of his own voice. If Adcock didn't cut him off—"So what's with the navy now?"

"I don't know, Resty, not exactly. Whatever they do here they keep dead quiet. Maybe it's testing—weapons, bombs, chemicals, who knows. But lately there's been a rumor of something in the air—"

"Germ warfare?"

"Oh, no, I don't mean that. They know there are people downwind over in Utah."

"That didn't stop the government in the past."

"I'm not saying our government's into chemical warfare," Simkin raced on. "They're not testing anything like VX or sarin, the stuff the terrorist tossed in the Tokyo subway. No, I don't think it's anything like that."

Adcock almost smacked into the car, an old tan Ford, before he saw it. Before Simkin could open the driver's door, he caught his arm. "You're telling me what the navy's *not* doing. But they're into something that's making them nervous about visitors. What is it?"

Simkin hunched his shoulders over his barrel chest and lowered his chin as if to protect his words. "I don't know for sure, but whatever they're tossing up in the air, they're making damned sure no one gets east of them. I got a friend in Public Health who's always going on about the navy. He thinks they're testing vaccines against biological weapons, like anthrax, or worse—if there's anything worse than anthrax. They say a suitcase of that could wipe out Vegas. Biological and Chemical Agent Detection program, he says. Says they shoot these biological agents that maybe the Arabs will use against our guys the next time we invade Kuwait, shoot 'em up over the desert and then see how long it takes to identify them."

The operation was top secret, but Adcock had heard crazy talk about it from one of the docs he met at the Carson Club. "Sim," he said disgustedly, "they shoot up simulants, not the real stuff. We don't have kamikazes in this country. Who'd they get to collect the real stuff?"

"The guys they tested the vaccines on. That's the whole point. Come on, Resty, do you think they would trust sending the entire navy, army, air force and marines where they'd be exposed to viruses or germs or whatever when the vaccines they gave the guys were tested only against simulants? All those guys with their billions of dollars' of materiel? You think they learned zip from Kuwait?"

Adcock said nothing. There was nothing to say to that.

Simkin let a beat pass. *Enjoying his little victory*, Adcock figured. "Like I said, Resty, whatever they're blasting up into the air, they're very prickly about anyone getting downwind of it. Guy I had working on my cars last week drove down to the Breadfruit Park Saturday and it was closed. And that's this side of the testing ground. Upwind."

"Winds change."

"Yeah. My guy said it wasn't closed the week before. He saw a family going in there to picnic. But now the navy's all hot to seal it off. Who knows what they got in the air there. Now, maybe they wouldn't care about us here—we're more'n five miles west of the park—but we'd be smart not to hang around to find out."

"Right." He climbed into the driver's seat of the Ford truck and waited till Simkin got in beside him. "I'll drop you off on the highway."

CHAPTER

35

KIERNAN SQUINTED THROUGH the dirt-glazed glass trying to make out the road from the desert on either side. Desert that could hide another abandoned mine. Her nose was nearly against the windshield. In all directions the land was the same, a waterless nubby broadloom carpet leading to nowhere. The truck strained in first gear, jerking and coughing. *If it were a person*, she thought, *I'd be calling for a priest.*

She crested the hill. The headlights shone down the steep decline. The emptiness was immense, the hillside like great Brillo pads packed one against another. By now Connie could have looped back to town on an unseen road and be headed to bed. There could be nothing down this arid hill but scrub pines and sunbaked bones.

Or Connie could be in a cabin somewhere down there, feet up, drink in hand, smug little grin on her face. Kiernan stepped on the gas. Halfway down the hill a dirt road led off to the right and disappeared in the night shadows. She hesitated, checked the gas tank—quarter full—and turned right onto a narrow rutted path.

The engine sputtered and halted momentarily like a snorer waking himself up with the noise and affording himself a moment of silence in which he eased back into raucous sleep. In that silent moment she could hear the wind snapping the tough branches of the scrub pines and feel it battering the truck as she hit a curve.

The edge of the canyon was longer than it had appeared in the dark. The road slashed back and forth, turning suddenly, sharply.

Abruptly a driveway cut right, into a pocket invisible from the road. Now, close, she could make out a high wooden skeleton of a mining building. It and two other crumbling buildings stood around an open area. Even in the dark she could see between the burned-out roof beams of the nearest one.

She looked around for a pit, but there was none. The whole place looked as if it had been deserted for decades.

She cut the engine, got out, and made her way into the compound. Here the wind was not so sharp, but the cold more chilling. The dry, sharp scrabble crackled under her feet. No car was visible, and looking down, she could make out no tire tracks. She rarely carried a gun; she'd seen the devastation bullets caused in too many postmortems. But here, in this deserted spot, a piece in hand would have comforted her.

She moved off the loose scrabble. Sky showed through the burned-out beams of the nearest house.

The second place, probably once a miners' bunkhouse, was burned as badly. A rusted metal bed frame hung off the porch on three legs.

When she approached the last house, she sighed. Burned to a shell. Could she have been wrong about this mine? Maybe it was not a marvelous semblance of a deserted mine but was in fact a deserted mine.

Something gave under her foot. She looked down, saw

nothing, bent down, and fingered a fuzzy, faded green tennis ball. A shot of longing went through her as she imagined Ezra bounding down the beach corralling his ball with his feet in the wet sand.

Leaving the ball on the ground, she stood, turned around very slowly till she made out a dark spot on the far side of the compound. No light shone, but unlike the other burned-out buildings this one was solid. No sky was visible between its beams.

She knocked. "Open up. You know I'm here."

Connie opened the door. The spiky gray hair that had looked so adventurous in the Gattozzi saloon, was matted back as if from sweaty hands drawn through it again and again. In the flickering light her chiseled features looked sepulchral and her caramel-colored eyes shone. She was holding a pistol.

Kiernan smacked it out of her hand. The gun sailed across the porch. Connie dove toward her, but Kiernan was already halfway to the wall scooping up the gun. It was an old, long-barreled revolver and it felt heavy in her hand. She stood and glared down at Connie. "Stay right there on the ground. I could have died out there in that mine pit!"

"You should have thought about that before you screwed Jeff." Connie had landed on an elbow, and it was already swelling visibly, but she made no move to coddle it.

"You think I—"

"Now I don't care who Jeff sleeps with. But when he went off to Africa, I wasn't thirty years old, and it mattered."

Kiernan took a breath, acutely aware of the cold wind blowing across her back. She stared down at the tough, wiry woman now sitting up, back to the wall. "You're Jeff's wife? I don't remember—"

"Don't remember me from his med-school years?

There's a surprise. Those were the four most isolated years of my life." It had been over a decade since then, but her anger sounded fresh and triumphant, as if she had always known this moment of vindication would come. Her face was flushed and her eyes moist, and in that moment she bore no resemblance to the no-nonsense woman in the saloon.

Kiernan waited till she caught her eye. "For that you were willing to kill me?"

"Kill you?"

"You led me into a mine hole."

"I didn't lead you anywhere."

"You didn't come back when my headlights disappeared. No one does that on an isolated mountain road."

"You've been here less than a day and you're giving forth the commandments for mountain driving?" The vulnerability was gone from her face now.

Kiernan shook her head. She couldn't tell what was behind Connie's sarcasm—guilt or just anger. There would never be any proof of her intentions. She would never know whether Connie Tremaine would have let her die. Motioning the woman up, she said, "Jeff may have had affairs, but they weren't with me."

"Please. You go to med school together, you go to Africa together. It doesn't take scientific deduction to come to a conclusion."

"The wrong conclusion." It would have been easy to tell her about Hope Mkema, but somehow she couldn't bring herself to do that. "I'm not speaking of what Jeff did in Africa, or after. But I was there for less than a month and so sick I had to be airlifted out."

"But you went there to be where Jeff was, didn't you?"

"Look, here's the truth. I didn't like your husband in med school—he was a bore. I wasn't pleased to find him in Africa, where he'd become an officious bore. And I certainly wouldn't have come flying out in the wilds here for anything less than the threat of massive contagion that an officious bore wasn't about to report to the health department. I don't know what you and Jeff and the sheriff and God knows who else is involved in, but—"

"Jeff and I, we are not involved in anything together. All we share is a name."

"You were worried enough about him to find me a car and point me out of town. Jeff is missing. You've got a safe house here. Where else would he be?"

"I don't know. That's my whole point." She seemed to deflate back against the porch railing. "I don't love Jeff anymore. Love can be a flimsy commodity in a small town with few choices. But I've been around him all my life and I know him. Jeff never went anywhere without leaving word with his receptionist. But today he did. He's just gone, and for all I know he's dead."

Kiernan could see her shivering. "Let's go inside."

Inside, the first thing that hit her was the heat; it seemed to steam off the floor, off the threadbare Oriental carpet, from the tapestries that curtained the doors and windows, from the smiling nineteenth-century faces in huge gilded frames above antique love seats, inlaid mahogany, and pink marble tables. The wavering light of the oil lamps made the room almost alive. But if this was a safe house, the guests had cleared out any evidence.

"I'm going to believe you," Connie said, flexing her arm and eyeing her swollen elbow. In jeans and a heavy sweater, she looked as if she'd broken into this bastion of gentility.

"Do or don't. Your choice." The hastily stacked magazines on the marble tables and the streaked ashtrays announced a frantic cleanup. How many frightened, confused women were beyond the closed parlor door? She didn't ask. The less she knew about the safe house, or who

Connie was sheltering at the moment, the less danger she would be to them. Jeff Tremaine was not here, that she did accept.

The sofa beckoned. Suddenly Kiernan realized how exhausted she was. The troubled sleep last night after Tchernak's outburst seemed years ago. And now the soft cushions . . . She chose the one hard chair next to a marble table and lay the gun at her side.

Connie disappeared through a narrow doorway and returned with a bottle. "Drink? We could both use one."

"You go ahead." She wasn't *that* sure of Connie. "Just tell me what's going on here. Start with the dead woman."

Connie perched on the arm of the brocade sofa. Her free hand tapped hard and quick on her thigh. Her mouth tightened, and the lines around her eyes deepened as she studied Kiernan.

"I thought you said you'd decided to trust me."

"To *believe* you. Trust is too much to ask on a couple hours' acquaintance."

"I trusted you when I bought the truck."

"And look where that got you!" Connie laughed, and the fragility of that sound said more about her precarious state than had anything before.

"I didn't have any choice, Connie. And neither do you. I know you've got a safe house here. I don't want to endanger it, as long as it has nothing to do with the dead woman in Gattozzi."

Momentarily her jaw tightened, then she sighed. "Okay. I'll have to trust you on that too. The truth is I need to know what you've found out. If I don't figure out who that woman is, someone from the county or the state is going to start nosing around—"

"What do you mean? She was one of your—"

"No, Kiernan, she wasn't. That's the whole point. If a guest of mine had come down with a condition as horrifying as that woman's, I would have had her medevacked to Las Vegas even if it meant every reporter in the state crawling all over this place. No way would I endanger everyone here and in Gattozzi. I grew up in Gattozzi; I've known those people all my life. No way would I—"

"Then who the hell is she and how did she get into the morgue?"

"That's the question, isn't it?"

"Surely you know if Jeff—"

Connie lifted the brandy glass to her mouth and sipped pensively. "I don't know anything about Jeff Tremaine anymore. He lives in town; I live here. Oh, sometimes I stay in his house there for appearance's sake, so people don't wonder where I live. But it's a big house."

"So the dead woman could be someone he knew," Kiernan said. "But why is the sheriff involved?"

"Don't know."

"What about the naval installation off Route Ninety-three, the Admiralty of the Sands? Does Jeff have old navy buddies there?"

Connie laughed again. "One thing you can count on with Jeffrey Tremaine is that he has no naval buddies. Jeff was thrown out of the navy after a year."

"On what grounds?" Kiernan asked, amazed. "The military wasn't meting out general discharges for fraternization back then. Drugs?"

"Insubordination."

"Really?"

"You're that shocked? Insubordination—you can't believe he had it in him, can you? Poor Jeff would be so insulted."

"Well, no," Kiernan admitted. "Jeff Tremaine in med school wouldn't dare to have questioned authority."

"There he never got the chance. He was a middle-of-the-road kid in a very liberal environment. There was always someone else eager to leap first into the fray."

Kiernan nodded slowly. Her picture of Jeff Tremaine was still the stiff kid in med school. She assumed Africa was an aberration in his life. But the man Connie was describing fit the doctor in Africa, who had been stopped by neither rules nor customs. There, Jeff hadn't stepped aside for anyone. "Between med school and Africa Jeff was so insubordinate he got himself thrown out of the navy?" she said, still amazed. "Insubordinate about what?"

"Secrecy. He wasn't about to administer unproven drugs to unsuspecting sailors. Gulf War kind of thing."

"So, then it's a safe guess he's not involved with the local navy?"

Connie picked up her glass and started to the kitchen. "There's very little I would swear to about Jeff. Maybe that he'll always be sneaking off to some woman. Surprisingly, that he's a good doctor. And definitely that he's not in league with anyone in the navy. Hundreds of acres of land right next to his town being off-limits and the government refusing to say what's going on there—it bugs the hell out of him."

"Does Jeff think they've got nuclear waste there?"

"Maybe. Whatever it is, it's top secret, and the navy's got more influence over what goes on around here than it should."

"By which you mean . . . ?"

"Well, I'll tell you how Jeff put it. It's like a battleship that gets separated from the fleet so long, the admiral forgets he's part of the country and starts thinking of himself as head of his own floating empire. Then any boat that comes near is the enemy."

"So you think—"

"Steer clear of it. You don't have time to get hassled. Believe me."

Kiernan followed her to the kitchen doorway. "Okay, but answer me this, then—the reason Jeff brought me to Gattozzi was to get me to take responsibility for the body, right? Was that because he was afraid of the sheriff?"

Connie's glass was in one hand, and a washrag hung suspended in the other. She turned and leaned back against the sink, oblivious of the precious drops of water splatting onto the floor. "I'm the last one to make excuses for Jeff. It probably doesn't look to you as if Jeff has much of a career, but he's active in the state medical association, the state committee on historic cities, the Carson Club, the Nevada Environmental League, the Anti-Nuclear Alliance, and who knows what else. This is his state and he's concerned about it. But the sheriff is another thing. And yes, Jeff's afraid of him."

THE ROAD WAS black: black macadam, blackness on either side. To his right, the Weasel knew, was Lake Mead, built by the WPA to create Hoover Dam and the zillions of kilowatts that made Vegas possible. He had been to the lake, had to tail a visiting Jersey punk there once. He'd had himself a good laugh watching the Hoboken hood staring at the lake shore. "Like they turned on the tap in a brown tub." That was one thing the little hood had been right about, there was no beach, no trees or shrubs or even grass, just rock, dirt, and water, and marinas every few dozen miles. But deep, and useful, as the late Jersey punk had discovered.

Now the lake was miles to the left, with nothing but turnoff signs to say it was there at all. And on the road, nothing else. Not so much as taillights. McGuire'd never admit it, but he didn't like empty roads. A nice red set of taillights ahead would have comforted him. A couple sets, on vehicles maybe weaving in and out, would have gone a long way to telling him he wasn't headed off the edge of the earth. Way in the distance behind he could see white dots. Made him uneasy.

"I'm a city guy," McGuire muttered to himself for the sixth or seventh time since he'd lost sight of the bright lights of the Strip in his rearview. "I get hired 'cause I know who's into who, and where 'who' is hanging. It goes down in Vegas, I know about it. But here . . ." The Weasel glared out at the offending darkness as if it were a line of hoods in black cravats and bulletproof vests.

There was a *sound* coming from the engine, or maybe the front axle. Metal grating on metal. It hadn't been there before, not till he got out on this road with no gas station for another hundred miles, unless he wanted to turn off and drive miles of unlit, winding, two-lane roads and hope one of the marinas would have something besides a self-serve pump. Was it getting worse? He couldn't tell. If he got stuck out here . . .

It could have been there before, he told himself, knowing he was grabbing at straws. He hadn't taken the 'Cuda out of town in a couple years. Hadn't hit—he glanced at the speedometer that was stuck at fifty—hadn't gone above fifty in years.

If he'd known about this trip into the desert when Adcock called, he'd have turned him down flat no matter— He laughed aloud. For ten grand he'd have walked across the atomic testing grounds. He wouldn't have believed the feds about no one downwind being in danger, he wasn't that blinded by cash, he'd just have figured that with his lifestyle he was lots more likely to see the end of ten grand than thirty years, or however long it took for those cancers to get you.

He slowed for the turnoff for 93, felt the 'Cuda pull against the turn, then ease into the straightaway. McGuire pushed pedal to floor, leaned back against the seat, and rested his hands loosely on the wheel. Nothing was going to change between here and the Doll's House. Nothing except an hour of time.

The metallic clanging in Louisa Larson's car was not in the engine. Her foot was nowhere near the floor. Her toes tapped on the gas pedal, giving the BMW a sputtering ride probably not unlike the miserable old rattletrap she was trying to stay behind. They said people grew to resemble their dogs and take on the personality of their vehicles. If there was ever a guy meant for a sleazy rust bag of a car . . .

Perspiration was so thick on her hands, the steering kept slipping. The rattling noise wasn't so loud, she knew that, but it was driving her crazy. She could have passed the thug—she knew his destination—but she didn't want to alert him. Tailing a car on an empty road should have been as complicated as prescribing ibuprofen for temporary pain relief. But this . . . Every time she came over a rise, she had to yank her foot off the gas. Once, she was almost in the guy's trunk, back when there was other traffic on the road. She was losing it. Damn Grady Hummacher, did everything the man touched turn to poison? Okay, so the boys didn't have the best of lives in Panama, but before Grady, they hadn't been kidnapped, infected, and likely to be murdered before the virus could kill them.

She could still feel the little thug's hands on her throat, and the knife slicing down her face. Automatically her hand went to the wound—rough, blood-caked—and she felt the panic and fury anew. Her back was slimy, her sweater wadded against her skin. Last year she had a growing medical practice, a spot on two NMA committees, and useful connections in the Association, in government; she was on her way. And now? Here she was speeding up a deserted highway after a vicious gangster. She had to get

to those boys before he did. The thug figured they'd be at
the Doll's House. Maybe. But that wasn't the only possibility, it was merely the most benign.

The rattling hammered on her head as if it were not
coming from the glove compartment but inside her skull.

She had driven this road often enough while finishing
off her scholarship commitment to know how long, how
frustrating, how endless it was. She floored the pedal and
passed the clunker so fast, it had shrunk to miniature size
by the time she could check the rearview.

Tchernak squinted against the lulling dark. He couldn't
afford to space out. It wasn't like the terrain was going to
tell him if he made a mistake. He cracked the window and
let the cool, dry desert air slap him alert. On this empty
straightaway it would be so easy to drift off, and then even
the fine new Jeep Grand Cherokee Laredo's four-wheel
drive wouldn't save him.

And those boys . . . Tchernak jerked awake. How
could Grady— But he knew only too well how Grady
Hummacher could go flying after a dream and never look
down at the consequences. Tchernak remembered the
week he'd spent hustling beds because he wasn't allowed in
his dorm room, because he'd been suspended from school,
because he had gotten caught in the Tasman Hall raid
Grady Hummacher planned. When the campus cops
stormed the building, Grady of course was gone. By the
time Tchernak got back in his room, Grady was a hero and
he, Tchernak, had pneumonia. But only a whiner would
have mentioned that.

Maybe nobody whined. Maybe Grady really didn't
know how nonchalantly he dangled people over the pit.

But Grady wasn't playing with undergraduates now.
Tchernak floored the gas.

CHAPTER
37

"TAKE A THERMOS of coffee with you, Kiernan. And gas for your truck? Do you need that?"

"Thanks, Connie." Her skin had that thick, heavy feel from lack of sleep. The coffee would only create a buzz in her nerves, but that would help somewhat. The hated thirty-six-hour rotations in med school had taught her well.

She took a final look at the faded gentility of Connie Tremaine's parlor in this isolated mine encampment. She could imagine Connie's ancestors four generations back proudly hanging the oil paintings with their great gilded frames and staking their claim, not merely to silver or bauxite but to the future of culture in the West. At night when they sat on the pincushion love seat and the brocade sofa, their feet on the bright, thick carpet from the Orient, and the gaslight sparkled on long silk dresses, one of them had probably sipped from the brandy glass Connie now used. When they'd imagined this place a hundred years in the future, what had they seen? Could they ever have conceived of it all coming to this?

In the silence she made out a low canine whine. The dog whose tennis ball she had spotted outside. It comforted her to think that Connie was not out here miles from town with nothing but a deep well dug in the days of gentility, a generator, and probably a cell phone.

"One for the road." Connie held out a cup of coffee. The china cup rattled on its saucer.

Kiernan took it and drank gratefully. Taking a second swallow, she looked appraisingly at Connie Tremaine. The woman was exhausted. Her tan camouflaged blotches, but blotches were definitely there. And her eyes were rheumy. "How do you feel?" she asked.

"Fine."

"No, really?"

"Fine," Connie snapped.

"Let me take your temperature."

"I'm fine!"

"You're not fine. Maybe you're just tired. But it could be more than that—"

"It's not!"

"—in which case you could be contagious. So if you've got anyone hidden here—"

"I don't!"

"—don't infect them. I'll get myself a thermos of coffee and the gas you offered."

"What? You're afraid to be downwind of me?"

Kiernan stared her in the face. "You got it." There was no time to argue, and no sense in minimizing the danger. If she was going to help Connie, she had to find the dead woman and find out where she had contracted the virus that killed her.

As she poured the coffee into the thermos, Connie handed her two Granola bars. "Still wrapped, so you're safe from me. And be careful out there. Back out. Don't drive over the courtyard."

"The *courtyard*?"

"Yeah. It's what we call the area between the buildings. There's a mine under there. Real shaky. Dangerous. You can walk across it without caving it in, but I wouldn't try it in your truck. You'd be fifty feet down before you got in gear."

Kiernan nodded in silent acknowledgment. "Take care of yourself, Connie. If you feel any worse, call a doctor you trust. I'm leaving you my number at home. If you don't have a doctor, call me and I'll get the right person here."

Connie laughed hollowly. "Which odds are better, me coming down with bleeding disease or you ending up wherever they've taken Jeff?"

Kiernan stepped outside. The cold was bone-chilling. The sharp wind reminded her she was on a desert mountainside where no tree grew tall enough to fight the icy blasts. She started the truck and headed out past the deserted buildings. In less than a minute she was beyond any sign of human habitation and the desert seemed drier and sharper for the brief period of safety behind her.

She couldn't help but like Connie Tremaine, who lived by her own rules out here alone with her dog and the unsolid earth. But could she swear Connie hadn't steered her toward the mine hole and wouldn't have left her there to die? No, that she couldn't swear.

How long before Connie could no longer think to get help? How long before anyone thought to look for her, if they knew where to look? Kiernan stepped harder on the gas, but the narrow rutted road allowed little speed. To her left were the mountains, to her right the drop. She focused straight ahead. Nevada didn't give second chances.

Thoughts of the virus, of the people threatened by it, flowed through her mind. The dead woman—what had drawn her to this desolate area? It was as if this were the

edge of the earth and she had come here to step off. And
no one cared.

Or did they? Her family and friends would be in Las
Vegas, or Reno, or somewhere farther. They would be on
the horn to the police there. It would be there that signs
with her picture would start to be plastered on kiosks and
utility poles.

And Jeff Tremaine. He was the key to the whole thing,
and he was gone. Connie assumed the sheriff was holding
him somewhere, but there was still no evidence of that.
And Kiernan wasn't about to rule out his leaving from
disgust, paranoia, or rage. A tree jutted out over the road,
throwing the surface into deep shadow. Kiernan yanked
the wheel, overcompensating and sending the driver's-side
wheels up over the embankment. It was a moment before
she righted the truck and breathed normally again.

Wherever Jeff Tremaine was, for whatever reason, one
thing was clear—he was the key to Sheriff Fox. It was Fox
who had the answers, and Fox from whom she was going
to have to get them. How to do that and not end up like
Jeff, that was the big question.

The road wound sharper and more suddenly than she
remembered, the rutted paths thwarting every attempt at
speed. At the crest she stopped and pulled out her cell
phone. When she bearded Fox she needed to be backed up
by every bit of evidence possible. Missing-person's lists
were one thing she could check. She could have
Tchernak—

No, dammit, not Tchernak. Well, BakDat— No, dammit, not BakDat anytime soon. And if Persis knew about
Tchernak quitting, she wouldn't produce the information
at all. Damn Tchernak. Why couldn't the man be satisfied
with his extremely well-paid job, his fine studio on the
beach, his superb wolfhound companion.

Ezra! Oh God, Ezra. She had left assuming she would

be back home by now to take him for his nighttime walk. She had asked Tchernak only to feed and walk him earlier. She could see Ezra's big wiry face, his huge brown eyes drawn in sad disbelief as he lay facing the door that didn't open. Ezra . . .

But no matter how pissed Tchernak was with her, he'd never desert Ezra. He still lived in part of the duplex. So as long as he was there anyway, there was no reason he couldn't get the latest missing-person's report. She clicked the phone on and it crackled to life as she dialed Tchernak's number.

The phone rang, and again. "Come on, answer! You've got to be home!" The phone kept ringing. And the answering machine didn't pick up.

She dialed her own number. The phone rang. Tchernak could well be in her flat with Ezra. He'd done that before when she was out of town. For Ezra, he had contended. She wasn't surprised he didn't pick up. He was, after all, no longer in her employ. He'd have no business answering her calls. And, as he would be the first to remind her, it was three-thirty in the morning, an hour when many people sleep. None of that would keep him from monitoring the message, though. For this call he'd make her eat enough crow for a family Thanksgiving, but she'd deal with that later. She waited for the beep. "Tchernak, it's me. Pick up. Listen, this is important." She paused. "I need a check on Missing Persons for the dead woman up here. Tchernak? Tchernak? Listen, this is crucial. People are dying. Pick up, dammit! Okay, I'll try you again in a few minutes."

How long had it taken from the infection of the index case of Lassa fever in Africa to villages of nothing but maggots? If only they'd gotten to that index case. . . . That had been the great what-if dream the medical team had played with night after night. Now she sat in the pickup cab, drank some of the coffee, nibbled on the Granola bars, and redialed Tchernak and then her own number. When he didn't answer this time, she shifted to Message Retrieval.

The first three messages could wait. It was the fourth that caught her attention. "Tchernak, Adcock here. That other number doesn't answer. Don't you even have a god-damn phone machine? What kind of detect—? Listen, I got a closer read on that number for you, but you're gone from the restaurant. You still in Vegas? Call me. Seven seven one, two seven seven two. If you don't get through, try me again. I'm going to check the hospitals again— something *you* could have been doing, Tchernak."

Kiernan smacked the Off button so hard she knocked the phone out of her hand. Adcock? Reston Adcock? The Reston Adcock who had demanded she drop everything to find his missing employee? Now he was dealing with Tchernak? What the hell did Tchernak think he was do-ing? Quitting without notice was bad enough, but abscon-ding with her case was something else. And to work for a sleaze like Adcock.

Oh, shit. Did Tchernak know Adcock would walk over anyone? He'd been right next to her when she told the guy she didn't deal with clients who had no ethics, but he was so busy pointing out that he knew Adcock's missing guy that he'd glossed right over the danger. And when Adcock called him and offered him the job, he'd have stepped right up like he'd been called in to replace the quarterback. And now he was missing! "Oh, Tchernak, what have you gotten yourself into?"

And now Adcock was calling hospitals. Again. Just the logical precaution in a missing-person's case? That couldn't have any connection to the dead woman's vi-rus. . . .

Surely.

She picked the phone up off the floor of the cab and dialed Adcock's number.

"Yeah?" The line was thick with static as if it was connected to another cell phone.

"Reston Adcock?"

"Hey, who's this?"

"Kiernan O'Shaughnessy here. I finished up and I'm here in Las Vegas. My associate, Bradley Tchernak, left me your number to contact him."

"Guy's got some sense of humor."

"Excuse me?"

"I don't know where he is, and now you, his boss, don't know either. If I handled my business like that, there'd be oil seeping all over the ground and not a bit of it marked."

"About the message you left on our California answering machine . . ."

"Haven't heard shit from him since then. It's like the guy's dropped off the face of the earth."

He wasn't here, he wasn't home. It was way too late for flights, so he wasn't in a plane somewhere. He would never have walked out on a case, particularly not his very first one. The only way he'd leave the field would be if he'd been carried off. This was worse than she'd imagined. What had Tchernak gotten himself into? He was too big to slither out a back window. Too decent, too eager to help. She stared out at the rumpled black mountains, dry and endless. Tchernak could be anywhere; his battered body could be lying a hundred yards off the highway and no one would find him. But if she picked up his trail from Adcock, she'd have a chance.

What about the dead woman? And Connie? And maybe Jeff and everyone in Gattozzi? Were they less important than Tchernak?

"Where are you, Adcock?"

There was a hesitation before he said, "Vegas."

She said, "Have everything you showed Mr. Tchernak ready at your office. It'll take me three hours to get there. You were calling the hospitals. I'm assuming you didn't find your guy."

"Not him or the Panamanians."

"Panamanians?"

"Jeez, didn't Tchernak tell you anything?"

"Adcock, you want to discuss business management at three-thirty in the morning? Just tell me who these boys are and why you think they might be in the hospital."

"They're seismic aides Hummacher brought in from Panama."

"Brought in why?"

"Only one reason, to keep the competition from getting to them."

"Give me what you've got on them too." She got the address, turned off the phone, and started down the mountain.

By the time she got to Vegas, it would be business hours in Atlanta. She'd call the CDC, track down someone who at least knew someone who knew her. She'd find credibility. She'd have to. How else was she going to convince them there was a threat of epidemic in a body that had disappeared? She'd *have* to convince them; no one here was going to take the word of an out-of-state private eye, not against the word of the sheriff.

But first she had to make it through Gattozzi.

CHAPTER

38

THE RADIO KNOB turned easily between Louisa Larson's fingers as she moved from one band of static to another. Bursts of song shot out, only to be shrouded in great hisses and grindings. She'd gotten a station up here at this time of night often enough before. Why couldn't she find it now when she needed the calming company of music, even music she didn't like? It had to be somewhere on the dial.

Unless the station had closed. Up here in the open, that broadcast could have been coming out of some guy's garage a hundred miles away. The "station" could close when he went out for a beer. She tried to remember if there had been commercials, newscasts, anything to suggest legitimacy. Of course she couldn't remember. If her mind were that clear, she wouldn't need to bother with finding music. She ground the knob to the left and clicked the car into silence.

Just as quickly the picture of Juan and Carlos was back in her mind. The symptoms they presented were close to Lassa, but—Louisa shook her head—her guess was de-

signer virus. She knew viruses; in her residency she had
learned enough to know she wanted nothing to do with
them. She could have applied to CDC or the military program. She had gone a hundred eighty degrees away, to
family practice.

But it didn't matter.

Bright lights burst out of the dark. The Doll's House.
She slowed, checking the parking area for Grady's truck.
Not there, as far as she could tell.

She pictured the boys' feverish faces. Anything could be
happening to them. The thug figured they were in Gattozzi. But Grady could have met someone at the Doll's
House and passed them on, abandoning them up here like
he did in Vegas. They could be dead already. She pressed
harder on the gas pedal. She was already speeding, not that
it mattered on this road. She had to get to the boys.

Abruptly she braked. She was losing it. She'd driven two
hours and now she was just guessing. *Pull yourself together,
Larson! The little thug does know something's happening in
Gattozzi.* How far behind would he be by now, half an
hour? She could sit here by the side of the road in the cold
and dark and wait. Or turn around and go back to the
Doll's House. With that clunker of his he'd be rolling in to
the pumps on fumes.

Reston Adcock pulled off 93 five miles north of the
Doll's House. The unpaved road paralleled the highway
and would take him right up to its back door.

The car bounced into a pothole. Adcock held the wheel
steady and let the car slow. His headlights looked like bea-
cons in the dark. If he'd been more than a few miles away
from the Doll's House, he'd have been pissed, but this he
could handle, and it was worth it for the cover it gave him.

He was real tempted to cut back onto 93 and assure

himself that that do-nothing Tchernak's boss was speeding
south. All he needed now was her to deal with. The Weasel
could handle Tchernak. Tchernak was twice his size, but
that's what weapons were for. Could he count on McGuire
to take out a woman? One thing you learned in the oil-
exploration business was you do what you have to.

Cecil McGuire had had ample time to contemplate
Grady Hummacher and Reston Adcock as his Barracuda
moved steadily up 93. The car had picked up speed on the
straightaway. He was almost at the Doll's House now. He
didn't know what he'd find in the next few hours, but he'd
been around enough to know it wasn't going to be pretty.

Cecil McGuire, the Weasel, had come to a very satisfying conclusion. Ten thousand dollars was hardly a substantial total payment for what this job was turning into.
Reston Adcock needed him. When he got to this place,
he'd make it clear to Adcock that ten thou couldn't be the
total payment, it was just the opening bid. This case was
the chance of a lifetime. Only a fool turns his back on a
jackpot. Once Adcock saw his work, he'd realize the danger of saying no.

He peered into the distance. Those red lights could be
taillights, but more likely they came from the Doll's
House.

CHAPTER

39

RIGHT FOOT ON gas, left playing the clutch, Kiernan barreled down the narrow mountain road above Gattozzi as it followed the whims of the black hills.

Tchernak could be anywhere, following any kind of lead. He had insisted he could second-guess Hummacher. Maybe. As for figuring Tchernak, well, no one knew him like she did.

The road dead-ended. The truck quivered madly and for a moment she thought it was going to stall and die at this elbow between hill and town. She sat catching her breath, checking the darkness, thinking again of Tchernak.

He had met with Adcock, then begun the search for the oil explorer, Hummacher. He'd have called BakDat about Hummacher, and if he'd learned anything at all in his time working for her, about Adcock too. He'd have ordered those backgrounds before he left La Jolla. And favored child that he was with Persis, he'd probably have had the results as soon as he could find a fax in McCarran Airport.

She turned left and started up an unlit residential street. Tchernak would have checked Hummacher's house or apartment, the neighbors, and, well, gone on from there. But first he'd have—he *should have*—cornered Adcock and gotten the skinny on that meeting that Hummacher didn't make. How much money was riding on that? How much could Hummacher sell his knowledge for? And who were the likely buyers? What did the two Panamanian seismic aides know that was so vital, he had to whisk them out of their country?

The first right turn was Main Street. She slowed almost to a stop, peering in both directions for the waiting sheriff's department car. The street was empty. Too good to be true. Uneasily she turned, hoping to get out of Gattozzi unnoticed. The highway was a quarter of a mile away. Restraining the urge to speed to it, she kept her foot steady and checked the rearview mirror. And when she came to the highway, she headed south with a relief unwarranted by common sense. She wasn't freer, she reminded herself, just moving faster in the cage.

What kind of boss was Adcock? Bad enough to create the notorious "disgruntled employee"? Had Tchernak gotten an employee list? The names of the recently resigned or fired? Surely, yes. Would he have spotted a telltale blink or twitch in Adcock's face when he spoke to him? Had he coerced him into full truth—as she would have done by what she thought of as refusal to come up empty and what Tchernak called pain-in-the-assedness? A spike of fear shot down her back. Investigating was like being an all-pro lineman; it took more than raw talent, it took years of training. Training Tchernak had barely begun.

The highway was flat and empty, lulling drivers into complacency, luring them off into rolls and crashes. She glanced at the speedometer and lifted her foot till it settled back to eighty. No need to give them an excuse. Oh, shit, she was beginning to think like Tchernak!

She turned on the radio, forced herself to listen through

the static. Her reward was bits of the same report she had picked up earlier, the tale of casinos rising faster than the dawn. And how much would it benefit a local sheriff to destroy the evidence of epidemic? She snapped off the radio, grabbed for the cell phone, and dialed BakDat.

"BakDat, the professional search network. Thorough, fast, reliable. Leave a message, and one of our many investigators will get right back to you!"

"Persis, this is Kiernan O'Shaughnessy," she said, relieved that the call had gone through. "I'm calling for Tchernak."

No response.

"Persis, pick up. Open your eyes and reach the hand of all your many investigators to the phone. This is important!"

Still no response. For Tchernak she would have flown out of the bed and had the computer up and running already.

"Tchernak is missing."

Still no response. Maybe Persis really was out, or really asleep. More likely she was just lying on her bed in an orange muumuu, fingering thin, dry dyed-red hair, listening to the phone and laughing.

"Okay. Listen. I'm on the move. I don't know when I'll get another chance to call you. In the meantime get me whatever he wanted from you in the last day. And Persis, if anything happens to Tchernak, you've got only yourself to blame."

Dammit, she could not charge into Adcock's office empty-handed. Without leverage all she was doing was wasting time. She could get Hummacher's address—probably listed—and see if Tchernak was there. What car was he driving? Had to be a rental. There were a dozen rental companies. If she had to call every one of them . . .

No, that was the wrong end of the snake. "Start with

the end you can put your hand on," that's what she'd told
Tchernak each time she'd given him a lead to track down.
Her own hand was nowhere near slimy scales. But if she
were to make a grab?

She'd grab on to Tchernak's modus operandi. What
would he do after his initial call to Adcock? Make plane
reservations . . . on Southwest, just as she had.

Headlights came up behind her fast. She was doing
eighty-five, pedal to floorboards, but the lights had to be
doing over a hundred. No red flashers, though. As the
lights came closer, she could make out their height—truck
lights on an eighteen-wheeler. She let out a great sigh as
the truck pulled out around her and swept by. She dialed
information, and then Southwest. "Listen, we've got this
rental car we booked through you guys and we left all the
papers in the motel yesterday morning. We've been driving all day, and, well, this is embarrassing, but we can't
remember where to return the car. You've got some record
of this, right?"

"I can't give you directions, but you could call Budget
direct for that."

So far so good. But she was holding her breath. Now
for another way of asking, "What am I driving?" With
Tchernak it wasn't likely to be a compact. Or a midsized.
At the client's expense? "Just one more question. I think
they said they had a special drop-off for off-road vehicles.
Can you check on that?"

"I'll ask."

It was a minute before the voice came back on the line
to tell her he didn't know.

She slowed and dialed.

"Budget Rental Cars."

"What kind off-road vehicles do you have in Las
Vegas?"

"Jeeps."

"What colors?"

"Gold, white, and blue. Which would you like?"

"Thanks." She hung up, checked the road, and redialed. "Budget Rental Cars."

"Listen, I am really embarrassed to be calling you about this. If my husband back in the hotel room knew this, he'd never let me out alone in Vegas again. But the thing is I went to the casino, you know the big green one?"

"Mmm."

"Well, you know it's got a parking lot the size of Dallas, and it's not like I had anything to drink, I just got caught up in the quarter machines and wandering around and buying those cute little dog magnets, the ones you put on the fridge door? And I was playing different machines after that, and well, I got all turned around, and now I can't remember where I left the Jeep Brad and I rented from you. Hell, I couldn't even swear what color the damned thing is. I wanted the white, but you didn't have that."

"Do you have the license number?"

"Oh, jeez, no. All the papers are in the car. But you have the paperwork on file, right? Bradley Tchernak. We just got the car yesterday morning. We told you we might even turn it in last night, which we would have done if Brad hadn't gotten lucky and we figured 'go with it.' And that was right. He's three hundred and forty dollars up. 'Course he spent a good bit of that celebrating, which is why he's sacked out in the hotel room right now. Not bad, huh? At least not bad if I can find your Jeep. But, listen—"

"It's gold, Mrs. Tchernak. A gold Jeep, Grand Cherokee Laredo."

As she turned off the phone, she wondered if he would have given her the license number, too, just to stanch the flow of chatter.

Coming at her, headlights grew fast and were gone before she had time to guess the make of the car. Not the sheriff. Where was the sheriff? What was pressing enough to drag him away from the woman who could tell the world about Gattozzi fever? Questions better considered across the Clark County line in Las Vegas.

She checked the speedometer—eighty—and stepped on the gas.

CHAPTER

40

TCHERNAK CAME OVER a hill and there it was! After the hours of unbroken darkness the burst of bright lights ahead could have been the Emerald City, except that they were red and yellow. As he drew closer, he could differentiate between the glowing square of red and yellow dots atop a tall pole, the yellow dots in the bed of white that might indicate gas pumps, the yellow against yellow around the big square blur he figured was a building. Was this the great mecca of Gattozzi? He had slowed for a couple of modest signs to towns miles off the road, but for over an hour there had been no mention of Gattozzi. If he hadn't seen the highway sign when he first turned onto 93, he'd have wondered if Adcock had been shitting him. But Gattozzi or not, this was the only place open in the middle of the night, and he was damn well stopping here. If this was the gateway to Gattozzi, it didn't bode well.

He slowed, now able to see the light-blurred windows in a cafe, a couple of vehicles parked in front. To the right stood a motel. The whole prefab affair looked like a group of giant cardboard boxes that had been dropped on the hard, bare ground one morning and opened for trade by dinnertime. Motel 4, or maybe 3 ½.

Tchernak saw the taillights and slammed on the brakes before he took in what was happening. Idiot flying out of the parking lot, that was what was happening. A bit too far away to clip the bumper of the gold Grand Cherokee Laredo, but it wasn't like the guy slowed down to check on unimportant minutia like other vehicles. How desperate was he to get away? Probably some jerk who'd got chucked out of bed by a girlfriend who'd had enough. Or hadn't.

Tchernak flicked on his blinker before making the right turn into the sprawling parking area, even though his was the only vehicle moving now. He looked around at the buildings and the dust swirling in his headlights and suddenly felt the weight of the long day. The place was just a motel and cafe, not Gattozzi. His first case and not only could he not find the missing person, he couldn't even locate the proper town to look in. What he had located was just another opportunity for bad coffee.

But somebody in there would know where Gattozzi was. The weight eased off his shoulders and he aimed the Jeep toward the cafe. While he was asking directions, he could get a piece of pie, maybe apple. Probably be awful. For an instant the memory of the cherry-kumquat tart he'd made for dinner Thursday was so real, the sweet and sharp smell wafted by his nose. He'd gotten the out-of-season cherries from a hothouse outside of Olympia, and the kumquats . . . Was that only three days ago? He shrugged off the question and focused on the cafe sign: Doll's House. In a spot like this there was always the chance of home cooking. Apple was the safest.

Unbidden, he found himself glancing at the motel and thinking of the asshole who'd almost taken off his fender. Fight with a girlfriend? Guy that pissed could have left her with a jaw broken in eight pieces. He half expected to see a tiny, bloodied woman staggering out of one of the units. But it was none of his business. Still, he found himself turning not left to the cafe but right to swing past the motel doors. He hadn't realized at first that there were two prefab rectangles, one behind the other, both with doors facing the road.

Not a car in sight. No light coming from a window. Maybe he had been wrong about the fight, maybe the rubber-burner was the night cook at the end of shift, or some local who had dumped trash and fled, or—

He almost missed the six-inch opening in the doorway of the last unit.

It was none of his business, and he had a pressing case that needed to be solved.

Or maybe it *was* his business. Long shot, but still . . .

He pulled up by the motel room, got out, and eased the Jeep's door shut. The wind slapped his jean legs against his shins, pulled his shirt out from his chest. "You okay in there?" he called through the dark doorway.

The light didn't go on, but he could hear something inside. "Excuse me?" He leaned closer to the doorway, scrunching his ear, but it was no use. On this desert the wind came too crisply, splattering sand and dirt, rattling all the corners of fixtures, smacking detritus left from who knew what against the tinny motel walls.

"Look, I just want to help. I can call a doctor if you need one. If you're okay, that's great. Just tell me and I won't bug you."

Still no words came back at him, but now he had factored in the wind and, leaning so close his head was almost into the doorway, he heard an irregular sound. Water. Not dripping. Running. And the smell—he couldn't place it, wasn't sure this kind of stench was coming from inside the room or was being carried on the wind from some unseen farmyard. But the water? You don't leave the tap open like that, not in the desert, of all places. "I'm just going to come in and make sure you're okay."

Tchernak slipped his hand around the side of the door. The chain jangled. The chain had been snapped.

Tchernak stepped to the side of the door and reached in till he felt the light switch. The light stung his eyes. He blinked a couple of times, then staying clear of the doorway, pushed the door hard and waited.

Seconds later he eased his head into the doorway. And stared. He was looking at a nightmare. He couldn't tell what color the room had been; it was blotched with the most disgusting colors, with gut-wrenching smells. It looked like a body had been turned inside out and splattered all the hell over.

A full minute passed before he noticed Grady Hummacher's body lying half off the bed.

CHAPTER

41

"YOU DON'T GET picked up for speeding in Nevada," Kiernan said aloud. Two hours and she would be in Vegas, the sun would be coming up, she'd be on the phone to the CDC and ready to beard Reston Adcock.

Two hours. Suddenly it seemed an eon, and the straight, dark road, a soporific. She recalled the lines of birds, dead beneath the power lines. How many noctural drivers joined them? As she came over a rise, yellow and red lights glowed in the distance. CAFE, the yellow sign shrieked. Did she dare stop? Just for the bathroom? And food. Food! How long would it take to grab a Hershey's?

Long enough.

She could see the cafe more clearly now—and the motel beside it. Even at this distance she could tell it was not exactly four-star. But still, the urge to turn in to the comforting light, to sit among normal people, where the biggest decision to be made was cherry or pecan pie—it was almost more than she could resist.

Suddenly she realized why she hadn't smacked into the sheriff on the winding up-country roads or the corner of

First Street in Gattozzi. Fox didn't need to watch those spots. The Doll's House was the place she had to pass to reach Las Vegas. A sheriff, of all people, would know the allure of the only twenty-four-hour cafe in hundreds of miles. No need for Fox to chill his derriere surveilling First Street when he could park it by the Doll's House's warm, fogged window and check out the half-dozen vehicles that passed. And if he was in the middle of a burger when she passed, well, plenty of time for a fine-tuned patrol car to catch the rickety truck before Vegas.

As she neared the cafe/motel, she eyed the parking lot. Yellow light paled down on the barren macadam. But patrol cars can be parked behind buildings. She checked the far side of the road. Nothing there. Dragging her attention from the seductive thought of food, she reached for the radio knob and had the power on before she realized what she was doing—mental wandering from exhaustion. If Tchernak were here, he'd have caught that mental disarray way before she admitted it. "You're too tired to decide to stop," he would say. Moving inertia, he'd labeled it. The last time had been heading home from L.A. after a long day following a lead that dead-ended and a longer evening explaining to the client. Tchernak had been driving. "Come on," Tchernak had said as he stretched his long arm across the back of the seat, "think with your eyes closed for a minute." Her head had nested so easily in the pocket of his shoulder, her own shoulder wedged against the cushioning muscles of his chest, her hand flopped comfortably on his thigh; the fresh smell of wintergreen he'd been using on a strained muscle soothed her, and the sound of her breathing—or was it his?—sucked her into sleep.

She shook off the memory. Maybe she was too tired back then, but now she was just fine. She was almost abreast of the yellow lights of the cafe. She slowed slightly—anyone would do that—and eyed the cafe for a telltale hood or fender poking out from behind. There was only one vehicle, too big and bright for a law enforcement vehicle, and it was parked not outside the cafe but by a motel door.

Reluctantly she stepped harder on the gas. She checked the rearview mirror for sudden headlights and a flashing red bar above. But all she saw were the tan buildings and yellow lights shrinking farther away until there was nothing but shapes and colors, tan and yellow and the dot of gold from the vehicle by the motel, till the whole oasis was a tiny amber bead on a black velvet table.

She crested a rise and it was gone.

CHAPTER

42

TCHERNAK HEARD THE whoosh of a car on the interstate. In the stone-still air of the motel room, it sounded like an eighteen-wheeler . . . driving through his head.

He forced himself to focus. He should do something. He had seen blood, plenty of it on the field. He'd seen legs broken, jagged ends of bone snapped through the skin. He'd been there when the whistle blew, the pile unpiled, and a body was left lying on the AstroTurf dead-still, and the coach and the trainer and the medical crew rushed on and hovered, and every player on either team and all seventy thousand fans in the stands remembered guys who had snapped their necks or smashed their skulls so hard that their brains tore loose. Those guys were friends a helluva lot closer than Grady Hummacher. But they hadn't been dead. And Grady Hummacher sure as hell was. Tchernak didn't need to get any nearer to his body to know that. He couldn't get nearer; his legs felt like they were wrapped in cement. Like they were dead.

God, and the smell! He had to get out of here.

But he couldn't do that. Not with Grady lying there.

From the looks of the room, Grady'd be lucky to have any blood left in him. Tchernak stared at Grady's back. He knew he should turn him over, check his face. But he just couldn't.

He'd check out the room first.

He stuck his hands in his pockets, safe from the danger of leaving fingerprints, and lumbered to the far side of the bed, running his gaze over the floor, the chair, the walls— anything but Grady Hummacher, who had been sitting in the airport bar with him talking about the girlfriend who was no longer a girlfriend and the teenaged boys he'd plopped on her.

Tchernak froze. The boys. Where were they? Teenagers? Thirteen years old, or nineteen? He was breathing through his mouth now, teeth together as if they could fence out the smell. He moved slowly across the room, keeping his back to the wall. There were no bodies on the far side of the bed. The bathroom door was open. Tchernak pushed it hard against the wall. Nothing behind it. He flicked on the light before he thought about it. And flicked it off as soon as he eyed the whole room. The boys were not here. Water gurgled in the sink.

Tchernak turned off the water and stood in the bathroom doorway. Last night Louisa swore Grady had plucked the boys from her office. That had to be true. No one else would have bothered with them. It had to be Grady who'd taken them. They trusted Grady.

Or so Grady had intimated.

Tchernak surveyed the swirl of blood and sheets one more time. Maybe these boys weren't so trusting. Maybe they got fed up with Grady coming and going, leaving them in a barrio apartment with neighbors they couldn't hear. They were boys used to fending for themselves in the jungle; given the alienation and frustration of their lives, the two of them could have snapped and beaten Grady till he stopped moving.

And then run off into the dark.

Or they could be lurking within spitting distance, panicked out of their minds, ready to lash out at anyone in the world they couldn't understand.

It was stupid to stay here at the death scene, Tchernak knew that. He had to get out. But he couldn't do that without checking out the body. He was a detective, after all. And he owed that much to Grady.

He swallowed hard, walked over to the body, and grabbed its shoulders. God, it was still warm. Still soft, like Grady was just sleeping. Like he wasn't covered with blood. Tchernak cut off all thought, all emotion, all urge to drop the body and run like mad.

His face was matted with blood. Even his eyes were bloody.

Tchernak dropped him so fast, he bounced. Then he ran outside away from the room and threw up his guts.

CHAPTER

43

KIERNAN SCREECHED INTO a U and headed back north on Route 93 and into the cafe parking lot. The gold Jeep Grand Cherokee Laredo had Nevada plates but no rental sticker. The Jeep could belong to anyone. Still, she couldn't ignore it.

She knocked on the motel room door. It swung open. The room was dark, but the outside light sent an ever paler trapezoid across the floor and onto the bed. She could see the jumble of dark blankets and sheets clumped together on the far bed. The air coming out of the room was hot. And the smell. Jesus, she knew the smell of bowels released, of urine shot in fear, of blood spurted and pooled. Of death.

Feet. Jean-clad legs. "Oh, God, Tchernak! No!" Her throat swelled closed; her eyes stung. She was shaking so hard she couldn't move. She didn't hear any sound till the door creaked behind her.

"Kiernan? What're—"

"Tchernak?" She looked from him to the body on the bed and back at him. Her throat tightened, but the knot inside evaporated. In two steps she was wrapping her arms around him, squeezing hard. He squeezed back. She could barely breathe. She pushed her head away from his chest, but he was still holding her like a football he was afraid of fumbling. "Jesus, Tchernak, you scared me. I was so worried about you. If you'd been dead . . . I can't even think . . . You are *alive*!"

Tchernak was saying something, but his words didn't penetrate. He was shaking. She pressed tighter against him. But he didn't grow still, and the initial relief she felt gave way to the smell of death. Now she did push free and turned to the beds. Both were caked with blood. On the nearer one, the body lay facedown. "If that's not you there, Tchernak, who—"

"Grady Hummacher." Tchernak left his hand on her shoulder. It was a big, meaty hand; his thumb rested on her clavicle. "Grady Hummacher, the guy—"

"I know, the one Reston Adcock hired you to find."

"Adcock's flying up here. But how'd you know I—"

She turned to face him. "Adcock left a message for— Oh my God, the blood! Did you touch anything?"

"Of course not."

"Blood, did you get it on your hands, even a speck?"

"No."

"Liar! Idiot! Look at your hands. They're covered in blood. Wash them. Wash every part of you. Oh, God, Tchernak get in there. Get the water running."

"Why? Is he infected?"

"He could be. A woman has already died, almost certainly of hemorrhagic fever. I've got Clorox in my pack." She ran for her truck and grabbed the small pack she'd brought in case of just this kind of emergency. She had figured it would take place in Jeff Tremaine's morgue with the dead body, not here in a motel room with Brad

Tchernak. Clorox was the staple coroners used to clean their autopsy rooms. It was the best she could do.

Tchernak was scrubbing his hands in the sink. She turned off the water, jammed the stopper in the drain, and poured in the Clorox. "Is the blood just on your hands?"

"Yeah. I turned the body over—"

"Did you touch anything else?"

"No. Well, only the door as I was running out to barf. And—oh, no, Kiernan—you. Look at your shoulder; there's blood all over it."

For the first time she eyed herself. Her right shoulder was stained from Tchernak's hand. "Let me see your shirt, Tchernak, where my face was when you hugged me." The shirt looked clear. She eyed his back where her hands had clutched him. "No sign of blood. But it takes so little, one drop in a cut . . ." She looked down at her hands in horror. They were still scraped from climbing in the morgue window. She stuck them wrist-deep in the Clorox. At least with the Clorox the bathroom smelled better than the death scene.

"Hey, this stings like crazy, Kiernan. You sure it's going to protect us? You sure Grady had a fever?"

"No and no."

Tchernak shook his head. "I touched him. His body was still hot. And his eyes, they were covered in blood. Whatever this fever is, he had it, didn't he?"

"I don't know. Hey, keep your hands in here!" She could hear the panic in her voice. "He could have what the dead woman had. Or it could be something different."

"But common sense says it's the same, right?"

"Tchernak, whatever it is, we're doing all we can. Okay, take your hands out. Wash them good. Shake them dry. Don't touch *anything*." She had never told Tchernak about those days in Africa, every time she swallowed watching for signs her throat was closing, checking her face every few minutes for hints of edema, waiting for fever and bleeding and death. At least then she knew it was Lassa fever that might kill her and that treatment was on the way. This was many times worse. All she knew was she and Tchernak could end up lying on beds with their eyes covered in blood.

"We're probably okay," she said with more certainty than she felt. "Viruses don't survive well in the air. *If* Grady had a virus. Whatever, we need to find out what he had and where he contracted it and if it's the same thing the woman in Gattozzi had."

Tchernak gave his hands a last shake. "Think like detectives, huh?"

"Right. Did anyone see you come in? Anyone follow you?"

"No."

"You're sure?"

Tchernak jolted up to his full six foot four. "Come on, it's pitch-black out there. How could I miss headlights?"

"Did you see anyone in the parking lot?"

"Yeah, but the car shot out of here so fast, I couldn't make out anything but speed. So that's good as nothing, right?"

"Damned suspicious, and useless, right."

"Did you notify anyone?"

"Not yet."

"But two strange vehicles in an empty parking lot, next to the room of a stranger . . . We might as well be advertising a circus in here. Watch the door." She turned on the light and started toward the body.

"The overhead? Do you want to announce us to the world? Don't you have a flashlight?"

"Right, Tchernak. It'd be so much better to be discovered lurking in here like burglars. If they're going to spot us, they've already done it. Now's the time for speed."

Blood was matted into the orange plaid bedspread all around Grady Hummacher's body. His was the outside bed nearest the door. She moved between it and its twin. "Tchernak, the blood's not just on his bed. It's all over the other one, much thicker there. Strange."

"Maybe not. He had two boys with him, Panamanians—"

"The seismic aides?"

"Two tribesmen he passed off as seismic aides. Adcock thinks they knew enough about his oil exploration that he didn't want to leave them behind. The boys are deaf and mute. He brought them back from Panama, stashed them in an apartment in the barrio, and when they got sick, his doctor friend, Louisa Larson, took them to her office and Grady snatched them out of there and disappeared."

"Wha . . . ?" Her head was swimming. She eyed the bloodstained bed. "Sick? Feverish, bleeding out?"

"The doc, Louisa, didn't say."

"You didn't touch anything of theirs, did you?" She could hear the alarm in her voice and felt him stiffening behind her. "Did you?"

"No. Probably not."

Again, fear spiked through her. How had the virus gotten here? Did it come from the boys? Could Grady Hummacher have been in contact with the dead woman? Or was this an epidemic much worse than she had imagined?

"Kiernan, we need to call the cops."

"In a minute." She turned from the bloody sheets to Grady Hummacher lying on his stomach, his face into the pillow. It was too late to worry about preserving the scene. The scene was already compromised, the body already moved. She bent over, looking closely at Grady's arm. No visible bleeding through the skin. But his head was a different story. The bush of sandy hair was caked with blood in the area of the right rear parietal bone just above and behind the ear.

She didn't move his head. Instead she took off her jacket, wrapped it around her hand, and pushed the pillow down until she could see what she knew was there: the entrance hole in his left eyebrow. She had been ready to discover him dead of disease, but this—a gunshot wound—took things to a different level of desperation. "He didn't die of virus. Grady was shot."

"Shot?"

"In the face."

Tchernak's "Oh" was so soft, she could barely hear it.

Tchernak needed time to recover from this second shock. But they had no time. "You haven't found the gun, right?"

"No. But listen"—Tchernak pulled himself up straight—"like I said, he had to have brought the boys up here. He snatched them out of Panama, brought them to Vegas, left them, then snatched them out of there and brought them here to this miserable motel room in the middle of nowhere. It was probably his gun. They probably shot him."

She shook her head. "Doesn't feel right."

"Why not?"

"That would be spur-of-the-moment. But Adcock was already worried two days ago. He had some reason for worrying about Grady."

Tchernak strode to the door. "This is insane, us standing here in a death scene. I'm going to call the cops."

"No! The local sheriff is in this neck-deep. He's the last man to call. The only people we can trust are ourselves."

"You're planning to leave the scene of the murder? How will that make you look to this sheriff?"

"The gun, Tchernak. Check the bathroom. I'll explain

the rest later." She looked under the bed, under the table, in the dresser drawers. "Nothing."

"Same in here. Look, you go out of your way to spite authority, but not me. I'm making a report—"

"Fine, you just stay right here and do that."

Before she could move, the door burst open.

"**WHO ARE YOU?** And what the hell are you doing in my building?" The woman's accent was local, her body tall and buxom in lime-green short-sleeved waitress blouse and black slacks. Her hair was short, wiry, apricot-colored, her square face set into an expression that said "Don't make me ask again." She was pointing a nine-millimeter automatic.

Kiernan planted herself in the doorway. "This man is dead. I was just coming to the cafe to call the sheriff." She was holding her bloodstained jacket in her hand. The wind had died down a bit in the few minutes she'd been in the room, and the air was colder. But it was fresh, and it felt good. "Are you Doll?"

" 'S no Doll. Cafe's 'Doll's House,' see, like 'dollhouse.' Husband figured this place for a hobby when I bought it. Supported him for twenty years now. Not that I hear, 'You were right, Faye.' " Her words had grown almost toneless in the retelling, and nothing in her tough-set face suggested she had any idea how inappropriate the anecdote was to the situation. She started forward.

"Don't come in here!"

"Hey, lady, don't you go telling me what to do in my own motel."

"Wait. The room's covered in blood. The man looks like he had hemorrhagic fever and bled out, though that's not enough to explain all that blood. But he didn't die of it, Faye. He was shot."

The woman's feet stopped; she had the look of a car idling, ready to charge forward.

Kiernan let a beat pass. "If you think there's anything I haven't told you, worth the chance of your contracting his virus, come on in."

The gun was loose in Faye's hand. I could kick it, Kiernan thought. Maybe.

"Were they contagious?" Faye asked.

"They?"

"Those boys of his, who else? He didn't have the woman with him this time. I believed him, dammit. I'm not one to be taken in. I know people, got to in this business. But this guy, Grady, I trusted him when he said the kids picked up the flu and could he stay till Monday when they'd be fit to travel. I figured what the hell, it's not like this is the height of tourist season. But I didn't give him the weekly rate," she added with a nod of approval, as if her decision restored her to commercial respectability.

Behind Kiernan the door opened. Faye had the gun aimed before Kiernan could say, "My, uh, colleague, Brad Tchernak. Grady went missing a few days ago. We were hired to find him."

"Uh-huh. He's the first thing you didn't tell me about in that room. You say you were *hired* to find him, huh?"

"You want to see my private investigator's license?"

"Yeah, yours and his."

"He doesn't have one; he works for me."

Faye assessed Tchernak and settled her gaze back on

Kiernan. "I'm holding my judgment on you two. Get your employee out of the way. The both of you, move back. Go on."

Kiernan jumped in front of the door. "Faye, look through the door first. You know how long we've been here. There's no way we could have done that kind of damage to the room. There's blood all over. We didn't create that. Grady's got a bullet hole in his head. If one of us killed him, would we be standing here unarmed? Think before you endanger yourself."

"Move, lady!"

Kiernan stepped outside and motioned Tchernak to follow.

A foot inside the door Faye stopped dead. "Jesus, Mary, and Joseph!" She backed out, turned to lean against the motel wall, then jerked away as if it, too, was contaminated. The color was gone from her face, and her apricot hair made her look clownlike. But she held the automatic steady.

Kiernan knew better than to reach out a comforting hand, even if that hand had not been medically questionable. Faye was the kind of woman with whom you didn't show softness. With her the battle of wills would be eternal. "Faye, why don't we go inside the cafe. Nothing more is going to happen to Grady, and Tchernak and I aren't going to run off." She eyed Tchernak and he nodded back: the proprietress of the only all-night cafe in the area was too good a source to pass up. As an ally she could be invaluable, as an enemy treacherous; and another enemy in this dark, arid land they didn't need.

Faye glanced toward the cafe, turned back to Grady's room, and was almost through the doorway again when she clutched her mouth, turned, and ran for the parking lot.

"Tchernak," Kiernan whispered, "we're not going to get another chance. What've you got?"

"Let's see. Louisa Larson. Office in a pretty shabby area, but she drives a blue BMW. Grady flew in from Panama City a week ago Friday. But he had a hotel receipt from down there for Tuesday night. His predecessor, Ross Estes, was killed down there three months ago. Last people Estes was seen with were Nihonco reps."

"Nihonco?"

"Japanese oil company."

"Whew! Was Grady selling out Adcock?"

"Could be. Adcock's hocked to the earlobes. And the two boys—"

"Where are those boys?" Faye emerged from behind the gold Jeep, still pale. The gun was now loose in her hand. "Grady said they were too sick to travel. Where are they? Who took them?"

"What makes you think they didn't shoot Grady and light off on foot?" Tchernak asked.

"Too sick. That blood in there, if it's not Grady's, it's theirs. Grady kept saying they had the flu, but I knew better. You don't bleed all the hell over with the flu."

"Did you call a doctor?"

"Didn't have to." Her hands were on her hips and she was nodding up at Tchernak. Chalk up another for his masculine appeal, Kiernan thought as she eased herself into the shadow and tried vainly to get her turtleneck tighter around her icy shoulders.

"Grady called Tremaine. Came into the cafe to use the pay phone—we don't have phones in the rooms. Thought he was being smart. Waited till I was busy with a party of four."

"So how do you know?" Tchernak's tone was almost baiting.

"How'd I know? Redial. It's not marked, but it's on the phone. Come in handy more than once."

"Did Grady call about the boys' being sick?" Tchernak asked.

Faye shrugged. "Redial only tells where, not what."

"Did the doctor come?"

"Not as I saw."

"Faye," Kiernan said, starting toward the cafe, "when did Grady make that call to Tremaine?"

"Soon as he checked in."

"And he didn't call again?"

"Nope. No calls to no one."

"And the boys didn't get better?"

"Not as I could see. Looked worse to me. But I wasn't in the room. I don't go in my guests' rooms, not 'less I need to. Makes it easier all around. But I'll tell you, I was tempted here. 'Tomorrow,' I told myself. 'If those kids aren't better by tomorrow, I'm going in.' "

Kiernan nodded, wondering what tomorrow would have brought—the doctor or chance at another tomorrow. If the boys lived that long. "Faye, who is it you think shot Grady?"

"His girlfriend."

"Louisa?" Tchernak said, moving in beside her.

"Oh, so he's got more'n one. Can't say that surprises me. I know men—see enough of 'em shacking up here— and Grady was too much a charmer for his own good. They only stopped for bottled water and picnic sand-wiches—"

"When was that?"

"Sunday morning, 'bout ten. Before the after-church crowd." Tchernak opened the glass door. Kiernan followed Faye inside through an almost visible curtain of grease. She didn't turn to see Tchernak's appalled expression, but Faye read it. "Yeah, mister, we get the after-church trade.

May not look like much, but I'm a damned good cook."
She moved protectively behind the counter and began
wiping the Formica.

The cafe probably sat fifty at the tables or the booths by
the windows. Now it was empty but for two egg-caked
plates and stained mugs on the counter. In one sweeping
motion Faye moved them into the dishpan and pocketed
the dollar-fifty tip. Somewhere beyond her a refrigerator
rumbled.

"You said the girlfriend's name was not Louisa. What
was it?" Kiernan asked.

"Irene. I remember because it's such an old-fashioned
name. But maybe that's only in the Anglo world."

"Irene was Hispanic?"

"Looked it. But she was dressed American, and by the
sound of her, she could have been from Iowa City."

"Wearing jeans? Nails polished a pale peach color?" In
her mind Kiernan could see those manicured nails with
skin grotesquely swollen around them.

Faye nodded so matter-of-factly that Kiernan had to
remind herself that she had seen a normal, healthy woman
with forty, maybe fifty years to live, a woman who had
stood by this counter and assumed that her biggest danger
was buying the wrong chocolate bar.

Faye squeezed out the rag and tossed it by the sink. "I'll
tell you, she had Grady pegged. She was already pissed."

"About?"

"Time. She was carrying on to get him to hurry. You
know the kind of thing you make a fuss about when it's not
the real issue. What the real issue was I couldn't tell you."
She stopped and her face puckered as if she realized the
ominous implications for Irene. "Is she the one who sent
you? You a friend of hers maybe?"

Kiernan shook her head. Irene could have used a friend.
Grady Hummacher might have seemed like a friend, but

he watched her get sick, dumped her off at the morgue, and called Jeff just once to find out what happened. Some friend. Jeff must have told him the disease's progress, and Grady would have recognized the increasingly ominous symptoms in the boys. But he didn't gas up the car and drive like crazy to Vegas or Reno or even St. George, Utah. He didn't even call Tremaine back. Grady Hummacher sat in his motel room and watched the boys dying. What kind of man was he? She shot an accusatory glance at Tchernak, but if Tchernak felt guilt by association, he wasn't showing it. He'd only said he'd known Hummacher; he hadn't said how well. And what about Jeff Tremaine? How, she wondered, did Grady Hummacher even know Tremaine?

But Faye's focus was still on Irene. "Where is she?" Faye insisted. "She didn't take those boys, that I can tell you, and she didn't look like a woman aiming to go on a picnic in the park. I know people, and she wasn't a woman all het up about kids, particularly those kids. I'd give you odds Grady never told her he was bringing them along on their date. You can see why she was pissed."

She couldn't let Faye go on ignorant of the truth, not if she planned for her to be an ally. "Faye, Irene is dead. She was dead before Grady was shot."

"Was she shot too?"

"Disease."

"What the boys had?" Faye asked slowly, as if keeping herself at arm's length from the words.

"Could be."

Faye looked slowly around the room. She had the look of a woman who had held herself together as long as she could and was fading fast. "I'll have to fumigate, the whole place. Be closed days for that—all today, and Wednesday too. Have to call"—she held up fingers on which to enumerate—"Tri-City Committee, before they head out of their meeting. Ministers' group. Wednesday. Tell the Carson Clubbers to head out to Vegas from somewhere else."

Kiernan was about to ask if the groups actually met in the cafe or just ate pie afterward. But Tchernak's announcement stopped her. "Carson Club," he said. "Grady Hummacher was a member of that."

Faye nodded, and glanced into the dark where the highway lay. In the silence that surrounded her hesitation, the growl of an approaching engine seemed to startle her out of her I-know-people persona. "Could be," she muttered, more to the window than to Tchernak.

The engine sounded smooth, tuned, powerful. Kiernan didn't have to look to guess who was driving. "You called the sheriff before you came out, right?"

Faye shrugged. "What did you think—I'd let you just drive off into the night?"

Right, what did she think? "Come on, Tchernak." She strode out the cafe door into the darkness that in a minute would be filled with pulsing red lights. Faye didn't follow. She had done her job.

"Tchernak, Jeff Tremaine was a member of the Carson Club."

"That could be how Grady knew him."

"Exactly. So, try this. Irene gets sick on their picnic, too sick to drive three hours back to Vegas. Grady calls Jeff and leaves her with him."

"And flies off to Panama and back."

"What that means is the call Grady made to Jeff Tremaine wasn't about the boys at all. It was about Irene."

"Sure. If he was worried about the boys, he'd have taken them to the doctor's office. Obviously he knew where it was." Tchernak hesitated. "So why didn't he?"

"That's the question. Because Jeff told him Irene was dead? Because Jeff panicked?"

"Or because Grady had some other plan for the boys when he brought them up here."

Kiernan nodded, impressed. "Maybe so." The patrol car was pulling up at the cafe. She stepped into the shadows and passed Tchernak her cell phone. "You said Grady arrived in Vegas a week ago Friday, was up here Sunday and back in Panama City Tuesday night. By Friday Adcock's so pushed out of shape about it he calls me and hires you. The questions are: why did Grady do an overnight trip, and why not on a commercial flight? Was he on a Nihonco charter? I'll keep the sheriff busy."

"Kiernan, I'll take him—"

"Right, and leave me to try to get something out of Persis? I'm better off with the sheriff. Go!"

She made it to Grady Hummacher's doorway moments before the sheriff slammed on his brakes.

CHAPTER

45

SHERIFF FOX SHOT out of his car and planted his ursine form in front of her. "Ms. O'Shaughnessy, you're under arrest."

She couldn't afford to be locked up somewhere while the virus spread—maybe through Tchernak, herself, and who knew who else. But the last thing she'd tell Fox was that she'd been exposed. "Sheriff, Grady Hummacher was dead when I got here."

"*Under arrest,*" he repeated, shouting over the whine of the gusting wind, "for breaking and entering the mortuary. What you've been up to here I'll deal with later."

From nearer the cafe behind her she could hear a soft groan, Tchernak's shorthand for *No taunting! No speeding! No defenestration!* She should be so lucky as to defenestrate! And as she would remind him if they made it out of Nevada alive, she wasn't diverting Fox just so Tchernak could spend the time critiquing her performance. If he didn't get through to BakDat, they were going to be running blind. "What proof do you have, Sheriff?"

"Fingerprints, for starters."

"Of course my prints are there, I was in the mortuary for an hour this afternoon. That's no proof."

"Hmm. Are you a lawyer, too, besides being a doctor and a detective? No? Well, then, we'll leave this question to the D.A." He turned to the patrol car and held out a thick arm. "In the meantime be my guest. Hands against the car."

"Why don't you charge me with breaking into the saloon too? My fingerprints are there. And in your jail."

"You won't have to break into the jail. This stay's on me."

She took a step toward him, hands planted on hips. "This is the United States, Fox. We don't do guilty until proved innocent here. You're talking false arrest."

"Hands against the car, miss."

"I need to speak to my lawyer."

From the shadows a form started forward. Tchernak. Racing in to protect his quarterback. She turned quickly and started into the parking lot.

Before Fox could grab her or Tchernak reveal himself, three dark cars cut into the parking area, tires screeching. They slammed to a stop in a row next to Fox's. "Stay where you are," Fox hissed at her as he strode toward the cars.

She shot a glance at Tchernak as he slipped back into the shadows. Did "buying time" mean nothing to him? The only reason he wasn't right here with his big hands on the car next to hers was Fox's lack of manpower. Now, with the arrival of three deputies, Tchernak's future freedom was limited to seconds. He didn't have time to dial Persis much less hear her answers.

Deputy Potter hauled himself out of the nearest car and opened the door for Jeff Tremaine.

Kiernan's breath caught. The door Jeff had emerged

from was the patrol car's back door—the cage. Connie had been right—Jeff was a prisoner.

"Ah, Jeff," Fox said, making no move toward him but signaling one deputy to circle the lot while the other one waited. "Tell me now, did you invite Ms. O'Shaughnessy to break the airshaft window and let herself into the mortuary tonight?"

The wind was flapping Tremaine's short sandy hair, and it was a moment before Kiernan realized he was shaking his head no—and avoiding her gaze. He turned toward the motel room, his back to her now. "Which room is the death scene?"

Where had she heard that wooden tone before? It was a moment before she recalled coming up behind him on the ward in Africa as he was assuring a terrified shopkeeper that his fever just seemed like Lassa. Two days later the man was dead.

She watched as Jeff walked to Grady's room, his movements as lifeless as his voice. His slumped back revealed no jerking in shock; he gave no audible gasp of horror.

Fox turned his attention to her. "Potter, pat her down and put 'er in the cage."

Kiernan turned away from the death scene and positioned her hands on the patrol car roof. It wouldn't be a new procedure for her. And Potter, while not swift, seemed less intrusive than some as he ran his hands down her legs. He stood, gave a weary sigh, and opened Fox's back door. "Okay, miss, you know the routine."

"Yeah, but not before I use the bathroom. That's what I drove in to the cafe for half an hour ago and I still haven't had a chance."

"I don't know. Sheriff? She wants to pee."

Fox stuck his head out of the bloody motel room. His face looked not the green she might have expected but merely scrunched in irritation. "What? You looking for another back window? Yeah, I know about that trick in the saloon."

"Sheriff, this is a legitimate request."

"Yeah, right. Okay. Go. Potter will be right outside. No, wait. Potter, come in here with O'Keefe and keep an eye on the scene. I'll take her. She clean?"

"Yeah, nothing on her. Probably all in that fanny pack."

Fox held out a hand, and with a sigh she gave him the pack. Her Swiss Army knife was not going to cut her out of here or uncork the identity of Grady's killer, but the loss of it underlined just how helpless she was.

"I could have left it with you, for all the good it'll do you," Fox said as he tossed it in the front seat.

"Yeah, you could have been the Dalai Lama too." She jammed her hands into her jacket pockets and headed to the cafe.

He chugged after her and she couldn't tell whether the gurgle of breath from him was a snort or just a sign of poor fitness. He moved in front of her. "I'm not even going to watch the Ladies' door. Go ahead out the window if you want. Walk as far as you want across the desert in any direction. But, word of advice, take a good long drink before you do."

"You major in sarcasm at the sheriff's academy?"

"Sheriff," a deputy called. "I found this guy out back."

"Kiernan!" Tchernak loped toward her and had his arms around her before his keeper changed gears. "Left Persis a message," he whispered, slipping the phone into her pocket.

"Hey, cut that out right now."

"It's okay, Sheriff," Tchernak said, "I'm her partner."

Fox shook his head. "Don't expect that to be a plus, fellow. Okay, Cioffi, put him in the cage."

"Yessir."

Kiernan was already at the cafe door. Inside, Faye stood

behind the counter like an admiral on the bridge. Kiernan veered left into the Ladies', and sighed at the age-stained yellow walls, speckled brown linoleum, and counter scoured down to the metal. The single window was large and low. A rhinoceros could have walked through it. But Sheriff Fox was right, the Doll's House was a landlocked Devil's Island, and all she'd get for her defenestration would be dehydrated. She used the toilet, then unfolded the little phone, hit Redial, and listened with relief as long distance beeped its way to California.

"BakDat."

"Persis. Did you get Tchernak's message?"

"Who's this?"

"Kiernan O'Shaughnessy." *As if you didn't know.*

"My business is with the Tchernak Detective Agency. As a reputable information service, I would never give out requested data to a competing detective."

She could see the blowsy woman plopping a bonbon between her over-red lips. "Tchernak's not going to be calling you. He's in a cage in a deputy's car right now. And if you don't tell me about Grady Hummacher's flights, Tchernak'll be there for a long time."

"Yeah, sure. Like I'd believe you."

"You think I'd lie? The sheriff found him standing over Hummacher's corpse," she lied.

A sharp rap on the door shook her. "Hey, hurry up in there!"

"I'll just be a minute."

"What was that?" Persis demanded.

"The sheriff. I don't have much time, and Tchernak's got less, so give."

"Okay, okay. I'll tell you. But, for you there's no cut rate. This time of night it's double-time."

If she hadn't been so pressed, Kiernan would have

laughed. "What carrier did Hummacher fly to Panama and back on?"

"Isn't one."

"Isn't a *commercial* flight?"

"No, there isn't. . . ." Persis paused as if she knew how infuriating that was. "Not one carrier, but two. I checked both commercial flights for both days. Hummacher wasn't on either. Only other one going from Las Vegas to Panama City was chartered to Nihonco Oil."

Kiernan nodded. So her guess had been right. Grady had been in bed, or at least on charter, with Nihonco.

"Come on in there!" Fox called before the requisite pounding.

"Just a sec, Sheriff." She shifted even farther away from the door and lowered her voice. "Persis, what about a Sheriff Fox from Gattozzi?"

"No request on him."

Of course not. Five minutes ago Tchernak hadn't laid eyes on Fox. "Fox, sheriff in Gattozzi, that's whose custody we're in. If you don't hear from us in a day, call my lawyer."

"Hey, I'm a data service, not a servant."

She said the magic words, "*Tchernak* is in danger," and pushed Off. Her cell phone wasn't the best, but it was the smallest. Even so, sticking it between her breasts created a telltale bulge—another misfortune of the small—and it was damned uncomfortable. Under her left arm, inside her bra wasn't much of an improvement, but not much was better than none. From force of habit she rechecked the entire tiny bathroom, under the sink, behind the waste can, but there was nothing likely to be useful.

Easing the door open, she glanced out, half expecting to walk into Fox's pounding fist. But the man was true to his word. He was not on guard inches away. She couldn't see him at all. It was his voice she heard.

"You expect me to believe you didn't see anyone go into that motel room?" he was demanding of Faye in the same "Hurry up" tone.

"Think what you like." Faye wasn't having any of that. "I had a bunch of teenagers in here, some I know, some I didn't. No way was I taking my eyes off them. You blink and you haven't got a catsup bottle left. Aliens could have landed in the parking lot and they wouldn't have drawn me out of here."

"No one else came in or out of the parking lot all that time?"

"I didn't say that."

"Stop screwing with me, Faye."

Kiernan expected her to snap back at him, but the voice she heard held a high quiver and the answer was disconcertingly quick. "There were cars, three of them. Didn't arrive together. I didn't see who was in them. Just cars." Had Fox threatened her?

Kiernan pressed her back against the wall and inched forward.

"Make?"

"Barracuda. A miracle it was still running. Didn't sound like that miracle would last. Then there was a pickup—"

"You recognize either one?"

There was a silent beat before Faye said no. Surely he noted the hesitation. Faye sounded just like the kids at St. Brendan's who didn't want to get their palms rapped with a ruler. If she could only observe their conversation . . . Kiernan edged to the corner, bent down to a level Fox wouldn't be watching for, and peered around. All she could see was the counter. Two vehicles? If Adcock flew up from Las Vegas, he'd have borrowed a car. It could be either, but odds were on the pickup.

"Third?"

"New. Foreign-looking. I'm not up on those. What-ever, I haven't seen it around here."

Had to be Louisa Larson, she thought. Tchernak said the woman doctor had a BMW.

"Any of them go to the motel room?"

"Behind the counter here I can't see the door. Maybe they all went in. All I can tell you for sure is the next time I saw the new car, the foreign model, it was at the edge of the pavement and a woman was throwing her guts up. If you think vomit's evidence, help yourself."

"Hey, don't you . . ." Fox paused as if he heard the hysteria in his own voice. "Never mind," he muttered.

Kiernan glanced from Faye to Fox, hoping to spot the reason for her fear. All she got was one sturdy woman with windblown hair and a weather-lined face, and big twitchy bear of a guy.

Kiernan stepped around the corner. "Faye, what order did those cars arrive in?"

"I don't know."

"Think!"

"What difference does it make?" Faye demanded. "Maybe the first one killed him and one of the others threw up at the sight. Maybe the first two saw the third coming and left. Anyway, it doesn't matter because I don't know."

"The teenagers?"

"Honey, for them the world ends at their elbows. Nothing outside this glass was going to get their attention unless it was another teenager."

Fox nodded toward the door.

"What do you think happened, Sheriff?" Faye asked.

"You said Hummacher had a couple of Mex kids with him. Maybe they got fed up being hauled around, or that foreign fever of theirs drove them crazy." He shrugged. "Shot 'im."

"And walked out into the desert you just warned me against?" Kiernan demanded. "And they're not Mexican, they're Panamanian!"

"Whatever."

"They walked off, sick as they are?" Kiernan demanded. "I'll take responsibility for them."

"And for Faye if she starts feeling feverish? And the maids who picked up their sheets?"

"Enough! Come on! In the car!"

She shot a glance at Faye as Fox shoved her though the door. The worried look on the woman's face assured her this incident wouldn't be forgotten soon.

She climbed into the cage. The seats were stiff with cold and the fear-drenched sweat of every prisoner who had ever been tossed in there. Like the boys would be when Fox caught up with them. Sick and terrified, if they weren't already dead. If they took their "foreign fever" to the grave the only civic reaction would be relief. A shiver shot down her spine. She pressed against the seat back, but there was no warmth there. The boys. Deaf and mute from an impoverished land, she knew what that meant. Without language, without the understanding of how society works, even their own society. Life constantly overwhelming, odds stacked sky-high against them. And then dragged into a foreign country. The awful aloneness of it overwhelmed her.

Turning to the window, she spotted Tchernak in the back of the last car, too far away to signal. The heater was off, and she looked longingly at her bloodied jacket before tossing it onto the floor. In the space between the motel and the cafe she could make out a line to the east. The black was lightening to dark gray. In an hour it would be dawn. She couldn't stop the shaking and she knew, as she had rarely known before, that sunup would bring nothing but a lack of cover.

It was fifteen minutes later when Fox climbed into the driver's seat, swung the car around, and pulled out onto the highway heading north. She looked out the rear window for Tchernak's deputy's car. The road was empty. There could be reasons for the delay in bringing him to the station, but she didn't bother guessing at them. She leaned her head against the cold seat and prepared herself for the Gattozzi jail forty-five minutes straight ahead.

Ten minutes down the road, Fox turned off.

"**WHERE ARE YOU** taking me?" Kiernan demanded from the back of the sheriff's car. The road was paved, but the desert sand and scree had almost covered it. In the dawning light it was a pale streak on the harsh desert floor. To the sides there was nothing but dirt and short, wiry tumbleweed.

"Fox, where are we going?" Kiernan waited through only a moment of his silence before whipping off her belt and clattering the buckle against the mesh.

"Hey, cut that out!"

"Where, Fox?"

"Okay, okay. You'll know soon enough. See that sign way up ahead?"

NO ADMITTANCE UNAUTHORIZED VEHICLES TURN BACK, it announced in bold print. In smaller letters beneath, it read U. S. NAVAL FACILITY. No guard station or gate reinforced the sign. "The Admiralty of the Sands? Is that it?"

Fox started to speak, and caught himself.

"You, Fox, are you the captain of the dinghy?"

"It's smart-asses like you that cause problems." It

sounded lame when he said it, and Kiernan suspected he had censored himself mid thought.

"And those boys; they weren't goading anyone. They were minding their own business. Aliens, without any language at all, minding their own business was all they could do. Why did you bring them here?"

"I didn't say *I* did."

"Why *here*, Fox!"

"Because, goddammit, we can't have aliens bringing foreign plagues on our people. If you're bleeding out from God knows what, this is the one place around here where they know about those microbes." He slowed at a kiosk long enough for the uniformed man to recognize him.

"Morning, Captain."

"Captain! Are you on duty here?" she demanded, but Fox busied himself with the dance of greetings before stepping on the gas. "You're on duty at this secret installation and you're pretending to be the county sheriff?"

"I am the sheriff."

"Sheriff reporting to whom? What are you, Fox, a spy, spying on your own people? Making sure they don't get wind of the nuclear waste here and kick up a fuss about deadly poisons in their ground?" Jeff Tremaine, with all his environmental connections, must have been the primo pain. But the boys, how did they fit it?

Of course nuclear-waste burial was only a theory. This place could house Intelligence or anything else.

The road ran so straight, Fox could have taken a nap at the wheel. After another ten minutes he turned left, following the arrow pointing to BIOLOGICAL AND CHEMICAL AGENT DETECTION SYSTEM FACILITY.

"Detection!" Kiernan cried. "What are you detecting? Incoming warheads? I don't think so. So, what, Fox?" Before he could speak, she knew the answer. "Oh no. Germ warfare. This is a secret germ-warfare lab. You're creating—"

"We are *not*! Terrorists all around the world are creating viruses that can wipe out a city. At B-CADS we're not creating, we are defending."

She had read about these installations in newspapers and magazines. "You're running experiments to identify these deadly germs—"

"Something wrong with that?" He twisted sharply right, glaring over his shoulder. The car jerked right and he had to yank the wheel to pull out of it. "You want us to sit on our hands till some nut sets off sarin in our subways like they did in Tokyo?"

"I want you to be up-front about what you're doing and not blame the virus you caused on illegal aliens."

"Right, and . . . Forget it. You'll have plenty of time to think your radical thoughts. This the kind of stuff you and Tremaine bitched about out there in San Francisco?" He let a moment pass before saying, so softly she had to strain to hear, "In your kind of work I'll bet you could be gone a long time before anyone worried."

"Fox," she said just as softly, "do you get a medal for bringing them two live cases of hemorrhagic fever to dissect?"

Her fingers were in the mesh, her mouth inches from his ear. She could have screamed till his ears rang, and she would have felt better doing it. And the boys would still be dying. Dying for the greater glory of research, where guinea pigs were more valued than human beings with no commercial value. She hadn't seen the boys, but she understood isolation and alienness, she who had spent most of her life apart from those around her. She had never had best friends. Her lovers had shared turbulent passions, never companionship. The closest friend she had was

Tchernak, and when all this was over, he could be dead. If these boys had each other, she envied them.

And if Fox and his crew let them die? Or worse yet, let *one* of them die . . . ?

"Goddamn you!" she screamed.

Fox tensed. "Sit back and shut up!" he screamed back.

His reaction wasn't enough. Nothing he could do would be enough. Even if he produced the boys in perfect health, it wouldn't make up for the arrogant servants of the people who used the people in the name of research, justified it in the name of the greater good, and denied any of it ever existed. She could have smacked him all the way to Vegas and it wouldn't have been enough.

Kiernan stared at the distant sky as stripes of morning gold faded to yellow, to beige, and into pale blue. It all looked so normal.

To the east she spotted green, intense green. It had to be the park Grady and Irene and the boys had been headed to last week.

"What's that?"

Fox kept his eyes straight ahead.

"To the right, that green area? It's what, about two city blocks wide? Is it some secret R and R spot for the Great Sand Admirals? Bunch of palm trees, some hibiscus, breadfruit, a big blue pool for the landlocked admirals to float around in with—what—battleships carrying rum drinks with umbrellas? Is that where the taxpayers' money is going?"

A laugh so spontaneous bubbled out of Fox that Kiernan shivered. "Ah, so it's ridiculous to even think of picnicking there? Why is that, Fox?"

This time he was better controlled.

Kiernan shifted forward to the edge of the seat. Fingers in the mesh, mouth inches from Fox's ear, she said, "Don't bother to answer, Fox, I'll do your part.

"Me: 'What is that park? Not a good spot for a country picnic ground.'

"You: 'No, ma'am, I reckon it's not.' You don't mind talking like a sheriff, do you, Fox? 'It'd be much too dangerous out there this close to the germ-warfare detection facility.'

" 'Why, Fox? What do they do here?'

" 'Just what it says, little lady. They run tests to see if they can detect viral and bacterial agents.'

" 'What kind of tests? Specifically what kind would affect that park?'

" 'Ah, very perceptive question.'

" 'Thank you, Fox. So you mean they do aerial testing? They shoot dangerous, potentially deadly bacteria into the air and then detect . . . ? See if they can detect it?'

" 'Very—' "

She stared out at the green square of park and thought of the farmers half a century earlier walking around on their land many miles to the east of here, milking their cows, unaware that they were downwind of a nuclear testing ground, drinking the milk and dying. But open air testing was a thing of the past—or so people assumed. Locals like Jeff Tremaine might be suspicious. But Grady Hummacher, who was off exploring for oil most of the time, wouldn't have thought twice about it. Here in this park—it had to be the place Faye talked about, the park Grady Hummacher took the boys—those two homesick boys would have run toward the first green trees and underbrush they had seen since they were hustled out of Panama. They probably thought they were in heaven, not a hellish outdoor laboratory where they breathed in deadly biological agents.

The game was over, her taunting tone gone, as she said, "Oh shit, Fox. You shoot microbes into the air, microbes for which you have no treatment and you hope—if you even care—that the microbes don't land on anyone down-wind. That's right, isn't it?" She banged both hands against the mesh. "That's right! And if someone happens to be in that park—"

"That park's off-limits. There are signs all over the place. And it's not a park, it's a testing environment. The only way you know it exists is if you work here."

"There was never any Panamanian virus, was there? The threat wasn't from dreaded aliens, the virus came from our own government. And so you carried off the dead woman's body—"

"To protect American citizens from disease—"

"To protect your secret project." The woman, Irene, was dead and her body removed from the mortuary. Grady Hummacher was dead. And now all that threatened that secret was the boys. Had Grady been shot while trying to protect them? She could see Fox, gun aimed, demanding the boys. She could see his finger squeezing the trigger. He'd signal his deputies to move the boys. . . .

The swollen, bloody faces of the dying African patients rushed back into her mind. It was years later and she could still see each face, faces she had seen only once, to whom she had never spoken nor could have called by name. But these boys—a squeak startled her, and she realized it had come from her own mouth. How long had it been since their exposure? A little over a week? If they'd had Lassa, they'd be dead by now, or almost. Irene had already been dead for days.

Why weren't they dead? Were they just genetically lucky? Had they somehow avoided the exposure she'd had? Only to be nabbed by Fox and his cronies?

But the sheriff's deputies wouldn't have touched the boys, not with their fevers and bleeding faces. Suited, masked naval personnel would have done it. As soon as

Fox had seen the inside of the motel room, he'd backed out. And sent Jeff Tremaine in.

And if the navy had taken the boys, she realized, they would have seized Grady Hummacher's body too.

"Fox, you don't have those boys, do you?"

"Not yet. We're counting on you to help us."

"Help you how?"

He didn't answer.

In the distance behind a denser, higher fence, a low, square building squatted in the surrounding dirt. She squinted to see the dark slits that broke up the tan facade. Windows? And the hollow in the middle—was that the entryway? The place looked like a space station on Mars. For all the chance of escaping, it might well have been. Despite the sun outside, Kiernan felt a chill colder than any during the night, and she didn't need Tchernak to tell her about her dire prospects. Military might and self-righteousness were a deadly combination.

No one was likely to find this place; it was hardly on the AAA map. Fox had been on target about no one worrying about her absence. Who would even know she'd flown to Las Vegas, much less where she'd gone from there? Was she counting on Persis to haul herself out of bonbon land and call . . . whom? God, she hoped Tchernak had had more sense than she had and gotten himself out of the deputy's car.

As they approached the gate, the pavement changed. It was newer, sturdier, a two-laned white road with actual curbs that led to nothing. Had they planned this facility for some other more accessible use, such as to be the head-quarters of the landlocked armada? The gatehouse was substantial, and the spike-post fence had to be ten feet high and was clearly electrified. Guard towers rose from the corners. Inside the cement block kiosk she could make out a uniformed figure. The place looked like a one-story

Leavenworth, or Lewisburg. Even the car facing away from the gate, a Miata much newer than her own Triumph at home, was painted military tan. It sat ready to speed the guard away the instant his watch was over.

Once inside the gate, she'd have no chance at all.

She eyed the guard, the guard's car. Distract him with sports car talk? Was there a way to get the guard chatting and . . . what? Nothing. That wasn't going to get her out of here.

Nothing. But there was nothing else. She hated to use the nausea routine; it was so juvenile, so trite, so demeaning.

The patrol car slammed to a stop at the gate. Fox stretched his legs but seemed in no hurry to haul her out. She turned toward the back window and spotted a trail of dust. A car coming. She watched until it was close enough for her to make out the driver. Another second and she realized Tchernak was locked helplessly in the back. "I really am going to be sick." She heard her own words before she realized she'd been speaking aloud, and to an empty car.

No other option. She banged on the window. "Fox, I'm going to be sick. Fox, you hear me. Fox!"

Fox ambled to the car, his ursine face drawn in disgust. "Old trick."

"I'm not kidding."

"Look, I'll bet—"

"You bet your upholstery? Another few seconds and you won't have a decision to make."

Fox shook his head. But he unlocked the door.

She started toward the side of the road.

"Eppers!" Fox called to the guard. "Keep an eye on her."

Kiernan staggered forward. In gymnastics, where flesh

was anathema, she had watched girls regurgitate. Later she had wondered if any of them had been among the young women subsequently who died of "unexplained" heart attacks. But back then, before the danger was known, how many ways can you make yourself throw up had been a hot topic. Picturing the worst possible fate had been her forte. Blood, guts, gore did nothing to unnerve her. It was the thought of tiny airless rooms that raised the bile in her throat.

Eppers was at her shoulder. He was five ten, thickly muscled, blond hair almost shaved, with a pale complexion that advertised his opinion of the desert. Mostly the kid looked bored. Eight hours a day in a cubicle without so much as a TV, who wouldn't be bored?

Behind her she heard the car that held Tchernak slam to a stop. Doors banged open and closed, first one and then a second. Tchernak was out. For an instant her hopes spiked. Then she spotted the handcuffs.

"That's Brad Tchernak!"

"Brad Tchernak of the Chargers?"

"That's him."

"Really?" Eppers looked over her shoulder toward the car, but he didn't move.

Kiernan lurched forward, gagged loudly, and threw up. Eppers took a step back.

God, she hoped she didn't have to do it again. She shivered violently, and forced herself into another gag. She had forgotten how revolting it felt as shame and fear mixed with bile, and even now she felt a wave of guilt.

Eppers moved closer to the second patrol car. "Brad Tchernak?" she heard him call out tentatively.

Tchernak's voice cut through the air. "You look like defensive line. I spent a lot of years staring you guys down." Tchernak was in his element.

She did a stagger step to the sports car. The key was in the ignition.

So this was how Fox planned on her helping him to find the boys. It had to be a setup.

CHAPTER

47

KIERNAN JUMPED INTO the Miata, fired up the engine, and was past the patrol car before it turned around. She ran the sports car through the gears in record time and floored the pedal. In the rearview mirror she could see the patrol cars still in place and Fox on the ground with Tchernak wagging his handcuffs over him.

Wind strafed her face in the open car. She squinted against the piercing sun and wind-borne sand. The new pavement ended. The car quivered, and she felt like she was sliding on her bottom over the rough surface. Once Fox gave chase, her little car would be no match for his high-powered patrol car.

If she were driving her own Jeep, she could cut straight across the brush. The Miata wouldn't go ten feet off the road before it ran aground like a pirate ship. There was no choice but to head straight west to the interstate and loop back from there.

No wonder Fox was in no hurry.

He had made his local reputation following an "escaped" suspect. Why wouldn't he try that again and let her lead him to the boys? Her escape attempt was a scenario with appeal to all parties. But she was not going to lead Fox to the boys. She'd turn right at the highway and drive to Las Vegas in first gear before she'd do that.

And die? She and Tchernak. If she couldn't force Fox to reveal the viral components, there would be no treatment.

Ahead was the gate. The crossbar was down, the guard seated in the guardhouse. He wasn't going to shoot. What would he do if she stopped? Well, Tchernak would be proud of her; she wasn't about to taunt. She had her role to play in the Great Escape. She ducked low and pulled her shirt up over her face as the crossbar skimmed the top of the windshield. The glass spider-webbed but held—for the moment. It would never last the miles to the highway. She held on to her shirt, ready to yank it over her face again when the glass flew.

As the road rose, she could feel the engine pulling. Some sports car! She hadn't even noted this rise driving in. Ahead to her right was a rocky mound a quarter of a mile from the road, and in the distance beyond it, higher, rough hills.

The road dipped and the car got a second wind.

She checked the mirror again. Still no cars behind her. She sped on, bouncing on the rough road, listening to the crackle of the bruised windshield glass. The highway had to be five miles away, maybe farther. She was leaning forward, physically urging the little car on. Every moment brought her closer to safety, to control. She felt as if she were pulling one end of an elastic leash, stretching farther, farther, willing the other end not to snap back at her. But when it did—when Fox sped close enough that she spotted him in the mirror—it would be too late. She had to disappear before that.

She thought of Tchernak back there in Fox's grasp, and pushed that dire thought away, focusing on the road and the mirror. Dirt behind. A mile maybe. Dirt kicked up from tires. Were they shifting cars at the fortress? Or coming after her?

If the sitting sports car was a setup, Fox would keep her in sight. He had the whole United States Navy behind him; he could reel her in anytime.

The only protection she had was that one small rise behind. Now or never.

She pulled the wheel to the right, angling the car down the slope toward the rocky hills, the obvious place to hide. She stepped full weight on the gas pedal and held it there till the speedometer stayed far right. Then she opened the door and jumped. She hit the ground rolling, but hit it hard. Pain shot through her body. She heard the metallic bang before she stopped rolling, and when she could lift her head, she saw the car a hundred yards away, both doors open, hood smashed into an outcropping, steam rising like a beacon.

Which was exactly how she felt.

No time to survey her wounds. Fox would see the smoke; he'd be here in minutes. She forced herself up, ran on will alone, whipping her legs faster, faster, away from the rocky hills, back across the road. The soft ground gave under her feet. She couldn't get a purchase. Pain stung her leg. Ignoring it, she ran across the wrinkles of sand, skirting low gray-brown plants. Her breath banged against her ribs; her throat burned. In the distance she could hear an engine roaring. A hundred yards ahead through the scrub was the dry streambed. In the distance was a rise, but she couldn't chance another dash. The streambed was too close to the road, too obvious. But she had no choice. She slowed, careful not to skid to a stop. Prickly branches scraped her raw flesh as she climbed down into the shallow bed. Thorns caught her sleeves and pant legs. She yanked them free. Covering her face with her hands, she lowered herself down.

She heard the approaching car squeal to a stop, then roll slowly over the rough terrain. Clearing a peek hole between branches, she looked back across the road and watched as Fox pulled up behind her car, got out, and eyeballed it. Steam still rose from the Miata. Behind it the rocky mound looked dark and ominous. At this distance Fox was a lump, a cutout. She couldn't read his body language. If he stayed put and called for help, she was sunk—sunk in this dry bed till some deputy or dog sniffed her out. "Go on into the rocky hills. You know you think I'm there," she muttered. "Do the macho thing; follow the scent. Go on!" Fox started forward, then stopped, turned around slowly, and came to a stop facing the road. He started toward his car.

"What's the matter?" she muttered. "Can't you handle one five-foot-tall woman by yourself?"

Fox hesitated, then turned around and headed toward the hill beyond the sports car.

Kiernan watched him till he was halfway to it. Then she pushed through the brush, up out of the ravine, and ran in the opposite direction toward the low rise.

She had figured the rise to be half a mile away. No such luck. Farther. She had to watch the ground, aiming around the scrub, leaping the strewn rocks. When she hit a flat spot, she half turned. Nothing seemed to move across the road, but she couldn't stop and look long enough to be sure. Her breath was coming in gasps, each hot inhalation searing her throat. The rise ahead didn't seem to be getting any closer.

She turned again. Still no movement. She ran on, not bothering to check again, knowing it would make no difference. If Fox spotted her, he'd be in his car and on her tail.

The rise that had looked fence-high from the road was taller than a second-story roof. Panting, she forced herself on till she was over the top. She skidded down the far side.

In the distance she could see a dirt road. And a car, waiting.

"**GET IN, O'SHAUGHNESSY**," the driver called across the seat of the pickup as she fell onto the seat. She was panting too hard to speak. The passenger pulled her in, and the truck rolled sedately toward the interstate. When she looked up, it was into the face of the driver, Reston Adcock.

Was this part of Fox's setup? Adcock and Fox in this together? Fox couldn't have guessed she would ditch the car and end up here. Maybe Fox had all possibilities covered, and Adcock was one player in a large cast. She leaned back against the seat, waiting till she could breathe normally. Adcock and Fox? And the guy next to Adcock?

The truck was an old blue Chevy, the kind that looked like a duck's head, and the bench was wide in both directions. Adcock was as well coiffed, well dressed in suitable outback garb, as the last time she'd seen him, giving orders no law-abiding private investigator would take. From the looks of him, he still worked out in a well-appointed health club. But the truck almost made her laugh. If Adcock were driving his own pickup, it would be a Mercedes, with leather seats. And he certainly wouldn't have this guy next to him.

The passenger was a decade older, and it looked to have been a hard ten years. Brown sports jacket, cheap, thin. Skin sallow and blotchy. He was the kind of street-smart guy who never intended to be in any vehicle off pavement.

If the two men had been seated any farther apart when she arrived, they'd have been on the running boards.

"So, O'Shaughnessy, what'd you find out from the navy?"

Of course Adcock figured she was back on his payroll. She was desperate for any ally, why disabuse the man? Still, she needed time to decide how much to trade to a man she couldn't trust. "Who's this?" she asked, eyeing the little man between them.

The hard-decade man had scrunched his shoulders inward, and shifted his feet onto the hump over the drive shaft. Everything about him said, *I'm just taking up space on the seat.*

"Forget him," Adcock said.

"Hardly."

"He's hired help. Hired not-help's more like it."

"Hey, Adcock, whadya want from me? I followed the doc up here, didn't I? I spotted her Beemer. I found the motel."

"Button it, Weasel."

Weasel. How apt. "Adcock, how is it you're right here waiting for me?"

"I followed you and the sheriff till he turned off. Then I circled back here and parallelled your dust. Like tornado spotting. Did you see the boys? Are they in the desert brig over there?"

"Slow down."

"What?"

"If you could follow the dust, so can the sheriff. He's

over on the next road." On this road it wouldn't matter how fast they went. All the sheriff had to do was call ahead for a deputy to wait at the interstate. Adcock would have to cut overland somewhere. But she wasn't ready to point that out. When he slowed the truck, she said, "I thought it was Grady Hummacher you were after. What made you shift your focus to the boys?"

"Now that Grady's dead, I'm responsible for them. I want to get them back to their own people."

The Weasel's snort was so muted, it took Kiernan a moment to realize there hadn't been merely a shift of weight in the truck. A retort was on her lips, but she kept quiet. When you're in the only vehicle in sight in the middle of the desert and the United States Navy is gunning for you over the rise, it's time for discretion. "How did you find out Grady was dead?"

"Walked in and saw his body. So much blood around his room, it looked like his fucking skin had been turned inside out. That answer your question?"

"Completely."

"So, O'Shaughnessy, the boys? Navy got 'em?"

"I don't think so."

"What about that green spot behind us? That'd be damned attractive to south-of-the-border kids."

"Jeez, Adcock, don't you think the navy would come up with that? Whadya think, you're the only one with a noggin?" With a louder snort the Weasel burrowed back down.

Kiernan nodded. "That's the first place they'd have checked. It's also downwind of their experiments. Not a place to go without a full bodysuit."

"I don't give a shit about the danger—"

"You want to end up with your skin turned inside out?"

Adcock kept the truck moving toward the highway. At the speed he was going, the three of them could have been any local family heading to the Doll's House for an early-morning breakfast before moseying on down to Las Vegas. But they weren't going somewhere as much as just moving, while Adcock made up his mind.

"Fine, fine. But if they're not here, where are they? I need to get them back before . . ."—he shrugged—"something happens to them."

"Let me think," Kiernan said. Adcock still assumed the boys were seismic aides. Did he think they knew where Grady's find was? Did he figure they could tell him? Was he planning on getting an interpreter to tell them to lead him to the oil?

She glanced at Adcock's face. Cured by the years in the sun, set-jaw lines etched deep, eyes that didn't waste time looking around—everything about him screamed impatience and a real small tolerance for dissent. She could see him stalking into Grady's room demanding the oil-exploration data. It was his right, after all. Grady Hummacher tells Adcock to go to hell. Adcock pulls a gun. A couple of escalations and Grady's dead. Adcock figures the boys will take him back to Grady's oil.

But Adcock didn't have the boys. So they were gone before he got there. The question was, where were they now?

"Hey, O'Shaughnessy, I didn't hire you so I could take you for a ride in the country."

"You didn't hire me at all. I'm only doing this as a favor."

"You expect me to thank you?"

"I'm doing this as a favor to Tchernak. Has he reported to you about Grady's midweek flight to Panama?"

"You mean after the Friday he flew in here?"

"Right. He came in on Friday, picked up the boys and a woman named Irene, and drove up here to a park—the one you spotted—Saturday. Monday he flew to Panama and returned to Vegas on Wednesday."

Adcock's jaw was clenched, but he held his silence. She remembered that about him, his ability to focus totally on the problem. "What'd he go for?"

"That's not the interesting part, Adcock. Both flights were on charters."

Adcock stared straight ahead, though she wouldn't have put money on his watching the road. The Weasel's body tensed, and Kiernan had the sense that he, too, was considering all the angles. But Adcock wouldn't have given him all the pieces those angles came off of. Adcock revealed nothing he didn't have to, and he played his cards so close to the vest that when she'd worked for him, only very fast talking had kept her out of jail. "Chartered to who?"

"Nihonco Oil."

He slammed the wheel; the truck jolted. "The bastard flew down with Nihonco? He double-crossed me? He sold me out? Is that what he did?"

"I only know he flew with them. He took the boys and Irene back to—"

"Irene? Irene Hernandez?"

"Who is she?"

"Head of subsidiaries for Nihonco."

Kiernan sank against the seat back. Somehow it seemed more horrible that Irene Hernandez's last day had been an extended business meeting. Maybe she liked the idea of a daylong trip to the tropical park, but chances were she'd have been happy signing the papers with Grady in the office. She'd have figured one more day was worth the millions Grady Hummacher's strike would bring Nihonco. She'd have been picturing a promotion, greater stock options, a bigger office, whatever fills executives' dreams. At thirty, maybe thirty-five, years old she had been a key executive with an international oil company, and once she died, Fox and the powers that be had taken a look at her Hispanic features and assumed she'd been merely a disease-carrying immigrant.

It was an odd relief, Kiernan felt, knowing that Irene Hernandez was no longer a nameless corpse with a distorted face. She was not so dispensable no one missed her. In her job sudden business trips would be the norm. No one would worry for another week or two.

Just as no one would worry about a private investigator gone from La Jolla.

"So, O'Shaughnessy, how do I get those boys?"

Over my dead body. "We've got a problem. Fox and the navy are looking for them. Fox let me escape. He's watching me. When we get to Ninety-three, he'll be there, or he'll have someone keeping an eye on us."

"It's not like we coulda turned off," the Weasel said.

Without bothering to brake, Adcock hung a U. Kiernan's shoulder hit the door. Her feet didn't reach all the way under the dash. To keep from being battered, she had to brace one foot awkwardly against the side panel and try to ram the other against the floor hard enough to get a purchase. Even the Weasel had stiffened his legs. Adcock's hands were tight on the wheel, his eyes were straight ahead.

"Adcock, that maneuver sums you up completely," she said, giving the Weasel a shove.

"Huh?"

"Where are you going?"

"There's a parallel road back this way. I took it to the cafe." He stepped on the gas. The old truck coughed and clattered.

Kiernan shifted her weight but kept her legs braced. "What does Louisa Larson look like? Like me?"

It was the Weasel who laughed. "Lady, she's twice your

size and blond. The only thing you two got in common is your sex."

"You were thinking of her as a decoy, O'Shaughnessy?"

"I was. That won't work. You'll have to be the decoy."

"Hey, I'm the one paying you. I'm going with you to those boys."

"You know where they are?" the Weasel asked as Adcock struggled to keep the truck from stalling.

"If I knew that, we'd all be back in Vegas. I have some leads, but I can't do anything till I shake off Fox. For that I'm going to need Louisa Larson. You have any idea where we can find her?"

She'd directed the question to Adcock, but it was the Weasel who nodded. "Gattozzi. That's where she was headed."

THE FIRST THING Kiernan spotted in Gattozzi was the sheriff's car in front of the station. "Empty," she said to Adcock and the Weasel, "but it didn't get here by itself. Get down out of sight, Weasel."

"It's McGuire, if you don't mind," he said as he slid down between the others on the old Chevy's bench. "Hey, my back's going into spasm. How long do you expect me to stay down here like a sack of groceries?"

Ignoring him, Adcock demanded, "How's this getting us to those boys, O'Shaughnessy?"

The one commercial block in town was more crowded than at any other time she had seen it. At nine A.M. Sunday morning cars were lined up in front of the whimsically-named 47th Street Deli between Jeff Tremaine's office and the mortuary. Gattozzians sat around the red-checked tablecloths, some solo behind a protective shield or newspaper, most clumped in animated discussion. Kiernan checked for Connie, Jeff, Fox, Milo—any familiar face. None.

The road to Connie's mine was so isolated, any vehicle

would stand out. The only vehicular advantage would be a good engine and four-wheel drive. It would be ideal to be making the trip at dusk in Tchernak's big new top-of-the-line Jeep. But there was no way she could stay out of sight till then. And Tchernak's Jeep was miles away at the motel.

"Hey, I'm dyin' down here."

"There! That blue BMW. Is that Louisa Larson's?"

"Weasel?" Adcock elbowed him, and McGuire poked his head up, nodded, and sank back down.

"She's the blonde at the window table."

The question in Kiernan's mind was—how to lure Louisa Larson out of the cafe and to a rendezvous.

But Larson seemed to be solving that problem. Her jaw dropped when she spotted Adcock's truck. She made for the door so abruptly, her napkin went flying. She had her keys out before she reached the car.

"What's with you guys and Louisa Larson?"

"The Weasel worked her over a bit," Adcock said matter-of-factly.

"Worked her over? How?" When the Weasel didn't answer, Kiernan rammed her elbow into his shoulder.

"Hey, whatcha doin'? Jeez, it's bad enough I'm ridin' on the floorboards—"

"What did you do to her?"

"Just a nick, just to draw a little blood. Nothin' a tea bag next to the eye wouldn't take care of."

She jabbed him again, harder.

"What's that for?"

"So you think twice before you cut a woman." To Adcock she said, "Make a left. Up hill. See that old bucket house at the top of the hill?" She pointed to the spot where she'd won Jesse's truck. "Head for that. As soon as you turn, hit the gas. That'll give us an extra half minute before Fox starts tailing. He'll be after us, but he won't want to be obvious about it."

Larson was behind them, closing the gap. Farther back an old truck meandered up the street and paused in front of the cafe.

"McGuire, when I'm gone, sit up just high enough so that your hair is visible."

"And you figure that'll fool the sheriff?"

"Only from a distance. It's the best we can do."

Kiernan looked down at First Street. The hillside road was more exposed than she had realized. What had protected Connie, Jesse, and the group last night was not the spot itself but the dark. "Slow down at that flat stretch up there. Don't stop. After I jump, pick up speed slowly."

"What about—"

She opened the door, braced her feet on the sill, jumped, and rolled. The ground wasn't as flat as it looked, and definitely not soft. Even after bracing for the fall, she hit her head on a rock. Sharp branches scratched her face and snagged her turtleneck. She pushed herself up in time to flag down Louisa Larson.

"Make a right," she said as she jumped in the BMW.

"Who are you? How did that little thug get you?" Louisa Larson's hand went to her face. She had straight blond hair and the kind of soft, even features that suggested concern. She would have been pretty had it not been for the ragged wound a fraction of an inch from her eye.

"He did that? McGuire? The Weasel?"

"Yeah, the little bastard. Took me by surprise. But go on about you."

Louisa Larson, the doctor who had provided the only consistent care for the boys, should be the one person to trust. But she didn't trust her enough to let on about her own medical background. "I'm Kiernan O'Shaughnessy, private investigator."

Louisa shook her head. "What is this? You and the big guy in the Jeep and the Weasel, you guys having a convention out here? Or are you working for him?" She nodded at Adcock's truck. Her voice was raw, her face lined with anger and exhaustion. She clutched the wheel too tightly and overcompensated on a curve. The woman was in over her head and too far gone to realize it.

"Tchernak, the Jeep guy, works for me. The Weasel"—mimicking Larson's tone—"I never heard of before I climbed into the truck. But you and I are both concerned about the boys. If we don't get to them now, they could disappear forever." With no trace of irony she added, "Trust me."

Between twists in the road Louisa Larson glanced over at her, automatically accompanying the movement with a social smile. "Tchernak I trusted. So I'm trusting you. I'm a doctor. I've got to find those boys before they're beyond help. Where are they?"

"Cut back to First Street. Make a right at the second corner past the sheriff's department. I've got to keep out of sight."

"Where are we going? The Weasel's still here, right? I've got a gun." No social smile here. "I followed that little thug as far as that miserable motel. I thought Grady and the boys would be there. I thought he might be sick by now but that he'd just be in the beginning stages. I was going to scoop up the three of them and drive like hell back to Las Vegas." She swallowed, her hands shaking so hard on the wheel, the car shimmied. "I never dreamed Grady would be dead. Or that someone would have kidnapped the boys. I mean, why, for heaven's sake? I took care of those kids. They're sweet, sad, wonderful, but let me tell you, they are one ton of work. They're like having puppies with hands. Whoever took them didn't know what they were getting into."

"They are deaf and mute? No sign language, right?"

"Backroom kids, that's what Grady called them. They

may have had skills in their tribe, but it's all useless outside a rain forest, and, you know, we don't have much in the way of big leaves and humidity here in the Silver State."

"So even if they were healthy, instead of being so sick they're throwing up blood, they'd still be useless, right?"

"Like I said, puppies with hands."

"Could you communicate with them? Get them to lead you somewhere?"

Louisa shook her head. "I don't know, or care. The bottom line is they're going to die without help, and it looks like I'm the only one who gives a damn. Well, you and me."

The BMW swung right onto the top of First Street. Kiernan slipped down onto the floor pad, feeling more vulnerable there where she could see nothing but Louisa Larson's inadequate shoes. If there was an "overland" to be done, Larson would not be the one doing it. "Are we past the sheriff's office yet? Any movement there?"

"No one coming out."

"How about standing inside the window, casually reading a map or talking or—"

"Oh, yeah. Big guy, drinking a cup of coffee."

"See if he comes out and gets in his car."

"Nope. This is the turn. Right, you said?"

"Right. The street looks like it dead-ends. Go all the way, the sharp right uphill. It's a road you'd never take unless you were headed for back country. Keep checking the rearview mirror."

"Are you on the run from everyone?"

"So it seems, huh?" She waited till she felt the vehicle turn and start uphill before pushing up onto the seat. "Louisa, you're a doctor. You've come all this way to save the boys. When you find them, what is it you're going to do for them? I saw Grady. He had already started bleeding out. What virus do they have? Is there any treatment?"

Louisa gave a little cry, and when she spoke, it was so softly, Kiernan almost missed her words. "Poor kids. I can't believe after all they've been through they can just die now. I was treating them, and their fevers were lowering."

"Treating them with what?"

"A derivative of ribavirin. I've got some in a freezer case in the trunk. If I can get to the boys in time, it could make the difference."

"This late?"

"The latest research indicates at least an ameliorative effect. Mixed with a drug called Cyro— But this is getting too technical. Trust me, what I've got is the best treatment there is. Whether it will be enough, I don't know."

Yeah, well, I do know. Ribavirin enhanced survival rates only if it was given early on. And only in specific arenaviruses. For Lassa fever it was a godsend. For Ebola, useless. In the case of an idiopathic condition, how could Louisa be doing any more than taking a stab and hoping? Why this particular combination—unless she knew the strains of virus that had infected the boys?

Louisa eyed the narrow, windy road, shot a glance at the gray soil and low prickly wild plants. "Just where are the boys?"

"A couple hours out of town."

"On a road like this?"

"Worse."

"But where?"

"I'll direct you, Louisa."

"I'm not a chauffeur! Tell me or—"

"Or what?" Purposely Kiernan kept her voice light and the aura of collegiality in place. "What do you want? I'm the only one who knows where they are. I'm taking you there. But it's not like there are street signs. I'll know the turns when I see them—I hope." She forced herself to add plaintively, "I'm doing the best I can."

"Sorry. Of course. I'm just edgy."

Plaintive always worked. It just galled her to use it.

Already the town was barely visible. The landscape, which she had seen only in the dark, was green and gray in all directions, dry and endless. She checked the rearview mirror again, but by now she expected the road behind to be empty. With all the resources of the county sheriff's department and the United States Navy, Fox wouldn't have to tail them. And if he did choose that low-tech method, he had plenty of time before there were any turn-offs.

She thought of the boys, but it was Louisa who put words to the worry. "Even in Vegas, where there's grass and shrubs and potted palms, Juan and Carlos looked stunned. What were they thinking—how do you think without words? But that's another issue. They looked as if a spaceship had abandoned them on Mars. To them this dirt and sand and air so dry it cuts your skin was as incomprehensible as living in outer space. I wanted to ask . . . everything." She sucked in breath, staring ahead at the empty road, hands white on the wheel. "And in the end I could *do* nothing for them."

"But you did arrange for them to go to the tropical park, didn't you. Grady said a friend told him about it."

Louisa's jaw tightened before she could smile. She clasped the steering wheel harder. "One of my professors in college had a project with government funding and he had to bring some of the specimens up here. He used to tell me about the park. It sounded so perfect for the boys."

"When was the last time you were there?"

"Never. I just heard. Why?"

"Because, Louisa, the park is downwind of the naval

testing facility. They shoot viruses and bacteria into the air
to see if they can identify them."

She gasped. "Microbes? In the air?" Her foot came off
the gas pedal; the car coughed; she fumbled with the gearshift and barely downshifted before the engine stalled. "It
used to be a park. That's what my professor said. It was
wonderful. And now it's what—poison?" She was shaking
her head. "Oh, God, you can't be right."

"I am."

"Oh, no. Is that where the boys got infected?"

Kiernan nodded.

Louisa was still shaking her head. She turned to
Kiernan, beseeching. "I thought . . . I thought it would
be nice for them. I sent them there, and now they're . . .
dying." As she swiped at her damp cheek, she scraped the
scar beside her eye and gasped. "I was only trying to do
something nice for them. You understand, don't you?"

Kiernan could have nodded and let her off the hook.
She didn't. She knew this type of woman who needed to be
liked and who used her charm as means of entree. Without
that acceptance she would be helpless, and desperate. Louisa Larson would have to work for approval this time. First
off, she'd have to answer questions. "The woman who's
caring for the boys was sweating, feverish. Was that how it
started with the boys?"

"I think so. By the time the neighbors called me they
were too weak to stand. They were having trouble swal-
lowing. If they'd gotten to me earlier—"

"That was the fourth or fifth day?"

She hesitated. "Could be."

"How long have they been symptomatic by now?"
Kiernan prodded. "A week, ten days?"

"Maybe a week. I don't know. Eight or nine days."

In eight or nine days Lassa patients were dead. *Let her be
right about her treatment.*

Louisa pulled the wheel hard, taking the BMW into a curve, and let the wheel slide back in the loop of her fingers and thumb. The familiar movements of driving seemed to pull her out of her shock.

She had to keep Louisa on edge. "The woman is dead. The boys were exposed at the same time—"

"No! Not necessarily. When Grady called that night— he wanted me to check on the boys—he told me he had car trouble. He found a sheltered spot, a sort of lean-to, he said. And for a couple of hours he fiddled with the engine before he finally gave up and limped the car to the gas station. He said the boys watched him, but he left them picnicking when he made the run to the mechanic."

"And the woman?"

"Of course Grady didn't mention her to me. But she could have been picnicking or exploring the whole time. How would I know?" She shot a glance at Kiernan. Checking for her reaction, Kiernan noted. Purposely she showed none.

"A week ago it was still hot here," Louisa hurried on. "In a desert like this it's summer for a long, long time, and then one day you wake up and it's winter. No fall, no warning."

Faye at the Doll's House had said the woman was already annoyed. Not the state of mind to spend hours handing Grady a wrench or a rag. Not when she could wander through southwest Nevada's botanical wonder— and never guess she was breathing in toxic particles. Did the boys get a smaller dose? Did they have a natural immunity? Or were they the first victims of person-to-person transmission from the index case?

It wasn't my fault! Louisa had insisted with each answer. *Trust me! Think well of me!* But that Kiernan could not do.

The only reason Louisa would have a specific drug would be because she knew what virus or viruses she was dealing with. And the only way Grady Hummacher could have gotten into the tropical park behind the guarded gate of the Naval Proving Grounds would have been if he'd had a pass. . . . If the woman who'd told him about the park had also given him her pass.

She turned and looked out the back window, squinting into the distance. The narrow line of road marked the rise and fall of hills going back and back till it became indistinguishable from the high desert on either side. There was no car, no person in sight.

Of course Fox wasn't following so close. He didn't have to. He could count on Louisa.

CHAPTER
50

KIERNAN SAT WITH her feet braced against the dash of Louisa's BMW. Snow had begun falling, scarce at first, now thick. Louisa clasped the steering wheel tighter; even so, the car skidded in the sharp curves.

"How much farther?" Louisa's voice was raw, any sociability gone.

"An hour maybe. Do you want me to drive?"

"No!" It was a moment before she said more calmly, "The place the boys are, is it on this road? Or do we turn off?"

"We turn. Soon, I think. But I've only done this route once, and that was at night. So I'm just going to have to be alert for landmarks."

Grudgingly, Louisa nodded, and Kiernan settled against the headrest, watched the road, and considered what she knew. Grady Hummacher had snatched the boys and driven through the night to the Doll's House. His one phone call from there had not been to inquire about Irene's health, as she had assumed. His goal had been to hide the boys. For that he called his sole contact, Jeff Tremaine, whom he knew from the Carson Club.

She nodded to herself. At one time she had speculated it was Jeff who operated the safe house. Of course Jeff knew of his wife's operation.

Maybe Grady was worried about the boys; maybe he just didn't want to be tied down as he auctioned his find in the oil world. If he was savvy, he intended to keep them out of the hands of his competitors and enemies.

"There, Louisa! Right!"

"Are you sure you know what you're doing?"

"Take it." As soon as the car swung right, Kiernan shut her eyes, willing a clear memory of the road. How long till she had left the pavement? Ten minutes, fifteen? "Speed up. We need to make time now."

"Because we'll be off the pavement soon?"

"Right," Kiernan admitted.

"This isn't a truck, you know, are you sure—"

"Louisa, what choice do we have?"

"If you'd tell me where we're going, maybe I could come up with another way. I've been around here before."

"No time for that." Kiernan spotted a road to the right. It was closer to parallel ruts than a map-worthy route.

She checked the road behind them, eyeing the horizon for a telltale plume of dust, seeing only emptiness and snow.

If Fox was following them, there would be no telltale dust now, not in the snow.

"There, turn left."

"On that! I'm going to have no transmission left. Can't we—"

"Turn, Louisa."

The car tilted and bounced as Louisa tried to find a path in the too-wide ruts from much bigger trucks. Kiernan braced her feet and thought of a whale-watching

trip she had taken to the Farallon Islands years ago,
twenty-six endless miles west of the Golden Gate, hours
on an ancient no-stabilizer boat watching a dot in the
ocean grow minusculely larger. All to discover that the
whales had moved on.

Now in the light she spotted lesser trails leading off the
rutted road. Each she discounted, each time hoping she
was right. She hadn't recalled the road twisting so much.
Last night the dark had blacked out the options. Now she
could see the seductive choices that protected Connie.
Louisa held the wheel tightly; she looked as if she were
hanging on as much as steering. Not once had she checked
the rearview mirror. Because of course she wasn't worried
about her compatriot Fox.

She was leading him there. Kiernan knew that and it
infuriated her. But what choice was there? She couldn't
lead Louisa away from the boys when Louisa had the drug
that might save them. And maybe save herself and
Tchernak. Here in the unforgiving desert she could neither
escape with the drug nor overpower Louisa and abandon
her beside the road to freeze.

Even with the heater on, the car was cold. Her cotton
turtleneck, inadequate before, now felt like paper against
her taut skin. Outside, the snow was beginning to stick,
throwing the landscape into an eerie black and white.
Kiernan leaned her head against the seat. Exhaustion blan-
keted her. How long had it been since she'd slept? She had
been trained on thirty-six-hour shifts in med-school rotations. This stint was still shy of thirty. No excuse for
drooping. She straightened up. "Do you have any food,
Louisa?" Before Louisa could offer a sarcastic "Help yourself," she had the glove compartment open and a chocolate
bar out. She didn't want to accept hospitality; she wanted
to grab the food as she would from an enemy. She crum-
pled the wrapper, dropped it to the floor, noted Louisa

biting back a complaint, and sat nibbling the chocolate as the windshield wipers cleared away arcs of snow.

"Keep left!" The mine hole came into sight as suddenly as it had the previous night. Almost as suddenly. Louisa had time to gasp, cut left, and skirt it with a yard to spare.

Now in the light the cavernous pit seemed even more horrifying. Nausea sloshed in her stomach. The skid marks from Jesse's truck were outlined in white now, two deep ruts running into the hole.

"Is that a mine?" Louisa slowed almost to a stop. "I've heard about abandoned mines collapsing, but I never figured them to be this size. They could put a cathedral in there."

Kiernan stared into the crater as long as she could see it, to remind herself of the vastness of the danger she had overcome.

The road wound, corkscrewed downward, narrowed, but the ruts remained too wide for the BMW. Kiernan's legs ached from bracing herself. In the daylight it was easy to see how well hidden the mine was. No one would go far on this road without a reason. What brush there was was short and provided neither cover nor silencing, and the reverberations of the engine and brakes echoed through the canyon. From the base a person could watch the car slowly descend like a pinball bouncing from turn to turn.

But Connie's mine hadn't been at the base, that much she was sure of. They passed the entry road before Kiernan realized it. "Stop. Back up." The narrow road angled back so sharply, Louisa had to make three cuts before she got the BMW around. Piñons grew so close, they scraped the car on both sides.

A quarter mile onto the drive, they spotted a derelict building in the distance. "You mean, that's it?"

"It's habitable inside."

Louisa stopped the car and pulled her gun-heavy purse onto her lap. "We'll get out here."

"All we'd get for that would be exposed. We're not surprising anyone. She'll be expecting something."

When the BMW rounded the last curve, Connie was standing, rifle poised. Kiernan hoisted her head and chest out the window. "Connie, it's me. The boys, are they still alive?"

Connie pointed to a half-collapsed outbuilding. "Get the car into the car barn. Quick!"

Louisa started to protest, but Kiernan held up a hand. In the silence she could hear the echo of an engine in the canyon.

"I'M A DOCTOR," Louisa called as she drove the car past Connie into the mine's outbuilding. "I've got treatment for the boys."

Connie waved the car in, just as the guard outside the tropical park must have waved in Grady Hummacher's car.

Louisa was out of the BMW before the engine was silent. "Where are they?" she demanded.

"Shhh." Connie pointed to the road. "Hear that?"

"I don't hear anything. Look, time is vital to these boys. You do have them here, don't you?"

Wind rustled through branches, snapping them against one another and scraping leaves into leaves. It whipped Connie Tremaine's short gray hair like wheat in a storm. Everything was gray, the dilapidated buildings, the sky, the scree from the abandoned mine that covered the ground. The snow was falling heavily now. Connie, deadly pale and sweaty, looked as if she could fade into the landscape with a thought. She eyed Louisa warily.

"Your answer is yes, then," Louisa insisted. "Look, obviously you've gone to a lot of trouble, danger even, for these boys." She grabbed Connie's arm. "Don't let them die now. Every minute counts."

Connie stood granite-still, arms across chest, face revealing nothing except the effort it cost her to remain standing. Watching her, Kiernan wondered how many times she had stood just so, assessing a husband or boyfriend, creditor or gunman who had tracked a runaway to her.

Snow speckled Louisa's blond hair, her soft, even features knit in concern. It was a look Kiernan had seen often in med-school rotation in the ER and on the faces of the staff in Africa. Louisa was shaking Connie's arm. "There's no time—"

Connie jerked free. "*Listen!* That vehicle'll be in our faces in a minute. Who's in it?"

Suddenly the wind slackened and the approaching engine thundered.

Louisa shot a glance down the drive. "There was no one behind us."

"No one visible," Kiernan said. "That's someone making up time."

"All the more reason to get the boys while we can."

Connie held up a hand to quiet the woman she didn't know and turned questioningly to Kiernan. "Your call."

There were a dozen questions she needed answered. Was the drug going to save the boys, or save the navy's experiment? Would the boys be cured or would it kill them—and the evidence of Louisa's connection be buried? Already the roar of the engine was louder, closer. There was no time. . . . "The boys have had this fever for days. Ten more minutes won't matter. We wait till it's safe."

Louisa wheeled toward her. "That's crazy. This drug's their best shot."

"We need to deal with the guy on our tail."

"But I could be—"

"A spy? A pawn? What's the right word, Louisa?" She was standing inches from the woman, shouting. "You've got a designer drug. The navy's researchers are the only ones who know what to design against."

"I couldn't—"

"You're still tight enough with them to have a pass into the park. You knew what they were doing there. Did you send Grady and the boys there just to spite Grady?"

Louisa jerked back as if she'd been slapped. "No! The experiments were different when I was up there. I never suspected . . . till it was too late." She swallowed hard. "But no one will ever believe me."

"Yeah, right," Kiernan snapped. "That's real hard to believe when you're leading Fox here. Why didn't you just offer him the backseat of your car and save him the trouble of driving?"

"I—"

Brakes squealed; the engine snored like a winter bear, paused, then grumbled forward. It made the turn in the driveway.

Louisa turned toward the driveway, her face taut with panic.

"What are you worried about? Your buddies will be here in a minute to back you up," Kiernan said. "Unless even you are frightened of them."

Louisa didn't answer.

"Maybe it's worth more than two dispensable kids to test their 'best shot' drug. Is that it, Louisa?"

"Hurry." Connie raced across the gravelly ground and disappeared into what looked like a pile of rotten timbers.

The truck was already in the driveway. No time to get to Connie. Kiernan raced back into the car barn, Louisa on her heels.

The driveway was ten feet away, visible between the boards. The wind hummed through the decaying wood, pricking at Kiernan's skin, its deep tone contrasting with Louisa's nervous huffs of breath. She was shivering so violently that even clasping her arms to her chest had no effect. She peered through the boards, through the falling snow, for the first sighting of Fox.

But it was Reston Adcock's pickup truck that screeched to a halt. He leaped to the ground, gun in hand. "Get out here, both of you!"

Louisa gasped. Her fingers went to the wound on her face; she started to move. Kiernan grabbed her arm. "He's looking around. He doesn't know where we are. He'll head for the house first."

"He's desperate. His hired thug has already attacked me. He's already killed Grady, what do you think he'll do to the boys after he's used them up?"

Or before, Kiernan thought. When Adcock realized the boys couldn't tell him where the oil was, he'd leave them here in the snow without a thought. But kill Grady? That was the last thing Adcock would have done, not when Grady was the only lead to the oil and the boys. Grady knew Adcock better than any of them. He would have let him in, offered him a seat, and waited to hear if he could top Nihonco's offer. If he'd been too feverish? Adcock would have scooped him up and raced to a hospital. What's a little biological danger compared with millions of dollars? Through the cracks she could see Adcock edging his way toward the house, gun poised, eyes wild. In the silence she heard a rumble in the sky like thunder. "Wait till he's inside. We'll have a little time to make our move."

"Move to what? From one pile of timber to another?"

"Shhh."

"No! Are the boys in the house? Is he going to find them?"

Kiernan shook her shoulder hard. "Quiet! Of course they're not in the house. Do you think Connie's an idiot?"

"Well, then where? If something happens to you and I can't find them—"

Adcock yelled, "I'm not after you girls, I just need those kids. Give me the boys and I'm gone."

He stopped halfway to the house. The whitening ground of the courtyard was in front of him, the pile Connie had disappeared into ten feet behind him.

Snow coated Adcock's shoulder as he looked from the house to the shed to the mine building and the car barn. Frustration and fury creased his tanned brow, and Kiernan could almost read his thoughts as he realized the impossibility of controlling all the buildings at once. Above him the sky was rumbling. It wasn't thunder.

Kiernan whispered, "As soon as he goes inside—"

"Get those kids out here! I'm giving you five seconds! I've got torches here. Five seconds! Then I start torching the place. You can all fry."

"He's not going to—"

In a burst Louisa was out the door. "No you won't, you bastard!" She aimed her gun and fired.

Adcock screamed, spun toward her, and shot.

She fired again and he slumped slowly to the ground, clutching his pistol as if it could heal him. He shot at her one more time as he fell.

Louisa grabbed her chest and sank. A gust fingered her blond hair, and Kiernan couldn't tell whether the weak cry was from her or the wind. Her gun had fallen inches away; she reached for it but her arm was rubbery and her hand fell ineffectually to the ground. "Help me! Help!"

Adcock didn't move.

"Help!"

Kiernan started toward her, then stopped. The porch door of the house creaked. Connie raced out. *Get back!* But it was too late for Kiernan to warn her. Running, Connie circled left, making a wide U on her way to Louisa. She almost reached the moaning woman when the shot struck her.

Kiernan looked to her right. Adcock was still lying on the ground. Standing over him, gun in hand, was the Weasel.

Above them was a helicopter.

CHAPTER
52

AS THE HELICOPTER blades drummed above, Louisa lay on the ground, moaning ever more softly. A few feet away Connie neither moved nor made a sound. She had just been trying to do the decent thing. Near the truck, Adcock, too, had crumbled to the ground. There was no way of telling whether they were alive. Snow was beginning to collect in the creases of their clothes. Kiernan had to keep herself from running to them. But there was no help she could give them, not now. She peered out through the car barn cracks.

McGuire was still out there, armed with his weapon and Adcock's. The wind whipped his thin brown hair, snapped his flimsy jacket against his ribs. His eyes were wild.

"Hey, O'Shaughnessy, it's the boys I need. Gimme them and I'm gone." He hadn't even looked up at the helicopter a hundred yards overhead. "Hey, I got no beef with you. This is a money deal. Gimme the kids. I sell 'em to Nihonco, I take my millions, and I'm gone. Gimme the kids and you got nothing to fear." He was shouting, but she could barely hear him over the beat of the blades.

Grady, Louisa, Adcock, and Connie, dead or dying, all
for the knowledge of the oil deposit the boys had no way of
transmitting. McGuire didn't know the boys had no language. By the time they could learn to communicate—if
they could do so at all—Grady Hummacher's oil would be
in gas tanks nationwide, via some other lucky geologist.
But the Weasel didn't know that. If he had, he wouldn't
have taken the chance of bursting through the chain on the
motel door and shooting Grady Hummacher.

"Hey, I don't have forever. This is my one big chance,
nothing's going to keep me from it. You got no choice,
O'Shaughnessy." For the first time, he looked up. The
helicopter was moving closer, shifting side to side. "Don't
think they're going to save you. Adcock was going to burn
you out. The torch is still here. The wind from that copter
will turn this place into an inferno. You'll be embers by the
time that thing lands. You and those kids if you don't get
'em to me. Now!"

Where were the boys? Had Connie hidden them so well
they would die before anyone else could find them?

"Hey, don't worry. Those kids are valuable property.
They'll get the best. Hey, I'll cut you in."

The helicopter was fifty feet up. She expected to hear
Fox's voice blaring from the sky, but he wasted no time on
words. The navy copter kept moving down, the vibration
from the blades growing progressively stronger. If Fox
took the boys to B-CADS, they'd be studied to death; if
the Weasel got them, they'd just end up dead.

The Weasel was eyeing the aluminum shed directly
across the courtyard from him. It was the one sturdy building in the complex, the logically safe place. To his right
was the house, to his left the car barn from which Kiernan
watched him. "The boys, O'Shaughnessy! Get me those
kids."

The copter was moving down fast. Fox was halfway out the door.

The helicopter was twenty feet above them. Fox was bracing himself, ready to leap the moment it hit ground.

The boards of the car barn shimmied. At any moment the whole building could collapse on top of her. She forced herself to wait, to gauge the right moment.

On the ground in front, Connie and Louisa shifted in unison. It wasn't them moving, she realized. The ground was shimmying.

"This way, McGuire!" She ran out under the copter. The maelstrom from the blades threw dirt and snow into her face. She ran, but the wind was so strong, it blew her back. She leaned almost horizontal, pushing off hard with each step. The Weasel was yelling, but she couldn't make out words over the frantic beating of the blades. "The shed, Weasel. They're in the shed. Come on, we've just got time." She bent lower, using all her strength to keep going. She was under the copter when she shot a glance back at the Weasel. The man wasn't moving. "Weasel, you want the boys or not? How many million dollars?"

She didn't wait for his reaction. The ground was snapping up and down like a trampoline. Like a tent roof. Like a skylight ready to crack. Beneath the thunderous clap of the blades she could hear the groan as the earth gave way. The mine roof was caving in. The helicopter blades skimmed her head, knocking her forward. She flung her shoulders back, desperate to keep from falling, being sucked down into the growing hole. She was almost across the cavern. The gray soil was rushing down all around. She grabbed for the edge of the hole, her legs pedaling like mad as the ground beneath her collapsed. She flung herself onto the rim and rolled.

Only then did she turn and look back. She could see Fox's horror-widened eyes. He yelled at the pilot. The copter jerked, head up. The engine screamed. Then it stalled and the copter smashed down on its side into the collapsed mine. The hole was fifty feet deep at the center, and soil was rushing in from all sides. Under the blade she spotted the Weasel, legs flailing against the rushing dirt. He wouldn't be coming out without help.

She needed time to catch her breath, but there wasn't time. Once the dirt settled, Fox and his pilot would get themselves out. "The boys!" Skirting the growing hole, she ran back to Connie. Connie lay two yards from the growing hole; she had pulled her arm under her head. Her face was gray. But she was breathing. Kiernan pulled her back near the grass. "The boys, Connie, where are they?"

"Hoist house." She pointed to the looming structure on the low hill. "Upstairs, trapdoor."

Ignoring the men's angry screams in the hole, Kiernan ran for the decaying mine building, clambered up the wooden stairs onto the tracks leading to the ore shoots. One side was blank wall, the other empty windows through which ore must have been poured. At the end of the open hall the ore bin stood empty, rusting. She slowed, looked down, kicking away the dirt till she spotted a metal loop handle.

The trapdoor lifted with surprising ease.

The room below was lit by a camping lantern. Wooden walls, wood floor, table, chairs, and in the shadows a cot with two forms, huddled together on it. Heat from the tiny space flowed up through the hole.

She lowered herself onto the rung ladder and climbed down. She was holding her breath. At the bottom she turned toward the boys. They looked so small, so wasted. But their fevers had broken and they were alive.

CHAPTER
53

BRAD TCHERNAK LEANED back in the seat of the fine gold Jeep Grand Cherokee Laredo. "So, Kiernan, 'after you got out of the burning pit,' as my father used to say—"

"Excuse me?"

"Well, he said it about those old Saturday-morning serials in the movie theaters, the ones that ended with the hero trapped in the burning pit and a promise of great excitement next week. Dad spent the whole week trying to figure out how the hero could possibly extricate himself. The next Saturday he would rush to the theater, ready to see the great escape. What he'd get instead would be the next episode starting with the hero saying, 'After I got out of the burning pit, I went on to . . .' So?"

Kiernan laughed. She was slumped in the passenger seat, and her bare feet were braced against the windshield. "I don't know how long it took Fox to get himself and crew—and the Weasel—out of the not-burning pit, but I moved like a whirlwind hauling the boys, Louisa, and Connie into Connie's truck. I knew I didn't have much time. I was afraid I'd have to spend most of it just shifting cars to get out of the driveway, and Fox would nab me right there. Or if I did get out, he'd have me intercepted on the road to Gattozzi. But I'd underestimated Connie. Her place was, after all, a safe house. The potential need for escape was always on her mind. Of course she had her truck at a hidden exit. Of course she knew other routes to Gattozzi. Even so it took so long, I was afraid Louisa wouldn't make it."

"But she did?"

"She won't be using her right arm for a while, but she's not dead like Adcock. And she's not bleeding out from contagious hemorrhagic fever the way you and I might have been."

"I'm glad you didn't mention that danger yesterday. Bad enough I thought I was going to be permanent navy property. Then, all of a sudden, I'm sent to the shower, my clothes are pressed—"

"Not cleaned, or deodorized, I note."

"Jeez, look who's talking. You could be Lot's wife. That's salt, not dirt, isn't it? But tell me. How did you get me free?"

"Connie Tremaine has connections in the fourth estate, and it would look real bad for the United States Navy to devote taxpayers' money to harassing a local citizen who was only caring for two disabled boys who'd entered the country legally. The boys' fevers had broken. There's no longer evidence they ever had an exotic virus. Anyway the virus-detection program is the second-to-last thing the navy wants on the front page."

"The second-to-last thing? What's the last?"

Kiernan laughed. "The picture of their helicopter half buried in the mine. Not exactly your recruiting poster picture."

Tchernak grinned. "Grady Hummacher would have

loved that. It's better than the Volkswagen in the staircase of Tasman Hall." When she looked at him blankly, he said, "I'll tell you later. But am I indebted to Connie Tremaine too? Did you both trade silence for my release?"

"Hardly. Not that I don't love you, Tchernak, but *silence*, really. We just got Louisa to give us the name of her contact at B-CAD. I pointed out to him that they'd be in deep enough shit without a kidnapping charge. Weak as Louisa was, she was still real anxious to minimize bad publicity. It's one thing for a local doctor to have worked on a project with the navy. It's quite another for that doctor to know that lethal bacteria and chemicals are being tossed into the air and citizens are not being notified. She's desperate to keep that quiet."

"Desperate enough to kill?"

"She didn't shoot Adcock over publicity. I think she really felt she was protecting the boys. Who knows? And would she have killed Grady if the Weasel hadn't gotten to him first? I doubt it. She's not a stare-you-in-the-face-and-shoot-you kinda gal. Whereas the Weasel wasn't knee-deep in qualms."

Tchernak laughed. "Like the lightbulb jokes: How many qualms does it take to overcome the smell of millions?"

Kiernan fished in the hamper behind the seat and pulled out two Cokes. Mexican Cokes, the kind with the caffeine-and-sugar kick that might keep her awake. They had been in Gattozzi all afternoon answering questions. For a while she was afraid she'd get another chance at a night above the Gattozzi saloon. But at dusk the county sheriff had said "Go," and they hadn't looked back.

She took a swallow of Coke. "Here, Tchernak, is Rule One from the Hostage Taker's Guide. Don't price your hostages before you check them out. McGuire had no way of knowing the boys had no language and were worthless to him. Adcock had Grady's geological exploration reports; maybe he could have gotten close enough to the oil for the boys to wander back to the site for reasons of their own. To anyone else they were useless. No one would take the boys back to Yaviza and devote years to following them around in case they might come across Grady's oil deposit—and pay the Weasel millions for the privilege of doing it. For that kind of investment you hire a seismic crew, string sensor wires, set off dynamite, and get yourself geologists to start evaluating the results. But the Weasel didn't think that through. He went after the kidnap scheme the same way he went at Louisa and then at Grady."

"You mean breaking the door chains and shoving his way in?"

She nodded. "No one else would have had to do that. For Louisa or even Adcock, Grady would have opened the door."

"I hope they . . ." Tchernak shrugged. "What'll happen to the boys?"

Kiernan smiled. "The fact that they're still alive is a good sign. I was afraid I'd find them dead in that hole. To have survived all they've been through . . . those guys are tough. Between Connie and Jeff they'll make sure the kids have the best shot, whether that's here or back in Panama. They'll start with a top-notch physical and see where that leads. Might be some oil money for tutors that could make their lives easier either place." She sighed. "You know, if Jeff had just been up-front—"

"Didn't I warn you about him? Who was it who said, 'Don't take that case,' huh?"

"You know, Tchernak, a more gracious person wouldn't have brought that up."

"Graciousness? Is this a new requirement in

O'Shaughnessy's Gracious Investigations?" He laughed, then took a deep swallow of his Coke. "You were saying about the taciturn doctor . . . ?"

"He could have leveled with me about his suspicions of Fox and B-CADS. But I guess after all his years of noting strange things he knew were connected with B-CADS and not being able to pin any of it down, it'd make the sanest person paranoid. And with his record with the navy, who'd believe him?"

She leaned back against the leather seat and looked out at the expanse of desert. The sun was crimson and shot stripes of gold above the western hills. In a few minutes it would disappear entirely. But for the moment it threw the land into high relief. In her two days here she had felt the vastness of the land, its emptiness, its inherent threat. Now its subtle changes filled her with awe. She could see why people like Connie Tremaine loved it.

She had been wrong about the danger. It didn't come from the land. "You know, Tchernak, we were lucky, this time. Whatever this virus was, its transmission wasn't airborne. It didn't survive in the air. You and I weren't infected. Jeff wasn't. Only Grady and Connie picked it up from live carriers, and the boys must have been barely contagious anymore by the time Connie touched them. Still, there could have been an epidemic. And Louisa was right about the danger of cutting a road through the Colombia-Panama rain forest. You do that and you set loose microbes never known outside a rain forest. You infect people like Grady Hummacher and then fly them all over the world and give those viruses new hosts who have no immunities. There are laws of nature; we keep breaking them. It's only a matter of time."

Tchernak finished his Coke and tossed the can in a bag. "But the boys didn't pick up the virus in Panama."

"No, they didn't. They got it right here in Nevada. And if they had been in closer contact with their neighbors in the barrio, they could have spread it to people who are afraid to go to clinics."

"No!" Tchernak put a hand on her arm. "Don't start on the dangers of denying people health care. I don't want to hear again about inviting epidemic. I'm not aruging. I am," he said, "just trying to figure how soon I can buy myself a fine Laredo."

"Ah, the hard life of the private eye, eh? Right down to the leather seats?" She plunked a hand on Tchernak's arm and laughed, taking the time to observe his craggy face and now fanglike mustache and those fine wide football shoulders. "So, Tchernak, speaking of fees . . ."

"Did Adcock pay me, is that what you're asking? You want to know how the competition is making out? Well, you learn lots of lessons in pro football, but none as important as: Get your money up front."

"You got the whole thing?"

"Well, no, not the per diem."

"The whole rest?"

"Well, no, not the payment on delivery."

"Well, then," she said, mocking his delivery, "what?"

"Thou."

"A thousand dollars? I wouldn't have hoisted out of my chair for that."

"You would if you weren't licensed."

"I wouldn't, but that's another issue."

Tchernak stretched a long arm around her shoulder. He didn't pull her closer; the Cherokee's seats didn't indulge togetherness. He stared straight ahead, and when he spoke, his voice was so impersonal he could have been reading the want ads. "I could become licensed. All I need is the hours."

She didn't respond, nor did she pull away.

"How many hours have I already worked for you, free of charge, I might add?"

"Instead of cooking as I paid you to do?"

"Yeah, well . . ."

Tchernak slung his arm across the back of her seat and she leaned into it. It felt cozy and warm and the desert reminded her that sometimes friendship can be all you've got. At times she had assured herself she was immune from the need for friends, for lovers, for anyone who tied her down. She hadn't been immune, just wary. People are demanding; they misunderstand; they leave; and sometimes they die. No matter how many cases she worked on, trying to explain a death, the explanation was never enough. It never blotted out death. She felt foolish even thinking about it. But that she wasn't about to admit, certainly not to Tchernak.

Her silence hung between them. When she turned and looked at him, he kept his eyes on the road. But his hand tensed on her shoulder.

She could manage without Tchernak, she told herself; she'd managed before him. She could hire another house-keeper, make arrangements for Ezra. But no one would care enough to badger and fuss like Tchernak. And if he was gone, she'd worry about him working all alone. And, well, she'd miss him.

"Okay," she said, "here's the deal. Get your six thousand hours with me. We'll negotiate pay. But you've still got to cook. And be available to walk Ezra—"

"Ez? This just saves me kidnapping him. This is terrific," he said clapping her shoulder. "So I'm going to be a partner."

She shook her head. "Tchernak! We haven't even finalized the verbal deal and already you're out of control.

You're not going to be a partner. You're going to be an apprentice."

"Oh, right. No problem." He was grinning. "No problem, *boss*. I can follow orders."

She was smiling, too, but a bit more skeptically than he.